Titles by Kim Boykin

THE WISDOM OF HAIR

PALMETTO MOON

Palmetto Moon

KIM BOYKIN

BERKLEY BOOKS, NEW YORK

THE BERKLEY PUBLISHING GROUP
Published by the Penguin Group
Penguin Group (USA) LLC
375 Hudson Street, New York, New York 10014

USA • Canada • UK • Ireland • Australia • New Zealand • India • South Africa • China

penguin.com

A Penguin Random House Company

This book is an original publication of The Berkley Publishing Group.

Library of Congress Cataloging-in-Publication Data

Boykin, Kim, 1957-
Palmetto moon / Kim Boykin.
pages cm
ISBN 978-0-425-27210-7 (paperback)
1. Marriage—Fiction. 2. Single women—Fiction. 3. Autonomy—Fiction. I. Title.
PS3602.O95P35 2014
813'.6—dc23
2014011728

PUBLISHING HISTORY
Berkley trade paperback edition / August 2014

PRINTED IN THE UNITED STATES OF AMERICA

10 9 8 7 6 5 4 3 2 1

Cover photographs: woman © Lee Avison/Trevillion Images;
background © amiloslava/Thinkstock; border © Volhat Manusovich/Thinkstock.
Cover design by Judith Lagerman.
Interior text design by Kristin del Rosario.

For Joan Gray and Peggy Boykin,
two of the most extraordinary women I know.

Acknowledgments

There's quite a story behind the writing of *Palmetto Moon*, but ultimately, everything this book is, I owe to my editor, Leis Pederson. Thank you, Leis, for your friendship and your support of my work. To Kevan Lyon, wonderful agent and friend, you're the best. And to my readers, most especially Doni Jordan, thanks forever. You've given me the greatest gift I could possibly ask for, and you make me want to be a better writer.

Publicity is a thankless job, but women like Erin Galloway and Jessica Brock at Penguin and Kathie Bennett of Magic Time Literary Agency toil away because they love books. Thanks to these three amazing women, more people know about my work and for that, I'm eternally grateful.

Have to admit I felt a little nervous about writing anything connected to the history of Charleston; the history hounds will rightfully nail you to the wall if you get it wrong. But during my research, I found there was a gap in Charleston archives throughout World War II and well into the late 1940s. So, I'm offering fair warning that with very little to go on, I have bent history a bit.

Most notably and deliberately, I altered the history of Middleton Place. Even today, the plantation is breathtakingly beautiful. If you get to Charleston, it is a must see. However, I want to be clear, it was never owned by the McLeods and has been in the Middleton family since 1741.

If you've never had Lowcountry cooking, you're in for a real treat when you get to the back of this book. *Huge* thanks to Executive Chef Frank Lee of S.N.O.B. for sharing your fabulous recipes. I am so grateful to Dick Elliott of Maverick Southern Kitchens and Susannah Runkle for coordinating this project to spread the gospel of Lowcountry cuisine.

Thanks to Charles Bierbauer and Elizabeth Quackenbush of the University of South Carolina School of Journalism for your support. So proud to be a product of that school. GO GAMECOCKS! Thanks also to Bob Webster and the good folks at Palmetto Moon across South Carolina. Yes, I borrowed my wonderful title from his clothing stores.

Author Harlan Greene, head of special collections of the College of Charleston, was gracious and helpful, pointing me toward historical support for Reginald Sheridan's character. Reading Harlan's work gave me a clear vision of what it might have been like to be gay in the south in 1947. Also a wonderful author, Valerie Perry, Aiken-Rhett Museum manager at Historic Charleston Foundation, is the truest lover of history I know. Thank you for answering my questions, for your generous spirit and friendship.

While Charleston is indeed the crown jewel of South Carolina, there are so many wonderful towns that add their own unique flavor, particularly in the Lowcountry. Thanks to Dana Cheney and his lovely wife, Bonita, for introducing me to the history of Colleton County and showing me around Walterboro and Round O. That you found "Miss Mamie's boarding house" now and circa 1947 is remarkable and still gives me chill bumps.

I'm forever grateful to my writers' group members—Wendy Oglesby, Mary Ann Thomas, Vera LaFleur, Claire Iannini, Kim Blum-Hyclack, and Susan Martin. Your love and support are invaluable.

Last, but never least, to Mama and Daddy, and to my family—Mike, Kaley, and Austin, I love you all. You are my heart.

·Chapter One·

CHARLESTON, SOUTH CAROLINA

JUNE 20, 1947

"Murrah?" Rosa Lee's eyes go wide and she shakes her head at me like I've forgotten the rules, but I haven't. Since before I was born, my parents forbade the servants to speak their native tongue in our house. Offenders were given one warning; a second offense brought immediate dismissal. I say the Gullah word again, drawing it out softly. "Why are you crying?" The hands that helped bring me into the world motion for me to lower my voice.

Rosa Lee's husband, Desmond, told me my first word was *murrah*. It was what I called Rosa Lee, until Mother made me call her by name. *"My own murrah."* The forbidden words bring more tears. I press my face into the soft curve of her neck and breathe in the Ivory soap Mother insists all the servants use, mingled with Rosa Lee's own scent—vanilla and lemongrass.

She holds me at arm's length, trembling, and I know I've done it again.

"You got to tell them," she pleads. "Make them see you can't go through with this."

I point to the door that leads to the elegant dining room where my parents are eating their breakfast. "I have told them. Mother refuses to listen, and I've begged Father. He says I *have* to do this." She looks away. Her body rocks, sobbing violently on the inside. "Rosa Lee, please don't cry. I can't bear it." She shakes her head and swipes at the tears that stain the sleeve of her freshly pressed uniform. "I won't do it again. I promise."

"When you're asleep, your heart takes over. You got no control, and it's gonna kill you."

She's right. Since I graduated and moved home from college two weeks ago, I've been sleepwalking like I did when I was a child, but these outings don't land me snuggled up in the servant's quarters, between Desmond and Rosa Lee. Most of the time, I wake up and return to bed without incident, but last week Desmond found me trying to leave the house. He said I was babbling about sleeping in the bay, which might not have been so disturbing if I hadn't been wearing five layers of heavy clothing. I knew what he thought I was trying to do to myself and told him not to worry.

Since then, Rosa Lee has insisted on sleeping on the stiff brocade chaise in my bedroom. Of course, my parents don't know she's there or that she's so afraid I'll walk to the bay or step off the balcony in my sleep, she's tethered my ankle to the bedpost with three yards of satin rope she begged from Mrs. O'Doul.

"Maybe it will be different after the wedding." I love her enough to lie to her. "Father says I'm a Hadley and once it's over with, I'll fall in line the way I was born to."

"But what if Desmond hadn't caught you?" She threads her fingers in mine and kisses the back of my hand. A part of me wishes her intuition hadn't sent Desmond to check on me, that he hadn't found me. "And what are you gonna do when we're not there?"

"Don't say that." My knees buckle, and I melt into a puddle at her feet. Justin has made it clear he's happy with his staff and has no plans to add "two ancient servants." But living under his roof and not having Rosa Lee and Desmond with me is unthinkable, another high price of being the last Hadley descendant.

"You think it's not going to get worse after you're married? Who do you think's gonna be there to save you? Mr. Justin?" She hisses the last word. "You think long and hard before the sun comes up tomorrow, because I'm afraid down to my bones that you won't be alive to see it."

She collects herself and heads into the dining room to check on my parents. They won't look into her beautiful brown face and see she's been crying any more than they see this wedding is killing me, or at least the idea of being yoked to Justin McLeod is. Not because he's eight years older than me and, other than our station in life, we have nothing in common, and not because of his good qualities, although no one can find more than two: He is a heart-stoppingly beautiful man and the sole heir to the largest fortune in Charleston.

For over a hundred years, Justin's family and mine have built ships. And while two world wars made us rich, a prolonged peace threatens to weaken our family fortunes considerably. Somewhere in all that, my father convinced Justin a Hadley-McLeod union would position them to take over the world, at least the shipping world. And Father is certain nothing short of a blood union will keep Justin in the partnership.

Rosa Lee pushes through the swinging door and pours the coffee down the drain, her signal that breakfast is over and my parents are no longer close by. I smile, trying to reassure her I'm okay, that I'm going to be okay. She shakes her head and starts to wash one of the breakfast plates in slow motion, barely breathing. I hate those things, and after tomorrow, I'll own twenty-four place settings of them, part of my dowry. I don't give a damn about thousand-dollar plates, but I do care for Rosa Lee.

"I can do this," I say from behind her. My voice sounds sure, steady. "I will do this."

"You and I both know you can't walk down that aisle. Dear God in heaven, Vada, *tell them*." Her head is down, and she says the last two words like a prayer. "Make them see so they'll put a stop to this foolishness."

There's no point. I've begged my parents, told them I can't marry Justin, because I don't love him. I've told them I feel nothing for him, not love, not even hate. Even after I told my father about the other women, he shrugged and said I was being ridiculous. "There are no fairy-tale marriages, Vada. Know your place, your purpose. Marry. Procreate. Continue the lineage. That's your job."

This archaic arrangement is not the job I want or the one I applied for. My heart races at the thought of how furious my parents would be if they knew my favorite professor recommended me for a teaching position, not in a posh boarding school but a two-room schoolhouse near a tiny crossroads community. Mother would fume silently while Father would remind me that no Hadley woman has ever worked.

But it's 1947 for goodness' sake. What did they expect when they sent me away to college, that I would learn everything *except* how to think for myself? The swell of defiance is snuffed out by Justin's testy voice in the foyer. "Well, I am here now, madam. What do you want?"

I can't make out what my mother is saying and slip behind the dining-room door. From where I peer at them through the crack between the jamb, she looks tiny compared to him, but she emanates such presence. Justin has the posture of a rebellious teenager.

"It's about Vada, and I am not talking about this here." She points toward the study. He eyes her for a moment, knowing full well the drawing room is a woman's place, the study a man's domain for brandy and smelly cigars.

I can hardly breathe as she leads Justin into the study. Maybe she did listen. Maybe she's finally going to tell Justin the wedding is off. The door to the study is slightly ajar. I slip off my shoes and tiptoe across the foyer to hear her say the words I've longed for since I was fourteen and learned about this horrible arrangement.

"You have me up before noon for this?" Justin is glaring at her, but she's so strong, so beautiful. She's not intimidated in the least.

"You must understand that Vada is a young girl, barely twenty. I heard the things she told her father. Your carousing."

"My carousing?" He laughs and runs his hands through his short dark hair.

"Yes. The parties. The women. After the engagement, I thought you would change, settle down. Surely you don't expect to carry on as usual after the wedding."

Justin is no longer amused. His face is red, the veins in his forehead pronounced. "Let me remind you, madam, after tomorrow, I may be your daughter's husband, but I'll carry on at my own discretion, not yours, not your husband's, and certainly not your Vada's."

Their standoff is palpable. Mother throws her hands up in disgust. "I shouldn't even have to have this conversation with you, Justin, but Vada is extremely unhappy, and the very least you could do is try to be more accommodating."

"More accommodating?"

"Just tell me, what is it going to take?"

"I beg your pardon?"

"Your price. To be a proper husband. Doting. Monogamous." She draws the last word out.

"Trust me, madam, you don't have enough money." He stands and straightens the sleeves of his suit. "We're done here."

"Justin." My mother grabs his arm. He towers over her. "*Don't* hurt her."

Her steely look is returned with amusement. "My dear Mrs. Hadley, for Vada or me to get hurt, one of us would actually have to care about this union. Tomorrow we marry together two fortunes for the greater good. Nothing more."

"But you expect her to be a proper wife?"

"Of course. Why shouldn't she?"

"Your level of arrogance is remarkable, Justin, even for you. Get out of my house."

He makes an exaggerated bow. "Good day, Mrs. Hadley."

The door opens, and Justin stands there for a moment, looking at my tearstained face. He sighs and pushes past me. "Really, Vada, after tomorrow, I'll expect you to be more presentable in the mornings."

I've honored Mrs. O'Doul's refusal to talk about Darby for three years now, but with the wedding looming, the loss feels fresh, and I can't help myself. "I miss her."

Mrs. O'Doul gives me a hard look to remind me of our silent agreement not to talk about her daughter, my best friend. She nods curtly as she scrutinizes my dress, which she's had to take in, again, for the rehearsal party. "You'll be a good wife. You'll make your ma and da proud."

I shake my head at my reflection and the exquisite design that looks funny with my bare feet. "Maybe it's best Darby's not here. She'd be so ashamed of me."

"Who knows where that girl is now? And, to be sure, she'd be ashamed if she showed her face around here, but not because you're marrying Justin McLeod, I can tell you that."

"She's your daughter. You can't still be mad at her."

Another stern look reminds me Mrs. O'Doul lost more than a daughter when Darby was run out of town for her tryst with Mr. McCrady. But Mrs. McCrady didn't stop there. She made sure Mrs. O'Doul's wealthy clients boycotted her dressmaking business. Darby's mother lost everything: her daughter, her shop, her apartment. My parents fussed when I insisted on Mrs. O'Doul altering my trousseau, but Mrs. O'Doul said it brought some of her customers back, the only good thing that has come from this wedding plan.

She smooths her hands down the seams of the ivory bodice and inspects a tiny pucker. "Damn beads." She works the seam with her fingers until it lies flat, then steps back and inspects the dress. Her smile is thin, almost sad. "I remember every dress I ever made for you. And now look at you, wearing couture since you were sixteen. Getting married tomorrow in the finest dress I've ever seen."

She's right. I've always had a shameless love for beautiful clothes, even more so for shoes. But when Mrs. O'Doul made something for me, it meant going to Habberman's on King Street. She always said Darby and me went together like grits and gravy, she couldn't very well take one of us shopping without taking the other. While she selected the perfect material for my dress, we played hide-and-seek among the tall bolts leaned against the walls.

Sometimes we sorted through bins of loose buttons or rhinestones and talked about what our lives would be like when we grew up.

As I got older, I worried that Darby would be jealous of the dresses her mother made for me. I know I would have been. But Darby said she didn't care—they were just dresses, and we were best friends, the grits-and-gravy kind.

The other girls Darby grew up with wanted nothing to do with her after I went away to college. She gave up a lot to be my friend, and how did I repay her? I didn't make time to phone her or return her letters. I was so wrapped up in things that didn't matter, I forgot about the one person who mattered most to me. And by the time I heard Darby had been banished from Charleston, I was too ashamed of what I'd done, of the way I treated her, to try to find her, to tell her how very sorry I was.

"You're a stunning young woman, Vada Hadley, and that dress—"

"The clothes you made, they were just as beautiful, and they meant something to me."

She scoffs and puts her tools away, satisfied that my dress looks the way Jacques Fath intended when he designed it. "You'll not find the likes of this fabric on King Street, I can promise you that. And if you did, I wouldn't know where to begin to make something this . . . perfect. And your wedding dress? Even grander, Vada. Really." She pushes a strand of hair behind my ear. "You're going to be a beautiful bride."

All through the rehearsal and this ridiculous party, everyone has said those words to me, like somehow the way I look will determine the outcome of this union. But nothing changes the fact that this is a mistake.

The canvas of the massive white tent billows a little, and the night air is damp and thick. Well-wishing men dab at their foreheads with handkerchiefs, and little beads of sweat line the lips of pretty women who are sweltering in the late-June heat. But even their intrusions can't hold my attention from the Ashley as it flows past Middleton Place. I can't stop looking at the river, thinking about it. Where does it go? To Edisto? To Savannah? Does it matter? It's free, unencumbered by family and duty.

"Tears of joy?" Justin's famous second cousin, Josephine, dabs at my face. I shake my head and turn my attention back to the river. "Middleton Place is stunning. And while I do have El Dorado, in my bones I know this plantation shouldn't have ended up with the McLeods, least of all Justin. But the gods split the lot the way they saw fit. Perhaps they intended for it to be your consolation prize."

"Does it console you, Miss Pinckney?" I ask.

"Words console me."

"Of course they do, your books. The movie."

She laughs and shakes her head. "Yes, the movie. Well, I don't think *Three O'Clock Dinner* will ever make its way to the theater, my dear. I hear Lana Turner's off again, to Mexico this time, vacationing with Tyrone Power, and who knows who it will be next? Those Hollywood folks don't know what they want, not really. Besides, I don't *need* a consolation prize. But you? I'm not so sure."

Most of the women here would kill for Josephine Pinckney's lineage alone, much less her present status as the darling of the literary world. They comfort themselves with catty remarks and whisper that she's plain and was never beautiful. But even in the moonlight, there's something about her knowing look and those piercing eyes that make her stunning and powerful.

"Walk with me?" she says.

I nod and step toward the grassy steps that lead to the river and away from the party. Breaking a heel is the least of my worries, but instinctively I tiptoe across the boards that stretch out across the water, and Miss Pinckney does the same. The river makes a swishing sound and cuts hard around the posts that anchor the dock into the muddy bottom, and the waxing crescent of the palmetto moon dips low across the marsh grass. A fish skips like a stone over the top of the silvery black water, and for the first time tonight, I feel like I can breathe.

"*Run out—run out from the insane gold world, softly clanging the gate lest any follow.*" I'm not sure if she's quoting her books or one of her poems, but even in my hopelessness, I feel her silent prodding.

"I don't want this."

She's quiet for a beat. "What *do* you want, Vada?"

"What I can't have."

"Something you can't have. Really? The only child of Matthew and Katherine Hadley? I speak from experience as an *only* child born into the pinnacle of this caste system we live in, there's nothing you can't have."

"You're—wrong." The sob building inside threatens to turn me inside out, so everyone can see the truth that doesn't seem to matter to anybody. Not my parents, not Justin, and least of all the party lemmings.

"Then what is it?"

I'm shivering in this heat, teeth chattering, unable to answer. All I can do is point to the river as it flows away from this horrible mess and escapes toward the ocean.

"*You* are wrong, Vada Hadley." She wraps her silk stole around me and kisses my tearstained cheek. "You can have anything you want."

·Chapter Two·

Just before midnight, we arrive back at 32 Legare Street. Refusing to eat or drink anything has only left me feeling light-headed, drugged. As Desmond opens the iron gates, my father says something to me, but I don't answer.

"I'm speaking to you, Vada." I nod. "As I was saying, my great-great-grandmother's mother . . ."

"Oh, Matthew," Mother says, "you're not going to tell that story now. It's late, and we're all tired."

"Katherine, this is our history, Vada's history, so yes, the story bears repeating."

Mother rolls her eyes. She and I know what's coming.

"Maria Whaley was just fifteen years old in 1829 when she scaled this very gate to marry George F. Morris, and without her parents' permission, I might add."

"It's a legend, Matthew, a fairy tale for the young women to swoon over when 32 Legare was a girls' school. If it is true, and I highly doubt that it is, Maria Whaley was *escaping* the premises. That's hardly a tale to tell your daughter on the eve of her wedding," my mother says. "Besides, a colonial woman of good breeding, hoisting herself over the Sword Gates? Impossible."

"My point is, Maria Whaley had only met Morris a few times at dances, parties, and such. She barely knew the man and yet she put her mind to it and learned to love him so very much, and in such a short time, that she made her own miracle."

"Matthew. Please," my mother groans and massages her temples. "The story is inappropriate, and worst of all, George Morris was a *Yankee*."

Desmond pulls the car around to the piazza and lets us out. My father continues the lesson as I start up the main staircase, past menacing-looking oil portraits of my ancestors that used to terrify me as a child. I stop midway, and my parents push past me, arguing the merits of family history versus silence. Maria Whaley looks back at me, frozen in time with a thin smile. It feels like she's mocking me, reminding me that she escaped to marry the man she wanted and I'm locked behind these gates in a marriage pact I have no say over. I reach out and touch her face. Whether her story is fact or fiction, there's something about her that has lasted for over a hundred years. She looks brave, and, like Josephine, very wise.

I throw open the door to my bedroom, and I am immediately assaulted by my wedding dress. It hangs on a hook on the back side of my open closet door. Beside it, the cathedral-length train makes a wide river of white illusion across the room. A perfect pair of white satin Salvatore Ferragamo pumps glisten in the dim light. All of this is Rosa Lee's doing, a last-ditch effort to show me my future in hopes that I'll change things before it's too late.

Three trunks are packed for a monthlong cruise to Europe. The thought of being trapped on a boat with Justin cuts my legs from under me, and I plop down on the floor in the middle of the illusion. There's a soft knock at my door, and it opens. Rosa Lee stands there in her robe. Her hair, which is usually in a tight bun, is past her shoulders. As she steps into my room, I can see that like me, she's all cried out. She closes the door behind her and throws a large old suitcase on the bed. One of the latches sticks as she tries to open it, but it finally does, and the suitcase is empty.

"You got no more chances. Come morning, it'll start up and you won't be able to stop it, but you can now. Desmond's dressed and ready to take you wherever you want to go."

I hang my head and dissolve into the illusion.

"*Child*," Rosa Lee hisses, snapping me to attention. "I didn't raise you to go along to get along. Do you want to marry that boy or not?"

"*No*." I'm surprised how strong my voice sounds.

"Well, when folks who are supposed to love you won't listen, you got to listen to yourself. What's yourself telling you, child?"

Her words propel me off the floor. I grab four dresses out of my closet and stuff them in the suitcase. I unsnap the trunk that holds my shoes and take no time to labor over picking favorites. Three pairs of sandals and a pair of pumps will have to do. My heart stops when Rosa Lee takes the dresses out of the suitcase and puts them aside.

"Not like this. You'll be home in a week, and much as I like the sound of that, I know you won't be happy." She sets about rolling them up into tight long bundles so that I can have a proper summer wardrobe and two extra pairs of shoes. "I can fit two more dresses, maybe three if they don't have a crinoline."

She stuffs my makeup bag and my lingerie under the dresses, and when she thinks I'm not looking, pulls a little pouch out of her bosom and tucks it into the suitcase. "No, Rosa Lee, this is your *tredjuh*." Even though my parents are sound asleep in the opposite wing of the house, I whisper the Gullah word and try to give her treasure back to her.

"Child, I love you, but you don't have the first idea of how to make it out there in the world. You don't know what it's like, trying to make two ends meet." She closes my hand over the pouch and shakes her head. "Lord, I'm going to worry myself to death, so you take this money. I wish it was more, but it's all I've got, and you gonna need it."

I try to give the pouch back again, but she won't hear of it. "You fit in, you hear? You make whatever you do work to your good," she says through tears, "and if you don't need this, I want you to have it anyways. You're my child. Always gonna be my child."

Another soft knock at the door makes me freeze. "Rosa Lee?" She opens the door and pulls Desmond into my room. He looks at me and smiles. "Well, looks like we're going someplace after all."

I hug them both. My heart is racing like a hummingbird as Desmond picks up the suitcase. "Wait." They both look at me, afraid that I've lost my nerve. I grab a blue A-line dress out of my closet and dash behind the antique screen. I slip out of my gown and into the dress I bought before I graduated.

Rosa Lee zips me up and unhooks my grandmother's necklace. "Take this for sure, but keep it hid. You hear?"

"Yes, ma'am." I drop the necklace into the small satin pouch the garters for my wedding came in.

"Don't you keep that necklace anywhere but in your bosom. And nobody better be getting it there." She straightens my Peter Pan collar and tucks in my tag. "Sears. I knew you had the gumption all along." She turns me around to face her and is trying to look stern, but the tears and her quivering chin give her away. "Please, child, I beg you, promise me you'll watch for the signs like I taught you. Make them work to your good."

"I promise." I hug her close one last time.

She holds me at arm's length. "You'll be fine. You hear? I love you, child. I love you." My heart breaks as she sputters out the words. "Desmond, y'all best go. And hurry."

Going down the stairs, Desmond bumps the suitcase, and I freeze. "This house is so big, they won't hear a thing," he says and bumps it again to prove it.

We walk around to the back gate to the old truck Desmond sometimes borrows from his brother. He throws my suitcase into the back, and I'm in the truck before he can open the door for me. "Know where you're going?"

"The bus station."

"No, ma'am, you're not." He shakes his head at me. "Besides that and the train station is probably the first place they'll look."

"Please, Desmond, I'll take the first bus out."

"I'm not saying the man behind the desk is going to recognize you, but he'll remember your pretty face. Your daddy will track you down for sure if you leave by bus or train."

"I'm not going to get you in trouble. What if Mother or Father needs you to drive them and you're not there?"

"Middle of the night?" His hands knead the steering wheel, and he stares straight ahead. "That hasn't happened since the night you were born. You came so fast into the world, right as we were pulling in to the hospital. If Rosa Lee hadn't caught you, you would have plopped right onto the floorboard." He looks at me. "You stole our hearts that night, and if you think I'm gonna drop you off at some bus station, you got another thing coming."

"But there's an even greater risk—" He shakes his head. If something happens, if the wrong people see me with Desmond, it could cost him more than his job. It could cost him his life. I grab my purse and open the truck door. "I'll drive myself."

"Your shiny red Cadillac will for sure get everybody's attention. Now I'm gonna drive you and that's that." He puts his hand on my arm. "And don't you worry about me. No risk is too great. Now you close that door this minute and tell me where to."

"Round O."

He gives me an incredulous look but starts up the truck, and we escape past the Sword Gates into the palmetto moon night.

A little over an hour later, we roll into a crossroads community so small, it doesn't even have a road sign. The boardinghouse is there, just like my professor said it would be. Nothing fancy, but grand compared to the half dozen or so houses around. There's a long clapboard building that claims to be a diner, a general store, and a post office.

Desmond kills the engine. "I was thinking if you were running away, you might want to go a little farther from Charleston than fifty miles."

"There's a job here." I can't believe this is really happening. "A teaching job."

"Well." He looks around the place. "When your daddy starts looking for you, I can guarantee this is the last place he'll look."

I throw my arms around him and breathe in the sweet scent of pipe tobacco one last time. "You need to go before someone sees us."

"No, ma'am. I'll wait until this joint opens."

"No, Desmond. It's dangerous enough that you'll be driving back to Charleston so late. Look, there's a porch swing. The sun will be up in a few hours; I'll be safe there. Please, Desmond. For me."

He takes his hat off and fiddles with it. "Guess this is good-bye."

I nod and press a piece of paper into his hand. "For emergencies."

He stares at the paper, smiling. "Well now, you did plan this out."

"I had bits and pieces of a plan, but when I came home I stopped believing this was possible. I don't know what I would have done if Rosa Lee hadn't come to my room tonight, if you hadn't brought me here. I owe you both so much, thank-you seems puny."

He looks at the boardinghouse address and phone number I've written down, rips the bottom half of the page off, and scribbles his brother's address. "You need me or Rosa Lee, just let Charles know, and he'll pass on the message. And don't you worry none. Your secret's safe with us."

It's just before three when Desmond pulls away. I lean my back against the arm of the porch swing, ball my knees up to my chest, and pull the store-bought dress down over my ankles.

The night air is thick and humid. Claire Greeley stands by the open window, bouncing her three-year-old boy back to sleep. She alternates between watching the two figures in the truck in the driveway and glaring at her older sons, Daniel and Peter, who are sound asleep in the twin bed next to hers. They look angelic in the bed they share with their baby brother, Jonathan, but right now, she'd love to pinch their heads off for telling the poor little guy stories about the boogieman.

Jonathan makes a little grunt, like he used to when he was a baby. The sound makes Claire feel lonely and reminds her of everything her husband has missed. She breathes into the crook of the boy's sweaty little neck, wishing she could catch a whiff of his baby smell just one last time. But at three, the scent is long gone, and when the child is awake, his sole focus is being a big boy like his brothers.

The idea of Claire's boys growing up leaves her exhausted, something she's grown accustomed to since her husband died in the war. She isn't exactly sure when the feeling set in, but she's felt this way for so long, it's hard to imagine what it would be like not to feel this way. At first, the exhaustion came from the grief, then anger, but at some point during the past four years, it's come from sheer worry. While she worries about normal everyday things, like who those two figures are in the truck and what they want at this ungodly hour, mostly she worries about her boys.

How long can they share this small room? One tiny bed? How long will she be able to make them follow all of Miss Mamie's ridiculous rules? Up until now, it's been easy to keep them in line. The fact that they're all terrified of the old bat helps, but what about when they get older? The worst question doesn't just keep Claire up at night; it follows her around every second of every day. How can she possibly make up for her boys not having a father?

She hears the truck doors open and pulls back the curtain to get a better look at the two people below. There is just enough light from the slight moon to see one is a white woman, the other, dark, maybe colored. Jonathan's breath stutters a little. Claire turns her attention away from the window and holds him a little closer. His gangly limbs bounce against her, reminding her how big he is, how big Daniel and Peter are, too.

The woman hugs the dark figure and then takes her suitcase

up the front steps. The man gets into the truck and drives away. Claire puts Jonathan beside his brothers, who lie straight and tall like sleeping soldiers. She goes back to the window.

She wonders who the woman is and why she came here in the middle of the night. From the window, Claire can't see the porch, but she can hear the old swing creaking slower and slower, until it stops. She imagines the woman has fallen asleep. Her intuition tells her the woman isn't trouble. Hopefully, knowing who she is and why she came to Round O tomorrow will confirm that. Her heart flutters a bit as she crawls back into bed. Claire hopes the woman is kind and maybe close to her age. It's been so long since she had a friend, a true friend, it's almost too much to hope for.

Something hard jabs at my ribs, and I awake to see an old woman poking me with a broom handle. "No vagrants here. Move along now or I'll call the county sheriff."

I wipe my mouth with the back of my hand, and the gray woman gives me another poke for good measure. "*Oww.* Stop that." I push the broom away. "I'm no vagrant."

The boxy gray-haired woman glares at me. "Who are you and what do you want?" The crusty tone of her skin matches her gray dress and shoes.

"I'm Vada *Hadley*," I say in a huff, stupidly, without thinking. This may be the shortest stint for a runaway in the history of runaways. I pause for a beat. My name means nothing to her. Elation bubbles up. *My name means nothing to her.*

She looks at my suitcase and mumbles something about it being a beat-up old piece of grip. "If you're here for a room, I've got none. Move on."

"But your sign says you *do* have a vacancy."

"You on my doorstep like a boxcar orphan first thing this morning? Who knows what kind of riffraff you are. I got a room, but not for you, missy."

"I know this may not look proper, but my father dropped me off early this morning, before you opened up. He didn't want to leave me here alone, but he had to get back to go work. I told him this looked like such a fine establishment, I was sure I'd be okay."

She starts to jab me again in the ribs, and I push the broom away. "I said, move on."

There's no place else to go, no hotel, not even a motel. And the town isn't really a town at all—just a spot where two country roads crisscross. A few tiny clapboard houses are scattered about, along with a lone church and some kind of business that claims to be a diner, a general store, and a post office all rolled into one. I look at the sign again, *Miss Mamie's Boarding House—VACANCY*. Okay, Vada, vinegar or honey? Honey or vinegar? Decide.

"Miss Mamie, I'm interviewing for a teaching position at the school on Monday."

"I don't care. You're not staying here."

"I'd greatly appreciate if I could stay until I have the interview. I'd pay you, of course, and if I get the job, I'll pay you three months in advance."

She looks at Rosa Lee's suitcase again and narrows her eyes. "I don't think you have that kind of money, but make it six months and you can stay. Twenty dollars a month, five a piece for tonight and Sunday. No job, no room, and you move on like the vagrant I'm sure you are."

"Agreed." I reach to shake on it, but she turns on the heels of her awful shoes and goes back inside.

"Room's at the top of the stairs. No drinking. No smoking.

Breakfast is at seven," she yells over her shoulder before disappearing down the hallway. "If you're not there, you don't eat."

I open the screen door and step into a large parlor with drab burgundy furniture. There are no pictures over the fireplace and no personal items that might make the house look like a home. A telephone table is to the left of the stairs, with a cardboard sign that says, BOARDERS MAY NOT USE THE PHONE. From the clatter, I'm guessing the hallway from the living room leads to a kitchen and, maybe, a dining room. I take my suitcase upstairs, looking for some clues about Miss Mamie, something I can use to butter her up, but there is nothing.

The room she assigned me is fine, really, although the bed looks more like a cot. There's a basin to wash up with and at least one bathroom that I saw in the hallway. Yes, this should do just fine, but I can't decide if unpacking is confident or bad luck, so I put the suitcase on the luggage rack and lie down. Just for a moment.

"Pretty." I hear a child's voice and awake to see three lovely boys inspecting me. The youngest, who is maybe four, strokes my hair again. "Pretty."

I prop up on my elbows and smile at them. "Hello, my name is Vada."

The serious one nods and grabs the little boy's hand. "I'm Daniel. These are my brothers, Peter and Jonathan."

"Jonathan," the little one echoes.

"It's nice to meet you boys."

"You missed breakfast and lunch," Daniel says. "Our mother told us to get you up for dinner. Her name is Claire. You'll like her."

"I'm sure I will." He nods and punches the middle brother, who said something under his breath. "What did you say, Peter?"

"I'm sorry, he was being rude." Daniel gives Peter another shot in the arm.

"*Owww*," he whines and hits his brother back. "I said you don't *look* like a reprobate, and you don't."

I laugh. "Good to know."

For three young children, they're awfully quiet as they make their way down the stairs. A lovely woman dressed in black, not much older than me, pokes her head out of the doorway. "You met my boys."

"Yes, they're adorable." I straighten my dress, which looks like a disaster after being slept in. It slips off of my shoulder and I push it back up. "I must look a mess. I'm Vada."

"Claire Greeley." Her smile is friendly. "You're very beautiful, Vada. I'm sure Daniel's already head over heels for you. He is at the age where he's noticing girls."

"What does his father think about that?"

Her smile fades and she looks at the floor. I say I'm sorry, but she shakes her head like she can't bear another apology that won't bring her husband back. She pinches at the shoulder seam of my dress and laughs when it falls down my arm again. "I could fix that for you, if you want."

"Really?"

"I take in sewing, alterations mostly. I'm happy to take your dress up, maybe after the boys go down for the night."

"Thank you, Claire, you're so kind."

"And so grateful to have another woman in the house." *Besides the horrible Miss Mamie.* We look at each other like twins, amused at identical unspoken thoughts. "Better come to supper, though. Miss Mamie normally doesn't care if we miss meals, but after you missed breakfast and dinner—"

"What?"

"She says if you miss another meal, she's going to throw you out for being sick."

"Can she do that?"

"I respectfully told her you're no Typhoid Mary, but it is her place. She does anything she wants."

Claire has a sweet face full of a thousand questions she is too polite to ask. "Thanks for telling me."

"Of course. I look forward to getting to know you, Vada."

The door closes behind Claire. In her absence and without the thrill of convincing the old bat to let me stay, I see the room for what it really is. The gray flowered wallpaper looks like it might have been lavender at one time. Wild roses meander in an intertwining pattern with plump cherubs, and I'm certain Miss Mamie was not the decorator. But if she wasn't, who was? When I sit up on the edge of the bed, the mattress dips into the slats that are too far apart. I run my hand over the small bedside table that smells sweet, almost like bourbon, and open the drawers. There's nothing but a dark brown stain, most likely evidence of how the last poor boarder survived, or the reason they were expelled.

A rickety-looking basin stand is beside the window with two threadbare towels folded over the spindle railing. My old suitcase sits on the luggage rack, a reminder of my old life and Rosa Lee and Desmond's sacrifice. I'm sure when my absence was discovered, they were lined up with the rest of the staff and interrogated, but if anyone had looked on the Harrington chest in the foyer, they'd have seen the note I'd debated leaving. It was short, but not because I didn't have time. I'd written it weeks earlier and stashed it in the pocket of my Sears dress. A lengthy explanation would have been a waste of ink and paper.

Dear Mother and Father,

I cannot live in the world you've planned for me, and regret circumstances have forced me to leave. Do not worry about me. As you've so often reminded me, I'm a Hadley. I will make my mark on the world.

Love, Vada.

It's hard not to think about Darby, what leaving must have been like for her. Did Mrs. O'Doul pack her suitcase like Rosa Lee packed mine? Did she hold Darby close and tell her she loved her before she sent her away? Did Darby land someplace dreadful, or was she too heartbroken over what happened with Mr. McCrady to even notice? No. Darby is too Irish not to land on her feet, and too brave not to grab life by the scruff of the neck and shake it until she gets what she wants.

The latches on the suitcase don't stick this time, and seven dresses rise and expand like fat colorful loaves. The modest chifforobe has the appearance of a pine coffin stood on end and only has four hangers. I loop two sleeveless dresses on each hanger. The tags scream the names I've grown to love but will never be able to afford in my new life. Dior, Chanel, Nina Ricci. My thumb skims across the large showy Hardy Amies label before I rummage through the contents of my makeup bag to find the cuticle scissors. My hands shake as my finger slips under the satin squares.

Knowing Darby is out there somewhere and she's made a brave new life for herself makes me believe I can do it, too. I snip away the small neat stitches that anchor tags to dresses that are so beautiful, they used to make my heart ache. The excitement buzzes in my chest and grows a little stronger as each tag falls onto the scarred pine floor. I keep at it until I've cut away my past for good.

·Chapter Three·

Frank Darling moves slower than a two-legged coon dog on a Monday morning. It doesn't matter that it is Monday, lately his days at the Sit Down Diner are all the same. He knows the feeling comes from the thud in his gut that came when he had to turn tail and come back to Round O, something he swore he'd never do.

When he turned eighteen, he tried to join the Navy to see the world. That was just before the war began, and with no boogiemen like Hitler and Mussolini trying to take over the world, there wasn't a really high demand for soldiers, but he joined anyway.

The Navy said he had a weak heart, a murmur. Nothing to worry about, the moonfaced nurse had promised as she stamped his file with thick black ink. REJECTED. His next physical, he coughed like he had the pleurisy and not just when he was supposed to. But the Marines, the Army, and the Air Force were all wise to that trick. Even the Coast Guard passed on him.

He was so torn up after that, he did the only thing he could do and came back to Round O. That was ten years ago, and ever since, Frank believes he can hear his defect mocking him. It happens on days like today, when there's a little breeze in the air, when the sky is fresh out of clouds, and the "Halls of Montezuma" sounds like a real place he'll never see from this hellhole.

Frank used to wish this place was the real Round O in Texas, but it's just some Podunk crossroads in South Carolina, a town where people live and die without much in between. Running the diner is as redundant as the name of the town, but Frank would rather die than wallow in public pity. Most days, he wakes up and tries to picture his life different, like if he tries hard enough, he can make it so. Every time he turns an egg or a hoecake on the griddle, he pictures his life turning, changing into something more than six days a week at the Sit Down Diner. Unfortunately, today is not one of those days.

"Two eggs. Spank 'em. Grits, extra butter. Biscuits. Bacon." Tiny's booming voice startles him; she seems to get a motherly kind of satisfaction out of getting his mind back on the griddle. "Today's just like yesterday, shug. Same as tomorrow." He gives her a dirty look, and she runs her hand through her hair so that only Frank can see she's giving him the finger. "Who went and stomped on your biscuits this morning?"

Frank nods at the order Tiny puts on the carousel and cracks an egg with each hand; they settle onto the griddle and begin to harden. Tiny pops her gum and raises her eyebrows at him, waiting for a wisecrack, but he's fresh out of snappy comebacks.

"You better spank those eggs and fry them hard, Frank, or you'll be doing 'em again."

Frank glances up at the next order and catches sight of the veiled image of a woman through the screen door. The morning sun outlines her small frame, and he doesn't have to see her face to know she's beautiful. He flips a salmon croquette and waits for her to open the door. It sizzles and he imagines what it would be like to love her the moment he lays eyes on her. Sure it sounds trite, but not compared to working ten-hour days at the diner. It's a good word to describe Frank's job, the diner. Hell, the whole crossroads is commonplace, as stale as yesterday's mackerel.

The woman is still on the other side of the screen. His heart pounds, but the murmur doesn't sound like it usually does, sloshy like an old wringer washing machine on its last leg. No, he feels the sound of each chamber opening and closing, strong, like a big bass drum, beating for the woman behind the screen.

Old Joe Pike clears his throat in a guttural way that always makes the ladies cringe, and even turns the heads at the back table, where the truckers sit. The woman hesitates like she's rethinking the sameness of her own life and stands in the threshold for so long, Frank panics. Maybe there is a God, and if there is, Frank's in trouble for thumbing his nose up at him for a multitude of sins, some of them his own. That last thought lays into Frank like a good stiff punch, and he almost drops the heavy skillet he yanked off the back burner the moment he saw her.

The door opens slowly. Even from Frank's cubbyhole, her face is luminous, a word never used about women in Round O, no matter how old or young they might be. Still, seeing the woman standing there, backlit by the promise of a new day, takes his breath away.

She looks surprised, maybe even a little embarrassed that Tiny knows she is new in the area, and blushes as Tiny sets about taking her order and prying into her business. Frank's daddy used to bawl Tiny out for being such a busybody. After he left the diner to Frank, there were times Frank used to get on the old woman good for being so nosey, but not today.

"Need a minute?" The woman shakes her head and Tiny seems satisfied with her bashful answers that can't be heard above the clatter. Frank wants to holler out from the kitchen for everyone to shut up so he can hear her voice.

"Crab cakes, grits, and tea—with milk of all things." Tiny winks at him, and he wills himself not to beg her for another morsel. "Single." She belts out the word and twirls the carousel so hard, the tickets nearly fly off.

If Frank wasn't so elated over the woman's marital status, he'd be mortified by Tiny's lack of discretion. "Vada," Tiny half mouths, half says under her breath. "Vada Hadley."

Every cell careens around Frank's body, crashing into one another, screaming her name. Straight away, he scoops up a handful of the crab cake he mixed up around five this morning, but then throws it back into the bowl. He should mix up a new batch and make sure they're the best damn crab cakes she's ever had, but that might take too long.

A bead of sweat drops off of Frank's forehead, and he misses catching it before it falls into the bowl, because he's distracted by the way she holds her cup with two hands. Her elbows perch on the table in a way that makes it look like perfect etiquette. She finishes her tea, adjusts the little chain that keeps her sweater around her shoulders, and shifts around in the booth like maybe she's rethinking her decision to stop in for a bite to eat. Looking around the place, then back toward the part of the building that is both general store and post office, her gaze settles on the exit.

Frank scoops up two handfuls of his daddy's secret recipe and throws them on the griddle with a little extra butter. In four minutes, they are on a plate beside lumpy stone-ground grits with a little puddle of yellow butter in the center. Tiny puts the plate on her forearm that has hardened over the years into the serving position by arthritis and repetition. A carafe of hot water for more tea dangles from her good arm. Frank prays that the cakes are done enough as she strolls her way toward the table.

"Frank won't brag, but his crab cakes are the best in the Low-country. Won't tell a soul what the secret ingredient is." Vada smiles and nods like she agrees, before she's had the first bite.

Even from the kitchen, he can see that her hands are pale and soft. Her lips part for the fork. He imagines them parting for his lips. She makes the face he wants to see every day for the rest of his life. Scrunched up like a young girl's, blissful like a woman's. Her shoulders rise and then lower slowly in approval as she takes another bite.

"Your hoecakes are burning," a voice says from the counter. Old Joe Pike points to his coffee cup. "Even when Tiny was running her mouth, your daddy never let nobody's coffee cup go empty. Burned them things good, you did. Serves you right."

Frank should throw him out of here, but the crusty old bastard knows he won't. Frank gives him the eye and barks out an order. "Tiny. Order up. And get Joe some more coffee. Pronto." Joe gives him the eye right back to let Frank know the two of them will never be square.

Frank snatches the cake off the griddle bare-handed and tosses it into the wastebin. His fingers throb in perfect time with his selfish heart, which has kept him in this awful town for one reason.

"You have to talk to the boss man." Tiny nods and winks at Frank. "He rents the postboxes. Are you month to month, or are you going to be here for a while?"

All sounds cease, and every customer turns to listen. Vada looks around the restaurant; everyone is frozen, waiting for her answer. Her eyes are the truest shade of blue Frank has ever seen. She blushes again and pushes a strand of wispy blond hair behind her ear.

"For the school year at least. I'm a teacher."

The clatter returns in a rush, and Frank can't make out what she is saying. All he knows is the breakfast shift is almost over, and in twenty minutes, he'll be face-to-face with Vada Hadley.

·Chapter Four·

The waitress seems nice and, with the exception of the scowling old man at the lunch counter, all of the eavesdroppers have kind faces. Still, her inquisition makes me blush. I don't have to look in a mirror to know the embarrassment is traveling down my neck, under the bodice of my sundress. Even my arms are pink. As soon as I say I'll be here for the school year, I know I've made a huge mistake. But it's too late. The diner noise gushes back like a giant wave, and every soul in here is satisfied that they know my business.

My stomach pulses to match the ache in my chest from the lies I told the woman about who I am and where I come from. While I am sure leaving home was the right thing to do, I hate that my body already hungers for the trappings of my old life. I recross my legs and sit up a little straighter, refusing to be the least bit sorry I ran away.

"I won't miss a thing about my old life," I whisper into my teacup, but my cheeks blaze, a telltale of another lie.

I *will* miss Desmond and my beloved Rosa Lee. Just the thought of her makes me ache for her to hold me close, to soothe me and set the world right like she has since the day I was born. But there are some things that even Rosa Lee can't set right. While she helped me pack, she made me promise to watch for the signs. By the time she helped me sneak out of the house, she was begging me.

This morning, when the principal said I got the job, he seemed genuinely excited, like I was the only person who had ever applied for the position. My first interview, for my first job? That's a really good sign. My face burned bright when he teased, "Now you're not related to those rich Hadleys in Charleston, are you?" I was sure the jig was up until he chuckled. "Of course not. If you were, you sure wouldn't be applying to teach in our little old two-room schoolhouse."

It was wrong of him to make the assumption that all people who come from my station in life thumb their noses at the small, the ordinary. Granted, Round O is no Charleston, but it's a nice enough place.

I can't wait to see Miss Mamie's face when I tell the old bat I'm staying. Besides, my small room at the boardinghouse isn't so bad, although I wish I didn't have to share a bathroom with the three gentlemen boarders, or Claire and her adorable boys. Aside from the children, the best thing about Miss Mamie's house is there are no haughty neighbors, no pointless parties, and, best of all, no ridiculous expectations because my last name is Hadley.

Just the thought of my last name conjures up images of Mother and Father's stern faces. I expect they are trying to salvage the marriage they planned before my birth. They probably sent Justin to roam the streets of my favorite cities to look for me, and he'll go, not to find me. He'll start in New York, at the Waldorf Astoria, because he loves the city and thinks it's my favorite hotel. He'll spend the afternoon searching the shops on Fifth Avenue.

Oh, Mecca. My fingers travel across the smooth blue gingham silk of my favorite sundress, a reminder that there will be no more trips to the boutiques in New York, and certainly not Paris. Yes, there was a time I thought I would die without the latest goodies in Jacques Fath's or Nina Ricci's salons, but I am giving up all of that for my new life, with a job, and dresses from Sears.

My foot peeks up at me from under the table, swathed in the most perfect sandals Salvatore Ferragamo could possibly imagine. He'd called them an artistic fantasy, a mirage of comfort, as he slipped them on my feet. The pang in my stomach hardens into the realization that, aside from a precious few people, what I'll miss most about my old life is the shoes.

The thought brings back that annoying look that frequents Justin's face that says he knows *everything about everything.* At this very moment, I'm sure he's sauntering into my favorite little shop on West Fifty-seventh, fully expecting to find me surrounded by doting salespeople and Charles Jourdan footwear. But Justin doesn't really know me, and he has never been the diligent sort. He'll order some custom-made footwear for himself, shrug off his failure, and head to Delmonico's. They'll know him because it's *his* favorite restaurant. After dinner and a show, he'll chase his failure with a brandy and a smelly old cigar.

Sometimes I think I hate Justin, but I don't. I know he doesn't love me, not the kind of love that makes a man search endlessly for a woman. If I were looking for love, that's the kind I would want. Could I have ever had that in Charleston, with someone other than Justin? Would I ever go back? If and when Charleston high society becomes less high, more practical. Reasonable. After all, who marries two names together without one care about the people attached to those names? It's barbaric; that's what it is; a betrayal of love itself, and unforgivable. No matter how perfect the match seems to everyone except me, I will never *love* Justin. Therefore, I can never *marry* him.

For all I care, Justin McLeod can keep right on looking. Not in a million years would he think of looking in a sensible place like Round O.

"More tea, shug?" The waitress's face is hardened from the years, but her eyes have the fire of a teenager's. She pours without waiting for permission. Mother would be mortified.

"Thank you."

"Frank'll be right out. You are still interested in the postbox, aren't you?"

"Oh, yes ma'am."

"How were your crab cakes? You like 'em?"

I wonder if her hearing is sputtering on and off, because she speaks in a normal tone and then shouts out questions like I'm the one who's hard of hearing. "Oh, yes ma'am, they're wonderful." But they aren't like Rosa Lee's.

If I miss anything about 32 Legare Street, it's her and the way she poured love into every morsel of food she made for us. And I miss hearing her say, *I love you, child,* out loud and often, making Mother and Father cringe. Not because Rosa Lee is colored. Because they don't believe in the kind of love that is so big, you can't hold it inside. Love, like everything else, is reserved.

My parents told me this when I asked them why they never gushed over me like Rosa Lee did. I remember asking them, "Reserved for what?" I didn't understand then, and I still don't. But one thing I am sure of, I don't want to love like that, and I don't want to be loved like that.

"Sorry, ma'am. My mistake. Tiny said you wanted—never mind."

I'm not sure how long the man has been standing there; his

lips are a thin line, and his green eyes are dark, almost sad. He turns to leave. I shake my head to bring myself back to the life I've chosen for myself. "Oh, dear, I'm sorry. I'm Vada Hadley, and yes, I do want to speak with you."

His face breaks into a smile, especially his eyes. He is handsome, tall, with broad shoulders, sandy-blond hair. When we shake hands, he cups his other hand over mine, and for a few honest seconds I see all I need to in him. Kindness. Sincerity. But there is something that is broken, and the connection from this simple handshake makes me want more than what is good and proper between two strangers who've just exchanged a handful of words.

"Frank Darling."

My face burns, and I pull away, folding my hands in my lap.

"Darling is my last name. But you can call me Frank."

"*Oh.*"

"Don't be embarrassed. Happens all the time. Can I sit down?"

"Yes, please."

"So Tiny tells me you need a postbox."

"I'm staying at Miss Mamie's, and—"

He nods and laughs under his breath.

"Does that mean something?"

"I know Miss Mamie—very well, and she's—" He shrugs. "Well, she's inquisitive, for one thing. Mr. Clip, Mr. Stanley, Mr. Mann, and Widow Greeley have had postboxes here for quite a while. So, what's your story, Vada Hadley?"

His smile is real and heartfelt. This time, I blush again, on purpose, and lean slightly forward. The old booth creaks like I weigh a ton. I unleash my hands because I talk best with them and explain to him that I need a good-size box. He follows their movements with the precision of a world-class musician as I tell him the brief history I've created for myself.

"—and a six-month lease will do just fine."

He tries to hide his disappointment by looking toward the kitchen. He's sweet.

"Maybe longer."

"Seven dollars for the year." That boyish grin. "Otherwise, it's a dollar a month, and if you leave early—well, if you leave Round O before that, I'll give your money back myself."

He puts a tiny brass key on the table. The engraving is nearly rubbed off; Box 24. I don't like even numbers. While I stymie my compulsion to ask him for an odd-numbered key, he extends his hand to shake on the deal. He has a callus on his palm, below his pinkie finger, that I didn't notice before, and two more at the base of his ring and middle finger. Rosa Lee and her husband Desmond have calluses like that. The mark of good people, hard-working people.

"A year it is—Frank Darling," I say and head back to the post office to send my new address to Desmond and Rosa Lee.

Vada's words are like sweet kisses blown into the air. Sure she's just repeating his name, but Frank imagines it different. *Frank Darling.*

What is wrong with him? Where is all the sap coming from? He was almost a Marine, for Christ's sake. But maybe it is possible to feel the way he does just from hearing this woman laugh, getting lost in those china-blue eyes. Vada walks back toward the store, picks up some note cards and stamps, and pays Hank Bodette for her purchases. Hank's all of ninety and comes to work every day to avoid dying. Still, he is utterly charmed by Vada and the womanly power she has but doesn't seem to be the least bit aware of. She scribbles off a note and gives it to Hank to mail, and by the look on the old man's face, you'd think she'd just written a love letter to him.

For as long as Frank can remember, he's wanted nothing to do with the crossroads. His mother was that way and left the place when he was seven. After that, his daddy put him to work in the diner, mostly to keep an eye on him, and he learned to hate this place, too. Yet this woman walks into this decrepit old diner that smells like a lifetime of lard fat and bacon grease, and there is no place he'd rather be.

His heart can't help but wonder what it would be like to have an everyday kind of love from blond, beautiful Vada Hadley and her soft pink lips. He imagines his hands lost in her hair and her eyes closing just before their lips touch. Suddenly, he is painfully aware that he is as hard as a cast-iron skillet.

The diner is nearly empty. Tiny has her back to Frank, so does Joe Pike. Mick Stallings puts a big tip on the table, hoping Tiny will see it, and saunters back to the postboxes to check his mail. If Frank stands up like this, Tiny Medford will turn around and make some crack about the tent pitched in his shorts. She'll be so loud that both Hank and Vada will turn around to see what the fuss is about, and Frank will die right here in front of Vada.

And Joe Pike? He'd like nothing better than to see the wanting in Frank's heart so he can squash it like a bug. Joe would do even worse if he saw Frank's private saluting Vada. Desperate, Frank does what he's always done at the end of every shift since he resigned himself to a life in Round O. He looks around the old place and asks himself the question that has haunted him since his mother left. *Who marries a diner to a general store to a post office? Who finds the woman of his dreams and then lets her go away forever? Who does that kind of thing? My daddy, that's who.*

The answer never fails to make Frank feel like he is being sucked into a destiny that is not his own. Unavoidable. Unstoppable. He doesn't have to look down at his pants to know he is shrunk down, way past cold-shower size. He stands without the embarrassment of a horny schoolboy and takes another look around the Sit Down Diner. For the first time in his life, he thanks the God he stopped believing in when he was seven for this old place, for sending the woman of his dreams his way. And if God's not too busy being mad at him, Frank prays He'll let her love him back.

The screen door on the opposite end of the building slams behind Vada and bounces against the frame a couple times to underscore the fact that she's gone. The thud in Frank's gut returns, a different kind of emptiness than when he came to work this morning. But he can almost see the promise of a new destiny and the promise that Vada Hadley will be back for her mail every day but Sunday.

"I'm talking to you, *boy.*"

Joe Pike stands and teeters a bit. His legs are bowed from birth, so Frank was told, although Joe swears different. He has a gimpy hand and likes to tell folks it got that way working cattle in Texas when he was south of fifty years old. But Frank knows different.

"Go on home, Joe."

Frank's words snap the old man's head back, and he looks at Frank like he just threw a glass of sticky sweet tea in his face.

"You better mind yourself, Frank *Darling.*"

"And you better mind yourself, too."

Joe pushes off from the table to get his old legs moving and whispers something under his breath so that only Tiny can hear it. Her eyes go wide and she blushes and Frank is terrified of what might come out of her mouth, because even though Joe Pike can keep his mouth shut, Tiny is completely incapable.

She walks over his way. "What was that all about?"

Frank buses Vada's table himself, slowly, wishing that he could linger all day over these dishes. But the stink of the past Joe Pike left in the air won't let him.

"Joe's never liked you much, but I've never seen him like that." Tiny's known Frank since before he was born and always knows when something's wrong. Her face softens. "Maybe he's jealous."

Frank looks at her like she's crazy.

She cocks her head to the side and smiles. "Maybe he saw her first."

Tiny has always said laughing and hard living would keep her alive forever. She lets out a cackle and wants Frank to laugh right along with her, but all he can do is nod at her and go back to the kitchen, clean up, and try to get back the part of the morning that was almost perfect.

·Chapter Five·

The post office door barely closes behind me and already I'm think-ing about Frank Darling and his cocky promise about the postbox. After getting my first job, I'm feeling more confident, too, and positively fly up the front steps of the boardinghouse, until I run smack into Miss Mamie.

"Good morning, Miss Mamie. I'm delighted to inform you I am gainfully employed, or will be when school starts after Labor Day."

"I heard, Miss Priss. Six months' rent. Now pay up."

I head upstairs and pull Rosa Lee's *tredjuh* pouch out from its hiding place and look at her money mingled together with mine. I wish I could call her and tell her about the job. She'd be so proud of me.

"If you're stalling because you don't have the money, you can pack your things and leave." Her manly voice catches a little, most likely due to the crow she's choking on. Starting down the stairs, it's almost impossible to wipe the smirk off of my face. I can feel traces of it as I hand her the money. She counts it twice and grunts in approval.

"You got a long-distance telephone call right after you left out this morning." She scrutinizes my face for a reaction with a technique that would put the best prosecutor in Charleston to shame.

"A long-*distance* call, how delightful. I'm so sorry I missed whomever it was."

"A man, and he sounded colored. I don't know why I bothered to write down his number. If you're cavorting with a colored man, you can pack your bags this instant." She looks at a slip of paper, presumably with the phone number on it, folds it back up, and slips it into her apron pocket slowly, like it's precious and worth keeping.

"I assure you, Miss Mamie, I am not cavorting with anyone." I pray my smile masks the horror that an emergency in Charleston has warranted a call from Desmond. I eye the note sticking out of the pocket of Miss Mamie's flower-sack apron that looks like she made it when she was a young girl. The stitches are uneven, and the apron is threadbare in places. But it is as formidable as Fort Knox, and I'd probably have to knock her senseless, or worse, to see the note for myself.

"Then why would he call? And what kind of decent woman receives calls from a colored man?"

She looks at me even harder. I look right back, not hard but not smiling anymore. This woman is just itching for an excuse to send me packing. Vinegar or honey? "I'm so happy I'll be staying in your lovely home. Long-term. And thank you for telling me about the call." I hold my hand out in hopes that she will hand over the paper with the phone number. She balks and pretends to brush something off of her apron and heads out the kitchen door for the garden.

Even with her back turned to me, I can feel her wicked smile. As the kitchen door closes, all the oxygen rushes out of me. Why did Desmond call? Is he calling to tell me my father knows where I am? No, if he knew I was here, he'd come himself and make me go home. Well, just let him try. I'm not under his thumb anymore. I have a new life and a job. He can't make me do anything I don't want to do, much less marry Justin McLeod.

Miss Mamie's ancient black telephone in the parlor rings loud enough for the deaf to hear, reverberating through my body like the buzz of a giant tuning fork. I was told boarders must ask for permission to use the phone, and we have strict instructions never to answer it.

"*Hello*," I whisper.

"Vada, honey? Lord, it's good to hear your voice."

"Desmond. Is everything all right?"

"I'm not sure, but Rosa Lee and I talked and decided you should be the judge."

"Is she there? Can I speak with her?"

"No, I'm calling from the pay phone, so I don't have much time."

"What's wrong?"

"A call came in late last night, after your parents went to bed, from a Miss Wentworth in Memphis. She demanded to talk to you. About Darby."

"Darby? She knows where she is? Oh, Desmond, that's wonderful news."

"I'm not so sure, Miss Vada. This Miss Wentworth woman sounds like a real troublemaker. We didn't give her your phone number or say where you are, but I did take her phone number down. Me and Rosa Lee went round and round about it before deciding to tell you."

"Oh, Desmond, maybe this is a sign that I'll find Darby and we'll be friends again." He rattles off the number, and I jot it down on the pad beside the phone.

"I don't know if it is or if it isn't. Are you doing all right, Miss Vada?"

"Yes, everything is wonderful. Please tell Rosa Lee I got a job teaching. It doesn't start until September, but I have enough money to tide me over until then."

"I'm so proud of you, Miss Vada."

"Thank you, Desmond, and thank you for telling me about Darby."

"We both love you so much. Promise me you'll think long and hard before you call this woman, and if you do call her, be careful."

"I will. I love and miss you both so much." Saying the words brings tears to my eyes.

The operator interrupts the call to tell Desmond he has one minute to deposit more money in the phone. I look up to see Miss Mamie coming toward the kitchen door with a basket of tomatoes.

"I have to go, Desmond. I love you. Please tell Rosa Lee I love her, too. Good-bye."

Miss Mamie doesn't get as far as the porch, sets a basket of tomatoes down, and heads back to the garden with an empty basket. I tear the note off of the pad and stare at the number. Should I risk placing a call? I have no doubt that if Miss Mamie catches me on the phone, she'll throw me out and keep the money I've given her. She has her back to me as she walks down a row of butter beans, feeling each pod to see if it's filled out enough to pick. Maybe there is enough time. I pick up the phone and wait for the operator to come on the line.

"Yes, Brentwood 649. It's in Memphis."

"Hold please," the operator says and connects the call. A gentleman answers.

"Miss Wentworth, please."

"Whom may I say is calling?"

I think about Desmond's warning to think this through, which I didn't. To be careful. "Just put Miss Wentworth on." Even my most intimidating voice sounds unconvincing.

"May I ask what this is regarding?"

"It's about Darby—O'Doul."

"Just a moment, I'll get her for you," the man says.

Even from the living room, I can look down the shotgun hallway and see Miss Mamie in the garden; her head bobbing up and down like a chicken scratching in the dirt. She stops and wipes her face with the long sleeve of the shirt she wears to keep the sun off her baggy old arms.

"Hello?"

"Yes, this is Vada Hadley." My voice sounds like a squeaky hinge.

"*Finally.* This may be a total waste of my time, and if it is, that little Irish bitch is going to regret her lies."

"Darby?" Her name gushes out of me with a mix of relief and excitement. "You know Darby? You know where she is?"

"Yes—no," the woman bites out. "She lived in my house for three years and ran up a considerable debt, always bragging about her rich sister in Charleston. That would be *you.* She even called you a few times, on my dime, I might add."

Darby called? Was I away at college? Why wasn't I told?

"Lucky for me I keep meticulous records, but the colored man at that number refused to give me yours."

"Is Darby all right? Is she happy?"

"She will be neither unless I get the money the little tramp owes me. Two hundred and fifteen dollars. Otherwise, when I do find that runaway, she's going straight to jail."

Miss Mamie straightens up and starts for the house with a basketful of butter beans on her hip. She limps hard when she thinks no one is watching and walks fine but slowly when she knows someone is. I try to duck back out of sight, but the phone cord won't reach.

"Yes. Of course, she's my sister. I'll pay her debt." Somehow.

"Wire the money to the Western Union here in Memphis. Make it snappy, and I'll consider the matter settled."

"No."

"*No?* Young lady, believe me, if I have to come down to Charleston and get the money myself, *you'll* be sorry. And if the authorities get involved—"

Miss Mamie struggles up the steps of the back porch and will be through the door any moment. If she looks through the panes in the door, she will see the phone off the hook and will promptly toss me out on my ear.

"What I meant to say, Miss Wentworth, is I'll bring you the money." After paying my rent, I have a little less than a hundred dollars, my grandmother's necklace, and no transportation. I try to sound honest, and not desperate. "Please. I'll do anything to find Darby."

"Fine, but I'm warning you, I want my money. I'll give you seven days, just until the Fourth of July. After that, I turn the matter over to the police, and when they find your sister, she'll rot in jail."

As she rattles off directions to an address in Memphis, Miss Mamie takes off her garden hat and hangs it on the hook just inside the kitchen door. "I have to go now," I whisper as Miss Mamie sets tomatoes, bottom side up, on the red-checkered oil-cloth. "I'll be there soon with the money. I promise. Good-bye."

My hand is still on the telephone when its shrill noise sends me dashing upstairs in my stocking feet, and I am halfway up the steps when I hear Miss Mamie waddling toward the parlor. I whip around like I was just now coming downstairs and smile at her. Maybe I should offer to help out around the house. Maybe that would butter up the crusty old broad.

Brrrring!

Miss Mamie lets out a heavy sigh as she trudges to the tele-phone table and picks up the handset. "Hello." The ancient oiled floor creaks under her weight as she shifts from one bad knee to the other. "*Hmmmmm. Hmmmmm.* She's right here." She glares at me as she hands me the phone. If Miss Wentworth has called to say she's changed her mind, all hope of ever seeing Darby again is lost.

"Hello."

"Vada?"

"Who is this?'

"Frank Darling, from the diner." His breathing is quick and nervous. Even after the unsettling phone call with Miss Went-worth, I can't help but smile. Miss Mamie is standing there, glar-ing, without the least bit of manners that would allow me a speck of privacy. He lets out a big sigh that spills out his words. "Well, I was wondering if you'd like to get a bite to eat. With me. Tonight."

"At the diner?"

"God, no. I thought I'd pick you up at six. I have someplace special in mind to take you on our first date."

"Thank you for the dinner invitation, I'd love to go." Miss Mamie stands there looking hard at me, like I'm some sort of hussy, before she shakes her head and toddles off toward the kitchen.

"We can have a nice meal, and then I'll bore you with my life story."

I hear myself laugh and hope that Frank will understand that I can't possibly tell him mine.

Everything Frank pulls from the chifforobe has grease spatters that look like big raindrops that will never dry. His shirtsleeves are rimmed with bright yellow mustard. His only dress shirt has a thin line of dust on the shoulders. He holds an underarm up to his nose. Even after a good washing, the diner smell never washes out of anything. Between the bacon and the rancid cooking oil, Vada will surely wish he kept his clothes in the meat locker. His father's clock chimes the half hour, reminding him he has thirty minutes to either find something presentable to wear or cancel. But he can't cancel. He won't.

Khakis are a constant reminder of the Army's rejection. He'd rather die than wear them. They're in the store, tucked away in the farthest corner from the kitchen, behind a tall bin with drawers full of seeds, so khaki-wearers know where they are but Frank doesn't have to look at them. What about dungarees? He can't take a girl like Vada out wearing dungarees.

He stalks across the yard in bare feet, which isn't a problem until he hits the parking lot and the loose oyster shell that's a poor substitute for gravel. The shells press into the soles of his feet. He picks up the pace, skimming across the tops of them so that he doesn't show up ill-dressed, with bloodied feet.

He unlocks the door to the store side of the Sit Down Diner and hurries toward the seed bin. There are only a dozen pairs of work pants on the table, smooth, the color of half-baked biscuits. The matching work shirts alongside them look too much like a day laborer's or, worse, a lowly private's uniform. Frank shoves the shirt and pants up to his nose and breathes in deeply. Satisfied the caustic smell of dye and starch trumps the diner smell, he takes both of them just in case his dress shirt doesn't work.

The screen door bounces behind him as he starts back across the parking lot, always three times. His mother believed everything good came in threes, and everything bad, too. She told Frank that the last night she tucked him in, before she left forever. Frank was only seven, too little to know she was leaving for good, so he didn't think anything of it when she told him she loved him. She kissed his forehead three times, and when he awoke the next morning, she was gone forever.

Not that he believes those kisses had anything to do with what happened. Life is what you make it, and he doesn't have to have three Vada Hadleys walking through the door of the Sit Down Diner to know how lucky he is. But his palms sweat and his hands are unsteady as he hurries into his dinky house, stripping as he walks through the door.

It hurts to admit the khakis look good with their razor-sharp creases, so stiff they can almost stand on their own. Bare-chested, he searches, desperate to find a brush to get the dust off of the shoulders of the white shirt so he doesn't have to wear the khaki one. A comb won't do, but he has a scrub brush under the sink he used on a black cast-iron skillet once. Instead, he finds his tooth-brush. He works the bristles over the fabric, sending a year's worth of dust scattering into the air. He has just enough time to comb his hair and use the brush on his teeth.

"Oh, God, why did I give up church? At least I'd have a decent Sunday shirt to wear." His conscience jabs him hard, reminding him why. He shoves the comb into his pocket and feels like he's forgetting something. He's sure he is, and maybe it's knowing just how fragile the next few hours of his life will be. He knows how women are. They shop for men, and though you'd be hard pressed to find a man who'll admit it, they do the same. Is she the right size? Is she smart? Is she pretty?

Frank has no doubt Vada will size him up like a new dress. Does she like him enough to invest in him? Will he be her favorite, or discarded in a few days, or hell, maybe hours, like an ill-fitting pair of shoes? Shoes. He picks up the stained brogans he wears every day of his life and slips them on, lacing them hard in disgust. He'll make sure this is the perfect date, so perfect, Vada won't even notice his damn shoes.

He tries to bring his breathing somewhere near a normal level, but after lying to himself about the shoes, it's impossible. "It's a date. It's not even a date; it's just dinner," he says out loud. But that's another lie. It is a date.

He sprints out the door and stops short of the shed. Until now, he was sure his car looked good, really good, but, standing here, it's clear that the paint is fading, that it's not a Buick, or even a Ford. It's a blinking Plymouth Mayflower, like the damn ship. A girl like Vada deserves better than this. He gets in and cranks the beast up and hopes she's not expecting much.

·Chapter Six·

As perilous as Darby's situation is, I am giddy with hope that I'll find her. Maybe she'll come back to Round O with me. We could share a room. After I start my job and make a little money, we could go shopping on Saturdays. Maybe Claire can come along, too. Of course, she looks nice in black, everyone does, but I'd love to see her in something striking. Jade or peacock blue. I finger the neckline of my flouncy chartreuse dress thoughtfully. There really isn't a good reason why a young woman like Claire, who doesn't look a day over twenty-five, can't mourn in a more flattering color.

Staring at my reflection in the cheval mirror, I remember Rosa Lee's warning to fit in, but I can't wear my Sears dress on a date. I won't. I clip my earbobs on and pinch my cheeks. Claire doesn't wear earbobs. Come to think of it, I've not seen anyone around here who does. I unclip the baubles and massage my earlobes until the red marks are gone. *There.* Small-town chic and ready for Frank Darling.

He seems like such a nice man, and he's very handsome. I wonder what that was, when our hands touched? I've never felt like that before, and certainly not with Justin, who always seemed genuinely shocked when I turned away his affections. But then he rarely took any notice about how I felt about anything, much less him.

Let all the darling debutants in Charleston swoon over him. They don't see what I see. The apple of Justin's eye is Justin. And the times he did touch me, the times his hands settled on my shoulders when he helped me on with my wrap or reached for my hand at dinner, I never felt that sharp current like I felt when Frank touched my hand today. I wonder if he noticed it, too.

"Pretty," little Jonathan coos at me as I start down the stairs. I scoop him up and start back up the steps. Miss Mamie only allows the children to play in their room, the front yard, or in the street. They're not allowed in the common areas downstairs and never anywhere near the garden in the backyard.

"You're the pretty one, sweet boy." I give him a little kiss on the cheek and he squeals in delight. "*Shhhh*, Miss Mamie will hear you." How that horrible landlady expects these children to grow up in this house without making a sound is beyond me. But Claire does a good job keeping them occupied and quiet enough to only warrant an occasional dirty look from the old bat. I knock softly on Claire's door.

She opens the door and reaches for Jonathan. "Ah, there's my little Houdini. Thanks, Vada. You've only been here two days and already I don't know what I'd do without you." The leggy three-year-old wraps himself around his mother and lays his head sweetly against her shoulder. "Did Miss Mamie see him?"

"Stop your worrying, Claire. I got him before he was halfway down the stairs," I whisper. "I wish the boys didn't have to walk about the house like they're in church."

"Me, too, but it seems all my wishes are ignored these days."

Last night, when I was porch sitting and making polite conversation with the three ancient bachelors, Mr. Clip and Mr. Mann told me that Claire's husband hadn't even been drafted until a few months before the war was over. Bobby Greeley had made it through hell only to have "a Kraut get him" a few days after the war ended and he was due to come home. Mr. Stanley, who is a particularly unattractive bachelor, didn't comment but said something about Claire. The words were nice, but the way he said it was so unsettling, I excused myself and went to bed.

"I don't have any family here in Round O and neither did Bobby, so we're stuck here," Claire says. "I keep wishing there was someplace besides this awful house for us to live, because I don't know how long I can keep them quiet. They are children. Boys at that. I'm not even sure it's good for them to be quiet all the time." Her older two, Daniel and Peter, read quietly in a corner of the room; they look up at us and then quickly back down at their books.

Her smile is worried. She is pretty and petite, with long jet-black hair pulled back with a tattered strip of satin that looks like it was white at one time. The room is as threadbare and shabby as mine, except there is a stack of other people's mending Claire takes in to pay her rent. This is no place to raise three children.

"I got the job. It doesn't start until September, but—" She stops me before I can say what I'm thinking.

"Vada, that's wonderful. Oh, you'll have Daniel this year; he'll be so pleased. I think he has a bit of a crush on you." The boy doesn't look up again from his book, but the only thing redder than his face is his ears, which are too big for him.

"Yes, well, I was thinking, since I'll have a little money coming in on a regular basis, maybe we could find a small house to rent.

Together. I could help out with the boys, especially during the summers, and I have a friend who might—"

"No." She looks mortified and not at all as excited as I was sure she would be. "We couldn't do that." She sets the little one down, and he toddles over to where his brothers are reading. He plops down hard on the floor with an empty wooden spool in each hand and begins to roll them across the floor.

"Why not, Claire? Between the two of us, we could swing it."

"You don't understand—" Her face is pale, her eyes look worried, as if little Jonathan had taken a tumble down the stairs.

"What's there to understand, really? It would be fun. I—"

"Lower your voice, Vada." Hers is barely above a whisper. "This is a small community, and you're new here. You've probably never even heard of the Chastain sisters, who weren't sisters at all. It was a scandalous Boston marriage, and they were run out of town on a rail when they were found out."

"A Boston marriage? I don't know what that is, but I think you've got this all wrong."

She pushes me out into the hallway and closes the door behind her so the boys can't hear what she has to say. "Two women. Living together. Not sisters." I cock my head to the side. Why do I feel like she's getting ready to wash my mouth out with soap? "Lovers," she hisses.

"Oh." I nod blankly. "*Oh*. No, not at all like that. I mean I'm not that kind of girl. I even have a date tonight. With Frank Darling."

"I know you're not," she says, her voice a little softer. "But people will talk. As much as I am not that kind of girl either, I'm stuck here until someone is crazy enough to marry me. And my boys."

I see her tears, the desperation I had expected to see from a woman in her position, but haven't until now.

"Claire, you're beautiful—"

She shakes her head and looks down at her hands. Her nails are bitten down to the quick. "Mr. Stanley has a pension."

I shake my head. "No." He's old and smelly and passes gas when he walks.

"He's made a proposal, of sorts."

Her chin is resting on her chest. I can feel the hope seeping out of her. She's actually considering this. Oh, God. "Claire. You can't. You mustn't. You're young and beautiful, and he—well, he's not."

"You don't know what it's like, Vada." She looks up at me with that kind smile that would melt the hearts of a thousand young men if it were her, just her. "I don't regret marrying at fifteen, having my boys. But Bobby's never coming back; I have to make a life for them." Resignation is etched into fine lines that she's too young and too beautiful to have. Nothing about this is right.

The doorbell rings. I hear Miss Mamie limping toward it, cursing under her breath but still loud enough for the whole house to hear.

"Your date?" Her smile is as genuine as she is. On the other side of the door, the older boys start to fuss. She raps softly on the door, and they are instantly silenced. "I hope you have a swell time. You look beautiful." She gives me a quick hug and pulls away, her face so achingly sad.

"We'll talk about this later, Claire."

"What do you want?" Miss Mamie snaps at who I am sure is Frank. I can hear his soft laugh. He says something to her, but all I can make out is my name.

"You better go, Vada." I nod, and just before she closes the door, she reaches for me. I can feel her longing and remember her face when I said I had a date, how for a sliver of a second she looked like a blushing schoolgirl full of hope and love. She lets go, and the resignation settles back onto her face. "Frank's a swell guy. Have a good time."

Does she know Frank? Does she want him? I suspect they are close to the same age, and yet he'd called her Widow Greeley, like she was ancient and that was actually her name.

"*Vada*," Miss Mamie barks up the stairs.

"Coming," I say. "Later, Claire. I promise." But the door has already closed.

I hurry, almost tripping over Miss Mamie, who stands like a sentry at the bottom of the stairs so that I have to wait for her to move. Frank looks at me, and I want to melt. I can tell he's trying too hard to keep a straight face in front of Miss Mamie. She finally steps aside, and he opens the front door for me.

As they walk toward the car, Frank's hand brushes up against Vada's, and he wants to reach for it, but he can feel the battle-ax watching them. Just the same, he looks toward the house as he closes the door of the Plymouth. Miss Mamie doesn't make any pretense of hiding. She holds back the lace curtains in the parlor, staring him down. He gives her a nod, not a friendly one, mind you, and believes her and Joe Pike would make a really good pair.

Vada leans toward the window, which is rolled down because it's so damn hot. "Frank," she says softly, and in his head, he puts the *darling* on the end for her. "It's so kind of you to ask me to dinner."

"I think it's pretty swell that you agreed to go out with me."

Her laugh is just about the prettiest sound Frank has ever heard. God, she's beautiful, but she's more, much more than just looks.

He hurries around to the driver's side and slides in, hoping to God the car doesn't do that hiccup thing it does sometimes. He almost apologizes to Vada for not picking her up in a Cadillac or something even better, if there is such a thing, but he doesn't, because the engine cranks right up. He puts his arm across the top of the seat to back out of the driveway. Vada doesn't move away, but she doesn't slide across the bench and rest her head on his shoulder, either.

He sits there for a moment, and she cocks her pretty head to the side. "Is something wrong?"

"Uh, no." He just has no idea how he's going to drive this car, because he can't stop staring at her.

She declares she's hungry. He would run all the way to China in bare feet to satisfy this woman, so he puts the car in gear and starts down the road toward Highway 17, grinning like a fool.

"Your food is wonderful, Frank. Why aren't we going to the diner?" Frank looks at her like she's got to be kidding, and she laughs again. He could get used to this, her pretty face, the easy way about her, the way she tucks her hands under her thighs so that they disappear underneath the sides of her pouffy dress. She's trying not to talk with her hands, but he wishes she would. He loves watching her long, slender fingers tell her story.

"No way."

"Where, then?"

"It's a surprise."

"*Oooh*, I love surprises. Can you give me a hint?"

"Afraid not, ma'am. You'll have to torture me to get it out of me." Sitting here with both hands on the steering wheel, unable to touch her, is torture enough. "But if you really want to know,

I'll tell you." She turns toward him and is a few inches closer than she was. She's nodding, grinning like it's Christmas morning. "I'm taking you to the best damn restaurant in Charleston."

"*What? No!*" She looks pale, like she might be sick. Hell, maybe she is. She's holding her stomach. He's positive the next words out of her mouth will be a demand to go home. The Plymouth limps over to the side of the road, and he puts the car in park.

"Vada, are you all right?"

She nods her head. "Why?"

"Well, I was worried about you—"

"No." She shakes her head like she's getting ready to throw up. "Why Charleston?"

Her cheeks are corpse white. He stifles the urge to run the backs of his fingers across them. Even dog sick, she's the most beautiful woman Frank has ever seen. "I don't have any idea what the best restaurant is, but I figured once we got to King Street, I'd ask around and take you there. I don't know much about Charleston. I've only been there once." He doesn't tell her it was to get turned down flat by the Navy.

Suddenly it occurs to Frank; she's ashamed of this boat he's driving. Maybe it's the khakis. Hell, maybe she's ashamed of him and would probably die if she saw someone she knew there. He ought to kick himself; of course she'd die if that someone she knew was her boyfriend. "The truth is, I wanted to take you there because Charleston is a pretty grand place. I thought you'd like it."

"Oh," she says softly, the color coming back to her face. "Really, Frank, we don't have to go that far."

Now he feels his face, blushing hot like a child's. "I guess I was trying to impress you." She puts her hand on his; his heart turns cartwheels against his chest. "Silly, huh?"

"It's not silly at all, but I don't want to go that far; we'd get back late, and we'd have Miss Mamie to contend with. Couldn't we just go somewhere else? Someplace closer?"

"There are a couple of good eating places in Walterboro, if that's okay. They even have a picture show."

"Sounds wonderful," she says, inching a little closer. He's glad she doesn't know he emptied out the coffee can for gas money and a fancy supper. He had no idea what things cost in Charleston, but he'd be damned if he'd not given her the moon and then some on their first date. She nods and smiles, and he's certain this will be the last first date for the both of them.

As he turns the car around and heads in the opposite direction, her smile puts the pretty blue sky to shame.

"I'm glad you asked me out, Frank Darling." His heart sings every time she says his name. "But you don't have to impress me."

"I thought maybe you didn't want to go there because—I thought maybe you had somebody there. A boyfriend."

"I don't have a boyfriend, Frank."

He grins at Vada, making her blush. "I'd sure like to fix that."

·Chapter Seven·

My breathing returns to normal. I smile as we pass a pretty field, but inwardly I am scolding myself for being so transparent. Why, I might as well have been wearing a great big sandwich sign that says, "I ran away to escape the tyranny of my parents." Just the thought of Father sitting behind that huge, gaudy desk in the study, planning my capture and marital demise, is enough to make me sick again.

No, he won't take my leaving lightly. Not at all. And when his pawn, Justin, comes back empty-handed, he'll take matters into his own hands. But even *he* won't think I'm actually working, something Hadley women do not do.

Besides, Father was never good at hide-and-seek. Not that he ever tried to look for me when I begged him to play. Father always sent Desmond to find me, because he didn't have the first clue as to where to look. Desmond always knew, just as he knows where

I am now. But he loves me like a daughter; he'd never betray me. The game is on a larger scale now, and I have the upper hand.

The car veers off the road for a few seconds because Frank looks at me a lot while he drives. Really, it's sweet, but I don't think it's very safe at all. The car groans to a stop at a stop sign. A woman at a tiny roadside vegetable stand looks up hopefully. A little girl is on her knees, playing jacks in the dirt, and another is chasing a pair of boys who look like twins. The children stop what they're doing and wave wildly, motioning for us to pull into the yard.

Frank lets the car idle. He's smiling at me, making me feel like a schoolgirl before he steps on the gas again. The woman cranes her head downward as she sorts through a basket of peaches. She's just like Claire, head down, always working. It's hard to imagine Claire ever felt the way Frank makes me feel, but I know she misses her husband, misses being adored, feeling beautiful, special.

"You're awful quiet," Frank says.

"That woman at the crossroads reminded me of Claire."

"A friend of yours?"

"No, silly, Claire Greeley from the boardinghouse. She's such a dear woman, and those children are adorable. It's terrible they can't live in a proper house, or at least someplace the children aren't encouraged to play in the street."

"Widow Greeley is nice—"

I press my lips into a thin line, trying to keep my mouth shut, but I can't. "Please don't call her that."

"Well, she is nice."

"No. Don't call her the Widow Greeley."

"Well, she is a widow, and her last name is Greeley. What would you have me call her?" He's smiling, teasing.

"Her name is Claire, and she's not much older than me. Widow Greeley sounds, well, old, very old, and she's not. Claire is young and beautiful."

I turn to face Frank. He almost runs off the road, so I turn around to watch the road for myself. He may be handsome, very handsome, but he is not a good driver. The car slows as we enter the small town. Frank turns down Washington Street and pulls into a space in front of Harold's Southern Diner and puts the car in park. "I hear Mr. Stanley is sweet on her."

"Really?" I spit the word out. "You can't be serious."

His look is defensive, but there's a hint of a smile. "I don't mean to rile you, but a woman in her position doesn't have many options. Especially with those three boys." I move away from him and his voice softens as he pleads his case apologetically. "I wish things were different for her, Vada, really I do, but that won't make it so."

I get my white tea gloves out of my purse and put them on absentmindedly. "I offered to share a house with her." Oh, this isn't a stuffy sit-down dinner. It's a diner, for goodness' sake. I yank them off.

"*No,*" his eyes nearly bug out of his head, "you can't—you don't want to do that."

"Yes. Yes, I know, the Boston-marriage thing."

Frank looks around and lowers his voice. "You know about that?"

"Claire told me because she was horrified when I offered to share a house with her and the children. But that doesn't matter, Frank—"

"But it does matter, Vada. Round O is a small community and you're a schoolteacher."

"Even if I was an actual participant in this so-called Boston marriage, which I am not, it wouldn't affect my teaching skills one iota. The whole idea of Claire trapped at the boardinghouse with the children breaks my heart, and I know it's breaking hers, too."

He rubs his knuckles across my cheek and smiles at me. I can't help but smile back. Without thinking that we are sitting in broad daylight, in front of a busy restaurant, he leans toward me. I can feel his warm breath on my cheek. I watch his lips moving closer to mine. A horn honks, startling both of us, and he sits straight up with a look on his face like he can't believe what he's almost done. I squeeze his hand to let him know I hope I won't wait long for our first kiss.

A *Charleston Evening Post* newspaper rack just outside the restaurant door catches my eye. I fumble in my pocketbook for some change.

"Allow me," Frank says. He inserts a nickel, opens the box, and hands me a newspaper. "Hope you're not so bored already you're planning on reading the paper during dinner."

I laugh and fold the paper in half and put it in my purse, intent on combing through it when I get back to the boardinghouse to see if there's anything about my disappearance. Although I am reasonably sure my father wouldn't use the police to find me; he'd use his own resources to be discreet.

I'm not sure if this place really smells better than the Sit Down Diner, or if I'm just hungrier than I was this morning after my interview. The restaurant is bigger than Frank's place, much busier, loud. The portly cook behind the counter wipes his round red face and turns up the radio. The whine of Bill Monroe crooning "Blue Moon of Kentucky" quiets the crowd a little. People look at us and nod, tapping their toes in time to the music.

We walk past the line of shiny red Naugahyde stools at the

lunch counter. Frank's hand brushes the small of my back, guiding me toward the only table for two, near the powder room, away from the clatter, the most romantic one in the diner.

He pulls my chair out for me. In the tight space, I can feel his breath on my hair, like he's breathing me in before he sits down across from me. His face is dreamy: high cheekbones, suntanned skin, blond hair slicked back with pomade. Quite dapper.

"I've thought it a million times all the way here," he smiles and my heart flips over in my chest, "hell, since the second you walked into the diner this morning, but I haven't said it—"

"Said what?"

"That you were beautiful." He shakes his head, then looks at me with those gorgeous green eyes. "You are beautiful."

Neither of us acknowledges the waitress who puts the menus on the table and waddles back toward the kitchen. I feel my face blaze.

"You're blushing like I said it for the heck of it, but it's true. Truer than anything I know."

"Thank you, Frank." I want to tell him I think he is beautiful, too, and he is, but it seems rather silly.

The waitress returns with her order pad and, without even asking, pours two glasses of sweet tea. "We got chitlins for the meat-and-three special." She looks back toward the kitchen and lowers her voice. "Don't order the meatloaf, and if you do, don't eat it. Y'all look like y'all need a minute," she says and walks off again.

"That's My Desire" comes on the radio, and the cook turns the music down.

Frank puts his glass up to his lips and takes a sip.

I breathe out a dreamy sigh. "I love Frankie."

Frank almost spews his drink. "Excuse me?"

"That song, before the cook turned it down. It was Frankie Laine's 'Desire.'"

"Oh." He looks relieved. He gets up and walks over to the kitchen. The cook doesn't seem to know him, but Frank says something to him and the man mops his brow with the towel slung over his shoulder and they shake hands. The man looks at me, smiles, nods, and then turns the song back up.

Frankie Laine's silky voice wraps around the orchestra's music, making me want to dance. Frank returns with a thin smile that makes me feel like he'd do anything for me.

Too soon, another country tune comes on the radio, and the toe tappers pick up their pace, nodding their heads to the music as they eat.

"I don't know this song, Frank."

"It's Moon Mullican and the Showboys. 'Jole Bion's Sister.'"

I laugh at the singer's hard twang and gross mispronunciation of the French words he's attempting to sing. The song is about a woman who caught a man's eye, until he saw her nine children. Could Frank be right about Claire, and there really are no prospects for her other than Mr. Stanley? Surely not. If Justin's looks can make someone overlook his myriad of flaws, I'm positive someone young and handsome will fall in love with Claire.

"I see those pretty wheels turning. What are you thinking about?" And before Vada can answer, Frank hears the chorus of the song and nods his head. "You're thinking about Claire?" Vada smiles because Frank called the widow by her given name. "If I could, I'd make the world what you want it to be." He reaches for her hand, runs his thumb across the soft ridges of her knuckles.

She squeezes Frank's hand like she believes him.

"Are y'all going to order? 'Cause if you're not, you'll have to leave. This place is for paying customers only." The waitress looks irritated. Frank looks down at the menu that is a minefield of bad choices. Cabbage and sausage? Gas. Spaghetti? He can smell the garlic all the way here from the back of the restaurant. Liver and onions. Definitely not food for lovers, but the chicken-fried steak and mashed potatoes looks safe. He switches out the side of grilled onions for green beans. Vada glances down at the menu for a second.

"Crab cakes," the waitress repeats after Vada.

Frank raises his eyebrows. Is this a challenge? Vada gives him a playful smile. "With grits, if you have them."

"'Course we have grits." The woman huffs. "What kind of place do you think this is?"

"Well, your sign out front says 'best eats around,' and to be completely honest, I'm not sure I believe it. The menu also claims your crab cakes are the best, but I had some stellar ones for breakfast this morning, so we'll see."

The woman hoofs it over to the kitchen, and the cook nods and looks at Vada like she's thrown down the gauntlet.

"Why, Miss Hadley, are you disputing Tiny Medford's word about my cooking? Tiny wouldn't take kindly to that, but, for your sake, I swear I won't tell her." She laughs. He looks into her face. God she's beautiful. He wants to know her, know everything about her. "So, where are you from?"

"I love this song." She ignores the question and sways to the easy beat.

He starts to ask again but gets distracted by her face, her smile, her fluid movements. "You want to dance?"

She stops and blushes. "Here? Now?"

"After the crab-cake contest. There's a dance hall at the end of the street. I've been there a time or two; it's a nice enough place."

The food is on the table too soon, and Frank can't eat until he watches her judge it. Her lips part for the fork. No scrunching shoulders or blissful face. She rocks her head from side to side like they're okay and eats. Frank's so proud, he's about to burst. If Vada Hadley doesn't know anything else about him, she knows he's a damn-fine cook.

He inhales his food to get on with the date, to feel her swaying in his arms on the dance floor. She takes dainty bites like she's in no hurry and sets her fork down.

"Can I tell you something, Frank?" She looks at him with those blue eyes, and all he can do is nod. "I have a secret."

Frank has a secret, too. He's fallen hard for Vada Hadley and her blue eyes, her soft pink lips that smile when she says his name. So damn hard. Could he possibly be the luckiest man in the world because she feels the same way?

"You can tell me anything, Vada."

She picks up her fork again and smiles as she pushes the food around on her plate, and he is completely lost. "I need your help, Frank Darling."

This doesn't sound like she's going to tell him she loves him back, but she did say she needs him. Sort of. At least she needs his help.

"Yes."

"What?" She blushes. "I haven't even told you what I want."

"Whatever it is, yes. I'll do it. I'd do anything for you."

"Really?"

He runs his hand through his hair, amazed that it's possible to go from feeling as old and codgery as Joe Pike this morning to being a lovesick boy. He weighs saying the words for fear she'll think he's moving too fast, that he's not sincere. But Frank's more sure of what he feels for her than he is of anything. "I'll do anything you want me to. But honest to God, Vada, if you don't hurry up and eat so I can hold you in my arms on the dance floor, I think I'm going to die."

She smiles at him and pushes her plate away like she's ready to leave, too. Without looking at the tab, Frank throws too much money on the table. As they wind back toward the entrance, she reaches for his hand. "Night," the cook snaps from the kitchen. When Frank asked him to turn Vada's song up, he made no mention of the jarhead's Semper Fi tattoo, like he might have if he wasn't out on a date. He didn't ask the cook if he'd been to war, so that he could tell Frank what he'd missed. Tonight is all about Vada Hadley.

The old lady keeping the door of the dance hall takes Frank's dime and nods them in. The dance floor is full, so many bodies jiving to a big-band tune, looking like one pulsing mass. A pretty brunette saunters up to Frank and asks if he wants to buy a dollar's worth of tickets from her. Before he can say anything, Vada pipes up, but her voice can't be heard above the music. The song tails off as the woman is leaning in closer to Frank so that he can see her wares. Frank loves the annoyed look on Vada's face. She holds their clasped hands up for the woman to see.

"Come on, honey," the woman coos, "a little variety will only cost you ten cents a dance."

"He's with me," Vada says above the noise, and the woman gives her a drop-dead look and slithers over to another guy. Vada looks at Frank with steely blue eyes for confirmation.

"*Yes, ma'am.*" They fold into the throbbing crowd and start moving as the band plays a snappy Dizzy Gillespie number. The other girls writhe around, sweating and red, but not Vada. Her movements are effortless and so graceful, her feet barely touch the floor. Frank struggles to keep up with her. She's lost in the wail of the orchestra, eyes closed, completely unaware of anything but the music until the applause at the end of the song brings her back to him.

She smiles and stands on her tiptoes so Frank can hear her above the crowd. "Do you come here often?"

He shakes his head. "Not in a long time. Anybody ever tell you you're a damn-fine dancer?"

"You just did." She grabs his hand, pulls him into the middle of the floor, and stutters out a few dance steps. He tries to follow but has a hard time watching her feet when he's so lost in her face. She takes his face in her hands and points it at her swiveling hips. "It's the jitterbug, silly." Holy mother of God. She leads. Frank follows and sort of picks it up until the last few bars of the staccato tune end.

The air is thick and humid with a thousand girlie perfumes, too much Old Spice, and sweat. Frank's shirt sticks to him, and it's hard to breathe, or maybe he's afraid to breathe, afraid that he'll discover this perfect date was just a product of too much wishing, hoping. Desire. But it's not just him. The whole room is so full of wanting, the couple next to them start making out on the dance floor like they are possessed. Two burly bouncers pull them apart and throw the guy out without warning. But the rules listed on the four-foot-by-six-foot piece of plywood on the way in strictly prohibit inappropriate public displays of affection on the dance floor.

Vada laughs and falls into his arms, breathing hard against his chest, and he's grateful a slow song starts up so he can keep her there. She rests her head on his shoulder; he rests his chin on her crown and prays that his private doesn't salute her again. She snuggles even closer, looks up at him, and smiles. A thin veil of sweat beads just above the most kissable lips Frank has ever seen in his life. He keeps shuffling his feet slowly in time to the music, wanting to be controlled, not wanting to rush something that he wants to last forever.

He doesn't hear her sigh above the noise of the crowd, but feels it against his chest. He can't take this anymore. "Do you want to get out of here?" His lips linger close to her ear and make her shudder. She doesn't look at him but runs her slender fingers down his chest like she doesn't want the embrace to end any more than Frank does. She looks into his face and nods, no warm smile, just longing tinged with something else.

Frank's choice is between the gazebo out back, overlooking a small pond, a place lovers go, and back to the car and, ultimately, Round O. He's not ready to take her home, so he takes her hand and leads her to the back of the dance hall. The bouncer opens the door. The night air is sticky and hot, but so much cooler than the writhing inferno inside. "Sure you want to step outside? You'll have to pay to come back in."

He looks at Vada to see what she wants; she smiles at him. "I'm sure."

They walk down toward the gazebo, draped with lovers making out, pressed up against the railings, sitting on hard wooden benches Frank is sure they don't feel. The moon is generous, and he can see Vada blush when they get close enough to hear the heavy breathing, the moaning, the whispered declarations of love and forever. Vada goes over to the side of the gazebo that's open to the pond below; she takes off her shoes, dangling her feet above the black water.

"I wouldn't do that if I were you." She stretches out her long legs and smiles at him, teasing before she scoops up a handful of water and flicks it on him. Frank laughs, and she laughs, too, shutting out all the lovers' sounds and the night sounds, too. He sits beside her and pulls her close so that her feet aren't dangling over the edge anymore. "See that?" He points out into the lily pads that are lovingly choking the pond to death. She peers out onto the moonlit lake until she sees the massive gator impersonating a log, and then she draws her knees up to her chest like a little girl.

"Vada?" She nuzzles closer to him. "Can I kiss you?"

She turns her face up to his, and her smile dissolves into yearning as they move toward each other. His lips graze against hers, nuzzling them so that when she runs her tongue across her lips it touches his. He can't help but be tentative, like she's breakable, like what they have is breakable, but the kiss deepens. Her breathing quickens, and Frank is sure he can feel her heart beating against his.

Floodlights come on, blinding them, and the old woman who took their ticket hollers that the dance is over and everybody has to clear out. Frank's forehead is still pressed against Vada's. He's afraid to move, afraid the spell will be broken. He helps her up, and she looks up at him and smiles. "Frank?" There's something monstrous and wrong about this night ending, about taking her back to the boardinghouse. Frank wants to take her away from here, but he doesn't think she's ready for happily ever after with him, at least not yet. She puts her hands on his face and runs her thumbs across his stubble. "Thank you. This was the most perfect evening ever."

They walk back to the car, hand in hand, looking at each other like lovers. He wants to be her lover, wants to be what she wants, what she needs. He opens the door for her; she slides in and over to the middle of the bench seat. He drives with his arm around her and doesn't give a rat's ass if Miss Mamie is watching when he pulls up to the house. He doesn't ask for permission to kiss her. He doesn't have to. She presses into him, and he feels that same current pass between them as when he first shook her hand, multiplied by a thousand.

"I have to go." She presses her forehead against his.

He gets out and opens the door for her, taking her hand, easing her out of the car without taking his eyes off of hers. She looks at the house and then gives him a little wave. "Thank you again, Frank, for a wonderful evening." She starts up the walkway ahead of him, her way of asking him not to walk her to the doorstep, not to kiss her good night in front of God and everybody.

"Vada?" She turns and takes his breath away. The familiar figure at the lace curtains raps on the window, making the panes rattle ominously. At the most, he is a few feet from her, but it feels like more. "What do you want from me?" The question didn't come out at all like Frank meant it to, or maybe it did. "Whatever it is, I meant what I said. I'll do it."

"After I tell you, you might change your mind."

"Never."

"Do you have to work Wednesday night?" Frank shakes his head and says the diner's not open in the evenings, and only for breakfast that day, like the majority of Christian businesses that close early for midweek prayer services. "Pick me up for church around 5:45. We'll talk after that."

The porch light comes on, and the front door opens. Miss Mamie comes out onto the stoop with her hands on her barn-size hips, giving Frank her best burn-in-hell look, and he just might for what he's thinking about doing if she gets between him and his girl. He nods his head at Vada and gets back in the Plymouth, knowing he won't sleep a wink tonight.

"You better watch yourself, missy. You being a schoolteacher and all. Staying out until eleven o'clock? I told you when you rented the room I wouldn't stand for any cavorting."

My body is still flush from Frank's good-bye, but I'd burn every last pair of shoes I own before I give this busybody the satisfaction of thinking she's shamed me. "Miss Mamie, I was not, as you say, cavorting. I was on a proper date with Frank Darling, who, by the way, is a perfect gentleman."

My tone is giving the old bat the vapors. "Furthermore, I overheard you on the phone this morning and know for a fact that you're having money troubles. I paid my rent six months in advance, and unless you're prepared to give that money back, I suggest you keep your opinions and your innuendos to yourself."

I turn to glide victoriously toward the stairs, but a huge mitt grabs my slender arm. I look down at the meaty hand, red as the old woman's face, and stare defiantly. Inside I'm terrified. And what if she throws me out? Where would I go? Back to Charleston? I don't want that.

Angry lines zigzag across the witch's face; her beady black eyes are no better than the gator's in the pond. "Watch yourself," the woman says hoarsely and lets go before retreating to her den.

"What was that all about?" Claire slips into the hallway in her bathrobe. Her hair is undone and hangs down below her waist. "Are you all right?"

"Yes. Honestly, I don't want to cause any trouble. But that

woman just gets to me." Vada lowers her voice. "Are the boys asleep?"

"Yes. Daniel was upset with me for embarrassing him." Claire smiles. "Says he'll never have a chance with you now."

"Oh, he's so sweet."

"He's smitten with you, Vada, as smitten as Frank Darling." Vada laughs and blushes. "I'm sorry, but I couldn't help but watch you on the walkway just now. I could feel the longing all the way up here." Claire peeks in on the boys, sprawled across the same cot, a mass of arms and legs.

"Come to my room, and I'll tell you all about it."

A door opens and Mr. Stanley looks out into the hallway. His eyes roam over Claire. Vada gives him a dirty look and steps in front of her. He shrugs and heads toward the washroom, farting all the way.

She looks in on the boys one last time and follows Vada to her room. They plop down on the bed like a couple of teenagers, giggling, shushing each other.

"So was it dreamy?" Claire asks.

"Oh, Claire, he is wonderful. Kind and handsome. And romantic, very romantic."

"I'm so happy for you, Vada."

While Claire is genuinely happy listening to the details of her date, the contrast with her own life makes her pull her robe around her a little tighter. Is Mr. Stanley her only option for getting the boys out of the boardinghouse? He doesn't even act like he likes her children, and the way he leers at her most all of the time is unsettling at best. Could she really endure that—or, God forbid, worse—on a daily basis?

The sound of the toilet flushing stops Vada in mid-sentence. Mr. Stanley clears his throat several times, like he often does when he gets up during the night, like it's some sort of mating call he expects Claire to answer. She can see Vada's heart breaking for her. Her own heart doesn't have that luxury. She has to make a better life for her boys. They deserve that and so much more, and if it means marrying Mr. Stanley, so be it.

"Claire, what you said earlier about—are you really considering him?"

"The boys are getting big, Vada, and I barely make enough to pay the rent for our room. I don't see any other options."

"Once I start working, I can help you."

"You're a dear, and your offer means more than you will ever know, but I need to think about a permanent solution."

"How about finding a better job?"

"There are no jobs here."

"I picked up a newspaper." Vada unsnaps her pocketbook, pulls the paper out. "There must be something." She leafs through the pages like she's looking for something, until she gets to the classified ads in the back.

"That's sweet of you, really it is, but even if there was a job there, I don't have enough money to move to Charleston or Walterboro, and I certainly couldn't commute."

"That's not fair. Most all of these jobs are for men." Vada's long, slender finger trails down the page. "Ooh, here's one, and it's here, in Round O. Housekeeper wanted for country estate. Funny, I haven't seen any estate around here."

"Must be the Sheridan plantation. It sits back about a half mile from the highway, down a private road; it's been closed for years." Claire grabs the newspaper and reads the ad for herself. "Apply in person at Barkley, Barkley, and Jameson, Attorneys at

Law, Pinckney Street, Charleston. Oh, Vada, this sounds perfect, but I have no way to get there."

"I bet if I asked, Frank would let you borrow his car. And I could watch the boys for you."

"Thank you, that would be wonderful. Speaking of the boys, I'd better get back to my room," Claire says, hugging Vada. "Do you mind terribly, asking Frank about the car?"

"I'll do it for you tomorrow, and I'll make sure he says yes."

I change into my nightgown, and the memory of Frank's kisses makes me blush and clutch my pillow to my chest. I can't help but think about how Frank and I started off this evening, headed in the wrong direction. How things had changed the minute I said what I wanted. Granted, I've had a very limited experience with men, but I have serious doubts all men are like Frank. Justin certainly wasn't. Even after having him thrown at me my whole life, I was never conscious of my own desires. I close my eyes and see Frank's jade eyes full of wanting. In my cotton peignoir, my face burns in the dark at the memory of the electricity that passed between us just shaking hands, our first kiss, and the thought of him seeing me now. What would it be like to undo the tiny pearl buttons, to slide the paper-thin fabric off my shoulders and give myself to him?

These feelings are exciting, but scary, too. They've awakened every sense in my body, so that good sense seems to go right out the window. Our first kiss left me so breathless, it almost made me forget about what I need from him, almost made me forget about going to Memphis. This thing with Frank is going too fast, streaking toward a place I've never been before, with little thought to the consequence of loving and being loved. Darby knows all too well about that, and Claire does, too.

I whip back the starched sheet, get down on my knees beside the bed, and bow my head.

Dear God. You've given me so much to be thankful for, a new home, a new friend, a wonderful date with Frank Darling. Forgive me where I have failed you. Please help me find Darby so that I can help her; it sounds like she's in a terrible fix, and I'm sure she'd be much better off here with me.

Please help Claire get the job here, and do send a good man her way, an honest man. He doesn't have to have money, but, as you know, it would really help with three boys. If at all possible, please make him handsome, and young, or at least closer to her age than Methuselah, and good. Very, very good.

I hear the horrible guttural sound of Mr. Stanley clearing his throat. He does it more than once, like he's trying to get Claire's attention.

And please, God, don't let her be desperate enough to open her door to Mr. Stanley. Don't let her sell herself so very short. Amen.

·Chapter Eight·

"You idiot." Saying the words doesn't make him feel any better.

Frank strips out of his work clothes and sits on the bed in his Skivvies. He can't believe he forgot to rinse the sweat out of the white dress shirt he wore on his date Monday night. And he is an even bigger fool for agreeing to go to Wednesday prayer meeting with Vada. He would have done anything she asked him to, but he'd rather swim out into the black water and kiss that big gator than darken the doors of the Round O Baptist Church.

Why can't Round O have more than one flavor of church? Maybe Methodist. At least they move their preachers around every three or four years. Reverend Gilbert Smudge has been thumping his Bible here since Frank was twelve, marking down sins in his own little book while assuring his flock God forgives and forgets. But not Smudge, not in twelve damned years.

Vada will probably have him prance right down to the front row, just so he can feel the spittle when Smudge screams at the top of his lungs that every living soul has been saved by the glory of God, *except* Franklin James Darling.

He could beg off, tell Vada he's too tired after work, or sick, but there's no good reason to put lipstick on the truth. Lying changes things, and not for the better. Shiftless people lie. Desperate people lie, and, knowing where Frank wants to end up with Vada, he's determined not to start out that way. She deserves better, and he'll be damned if he'll not give it to her. He puts his stinking shirt on, buttons it up, and tucks it in. The thin black tie feels more like a noose, and his shoes haven't changed overnight. But the last time he held Vada, he told her he'd change the world for her. Maybe it's time for him to change a little, swallow his damn pride, and take the two-hour butt whipping that's sure to come.

He walks across the crossroads to Miss Mamie's house. The bachelors are sitting on the porch, dressed in their everyday clothes, with no intention of going to prayer meeting. The widow's boys—Claire's boys—run out of the house and explode, laughing as soon as the screen door closes behind them. Miss Mamie waddles to the door and pushes it open so they can get the full effect of her mean face and giant form, which is shrouded in gray—to match her heart, if she has one.

Claire and Vada walk out of the house together, and Vada stops talking as soon as she sees Frank. Claire blushes and nudges Vada forward, and she glides down the steps and motions for Claire to follow her. Reluctantly, she does. Surely Vada's not thinking of dragging Claire to church with them. Maybe it would serve as a much-needed distraction, considering Claire quit going after her husband died.

"Ladies."

"Hello, Frank." As she pulls him aside, Vada looks like she

wants to kiss him in the best possible way, but Claire follows. "We have a favor to ask."

"Really, it's me who needs the favor, Frank," Claire says. "May I borrow your car to drive to Charleston? It's for a job interview."

Frank has never loaned his car to anybody, much less a woman who rarely drives, but Vada is looking at him like he hung the moon five minutes ago. "Sure. What's in Charleston?"

"A job that's here, but the interview is in Charleston. Would tomorrow morning be okay? I assure you that I am a very good driver."

"It's fine by me; I'll be working."

"Then it's settled," Vada says, and takes his hand, and they walk four doors down to the church.

Wiry old Mr. Legate hands Frank a bulletin before he looks up at him. He drops the whole stack like he's just seen Judas Iscariot himself. Frank bends and picks them up for him, desperately trying to catch his eye, to plead for a little of that forgiveness the sign out front claims they hand out so freely. But Mr. Legate just snatches the bulletins out of his hands and shoves one toward the couple behind them.

"He must be surprised to see a visitor," Vada says. "I'm so glad we could come."

Early in his life, it was clear that Frank was headed straight to hell just from being born to a half-Catholic father. And then, from the mortal sin he committed, at least in the reverend's book. It wasn't like Frank expected for folks to extend the right hand of Christian fellowship to him, but he didn't expect the looks he gets from regulars at the diner. He can't help but be distracted by their stares, and by the time he looks for Vada, she's marched herself down to the third pew from the front, in the dead center of the congregation.

After the pianist plays for a while, Vada looks over her shoulder at the people who can't shut up about Frank being there. She leans into him. "They're being very rude." He moves a hymnal's width apart from her, and the whispering subsides a little. She smiles at him and touches his skinny black necktie, setting their tongues wagging again.

The reverend makes his entrance from the back, shaking hands down the aisle and blessing people as he goes. Until he gets to Frank. Smudge stops and stares at him with his beady little Baptist eyes, and Frank stares right back. He will not apologize to God or anybody for following this woman into hell. Vada shakes his hand and he lingers, looking at Frank, not her.

"How nice to have a visitor in our midst." She gives a curt thank-you and pulls away, not fully understanding the meanness that is emanating from him. "I hope you find today's sermon . . . illuminating, my dear." The bulletin clearly says the sermon title is "The Servitude of Mary and Martha." But the minute that man tells folks to turn their Bibles to Second Samuel and the story of the *seduction*, Frank knows he is in for it.

Vada nods and opens her Bible, listening intently, letting the innuendo go straight over her pretty head. According to the reverend, Bathsheba was damned because she could have resisted the temptations of David but *he* didn't. Several times during the sermon, the reverend got his personal pronouns mixed up. By the time he was done screaming and hyperventilating, it was clear, by his own theology, Bathsheba and especially David were *both* going to burn in hell *forever*, for what they did. And for the first time in twelve years, questions about the rumors were put to rest, and every soul in church knew Mrs. Smudge really had seduced Frank at fifteen. Everyone except Vada.

If that wasn't bad enough, the closing hymn was "Oh Ye

Abomination," and Smudge had the congregation sing all six verses. Twice. Frank got some apologetic looks from people who'd openly snubbed him earlier. But everybody there was afraid to shake his hand in front of God and the reverend, so he headed toward the side door of the church and was grateful Vada slipped out behind him.

"That was an interesting take on the scriptures." Vada walked beside him, brushing up against his hand but not reaching for it.

"I'm sorry. I wouldn't know. I'm not much on church. But I did make you dinner before I picked you up," *and then showered, so I wouldn't smell like fried chicken.* "I'd hoped we could picnic down by the creek, but it's still hot. I don't know how you feel about being alone in the diner with me—"

"You sound like I should be afraid of you, Frank Darling." She laughs and reaches for his hand.

"No, Vada."

"After our last kiss, you won't hold my hand, Frank?"

"If you can't feel those churchgoers burning a hole in your back, look over your shoulder and see for yourself. I'll hold your hand all right, but not now."

"Don't be silly." She wants Frank to look at her, because she knows he can't deny those blue eyes anything.

"You're a schoolteacher, and we just went to church. People will talk."

"I don't see how this is any different than being alone with you on a date; besides, I smell chicken, and it smells marvelous." She opens the screen door of the diner, and Frank stops short. He can still feel people standing in the church parking lot a hundred yards away, watching them. He can't let her do this.

"I need to tell you something." She follows him over to the huge mimosa tree with three crates turned on end. Cigar and hand-rolled cigarette butts litter the ground from where the bachelors from Miss Mamie's congregate to solve the world's problems. He motions for Vada to sit, and she does, without a thought for her pretty pink dress splayed out on the ground. "It's about church today."

She looks up at him so that he is lost again in those blue eyes. He wants to remember her pretty smile that he will never see again. "The truth is, Vada, I haven't been to church in years."

"Oh, Frank, that's nothing to be ashamed of. To be completely honest, until today, I'd never wished for the boring liturgical Episcopal service I grew up with."

Frank sits across from her, because standing over her seems wrong; he should be down on his knees, so he won't miss a beat between his confession and begging for forgiveness.

"That sermon today was for me." She looks puzzled and starts to say something, but he cuts her off. "The reverend had good reason to preach it. When I was fifteen I . . . his wife . . . we—"

"Oh, Frank." She laughs until she sees he's serious. She reaches out and runs her fingers down the side of his face. He leans his head against her hand, sandwiching it against his shoulder for a few seconds.

"You mean—" She stops when he nods his head. "Oh, Frank, you can't be serious. You were just a boy."

He can't look at her. "It lasted about a year. She left after he caught us." But the good reverend didn't leave. He'll probably stay here until he dies, to remind Frank of what he did.

"And you think people think differently of you because of that?"

"I know they do. There were people there today who believe *they'll* burn in hell if they darken my door. They drive all the way to Walterboro for groceries and only come into the store if it's a dire emergency." He looks at her so she'll know he's sincere, that he's trying to own up to what he did. "I don't regret asking you out Monday night, but maybe I shouldn't have. I don't want to cause you any trouble."

"Did you love her?" Vada's face is serious.

"I thought I did. Lila was pretty, but she was always so sad." Except when she was with Frank and she seemed happy, in a desperate sort of way. "You're right, I was just a boy. A stupid boy."

She stands and brushes off the front of her dress. Her long, slender fingers pluck one of the mimosa blossoms that matches her dress. She twirls it around the tip of her nose, looking at Frank, deciding his fate.

"I wanted you to know—thought it was only fair that you know what you're getting into by being with me."

His breath leaves him as she turns and walks away. He can't move a muscle; besides, he has no right to go after her, to start something with her that might soil her good name. All he can do is watch her as she goes. She looks back over her shoulder and starts up the steps of the diner, a silent invitation. He starts breathing again, believing again.

·Chapter Nine·

He's put a tablecloth on the center table. There's even a mason jar with wildflowers from the field between here and the church. I recognize the tall, spritely buttercups and the pretty yellow and orange blanket flowers that trail gracefully out of the makeshift vase, but I've never seen the frilly blue flowers before. I take a seat, add my mimosa blossom to the jar, and prop my chin up on my hands to let Frank know I'm not going anywhere.

Just the thought of what that horrible man did to Frank today, and in a church no less, makes my blood boil. I'm sure the last thing Frank Darling wanted was to go back to that place, and yet he did it for me. And that awful woman who, well, I'm not sure what the word is for deflowering a boy. What about her? Oh, and the reverend, with his evil eyes, singing that last hymn at the top of his lungs? Why, *he's* the abomination, and his wife is not much better.

I watch Frank in the kitchen, fixing our plates. I can see the hurt on his face. Every once in a while, he looks up to see if I'm still here. I won't embarrass him further by saying the words out loud, but I'm staying put.

He sets two plates on the table, sits down, and starts eating. I bow my head, and he drops his fork. "Dear God," I say, reaching for Frank's hand, "bless us, your creatures, for the food we are about to receive and keep us mindful that you are a loving and forgiving God. Amen." *There.* I smile at him. "Let's eat."

The food is scrumptious, and the longer we eat, the better Frank seems to feel. He watches intently for my approval as I try his mashed potatoes for the first time, his black-eyed peas. "The chicken is wonderful, Frank. Did your mother teach you how to cook?"

"No." He looks taken aback, then pushes his food around his plate. "My daddy had this place, and his daddy before him. I'm not sure who taught them, but they taught me."

"What's the first thing you learned to make?"

He smiles. "Biscuits. I got them so wrong, the dog gave them to the field mice, and even they wouldn't eat them."

The biscuits are golden brown and look like they've been buttered on the top. I break one in half and take a bite. The next thing I know, my shoulders are up around my ears and I'm breathing out an *mmmm* sound. Frank's smiling his proud, beautiful smile. The world would be a perfect place if Frank Darling's biscuits married Rosa Lee's crab cakes.

"What about you? Who taught you how to cook?"

"Oh." I swallow hard. "No one, really."

"You must be a natural. What's your favorite dish to make?"

I can't help but laugh, knowing that if I made anything, the dog and the mice would be dead. "I can't cook. My mother did all the cooking." *My murrah.* "I'm hopeless in the kitchen, a complete calamity."

"I could teach you." Frank smiles, and I believe he could. "Now, as I recall, the last time we shared a meal, you said you had a favor to ask of me."

My turn to be penitent. I put my fork down and shake my head. It's clear, after church, that I'll have to take the bus to Memphis. The last thing Frank Darling needs is another reason to set tongues wagging. "Never mind. It was nothing."

"Vada." I love the way he says my name, like it's holy. "I told you I'd do anything for you, and that still stands." He reaches on the other side of the counter for two plates, each with a huge slab of chocolate cake topped off with dark, gooey frosting and pecan halves. After stuffing myself on the meal, I can't believe I'm actually salivating.

I put a forkful into my mouth and sigh. He laughs and starts in on his cake. "Frank, this is wonderful. How do you get it so moist?"

"Buttermilk and a little Coca-Cola. I'm glad you like it." He gets up and puts two cups on the table and starts to pour the coffee, and then shakes his head. "How could I forget? You like tea, with milk."

"I love coffee, especially with chocolate."

"Sugar?"

He laughs when I drop five cubes into the hot brew. "The meal, the flowers, the dessert, it's all so wonderful, Frank."

He pushes his cake away and takes my hand. "Enough with the compliments, Vada. Tell me what you want."

My eyes are wide from the reference that could mean anything from passionate kisses to more chocolate cake. With Frank being the only person I know with a car, I admit I'd considered him as a way to get to Memphis and back, a handsome, charming vehicle. But after church and the scrumptious meal he made to please me, I'm confused. I still must help Darby, but I'm not sure I'm prepared to ruin Frank Darling to get to Memphis.

"You can trust me, Vada. Please."

"As you know, I don't have a car." He looks hurt, like he's thinking, *Oh, great, she wants to borrow my car again.* "There's someone in Memphis—"

"Jesus, Vada." He runs his hand through his sandy-blond hair and looks at me. He's hurt, angry. "Who is he?"

"He's not a he at all, Frank. He's a she, Darby, my best and dearest friend. She's in trouble and needs my help." I can tell by his face that he's utterly confused, and as flustered as he is, I'm not completely sure how much I should tell him.

"What kind of trouble?"

"She owes a horrible woman a lot of money. If you can just take me to the bus station in Walterboro—"

"It would take at least twelve hours to drive there by car, no telling how long by bus, and I'm not putting you on a bus."

"Please, Frank."

"No, I'll drive you myself." His brow furrows with worry. "And then you're going to pay this woman off?"

"Of course I'll pay the debt. But the real reason for going is to find Darby and talk her into coming back here to live with me."

He lets out a frustrated sigh. "Hell, I can't let you go off by yourself, not like that. It's just not safe. But you saw the looks I got today, even after twelve years. Are you sure you want that? Because if you and I leave out of here together and don't come back for three or four days, that's exactly what you'll get, or worse."

"I don't care what those people think."

"You should. They're the same people whose taxes are going to pay you to teach their children, Vada, and this won't look right at all. Honest, I want to take you, but I'll be damned if I'll be part and parcel to your getting run out of town."

"You're right, Frank. I should care about those busybodies, but I don't. It's imperative that I help Darby, and soon." Looking into his eyes, I know he cares about me, and I'm tearing him in two. Who will take care of the diner? How can both of us leave town without looking like we're together?

"The thought of what this could do to your good name makes me say no, but I'm a selfish bastard. Even if I wanted to, I couldn't turn down two solid days with you." He leans across the table and rubs a dab of chocolate off my lower lip with his thumb. "The diner's closed next week, for the Fourth of July; I go fishing every year up at my cabin on the Santee Cooper River. I could pack my stuff and head out of town, same as always. Leave before noon, so everybody can see. Tiny can bring you to me the next morning. I trust Tiny, and you can, too."

"Lord, Frank, did somebody die? You got your hat in your hand." Tiny swings the screen door open to her little hole-in-the-wall and shoos the flies away that have congregated over her mangy old mutt lying in front of the door. "Just step over Sheba. She ain't feeling good today."

This house makes Frank smile, remembering his mother in a good light, which is rare and justified. He used to picture this place every time his mama told the story about the teeny-tiny woman in the teeny-tiny house. Mama'd wanted to be an actress her whole life, so whenever she told the story, she gave a grand performance that left her drained and sad afterward.

"You want some tea, shug?"

"No, I can't stay long."

"What brings you out this way on a Wednesday night?"

"Vada."

"Do tell, and you look like you've been to church, Frank."

"I have." She raises her eyebrows. "Got preached at for two hours. It was bad that Vada was there, but as embarrassing as it was, it was easier to take with her by my side."

"She's a pretty woman. Seems real sweet." Tiny leans over and pats his leg. "Have yourself a good time, Frank, and if it turns into something, all the better. You deserve it."

"Thanks, but I need your help." He tells Tiny the plan he hatched, and she doesn't flinch, just nods like she's jotting it down on the little green order pad in her mind. She doesn't judge him, which is one of the things he loves most about her. Tiny has never judged him. "Sounds crazy, huh?"

"What time are you wanting me to have her at the cabin?"

"You'll do it, then? Just like that?"

She looks annoyed. "I helped your mama and daddy out with you, changed your diapers, and powdered your behind. You ought to know better than to ask such a thing."

"I'd appreciate if you could have her at the cabin Tuesday morning. In case anybody asks, she's going to tell Miss Mamie you're taking her to the bus station in Walterboro to go home for Independence Day. I'll call you when we get back, and you can drop her at the boardinghouse so everything looks like it's on the up-and-up."

Tiny nods like she understands Frank loves this woman enough to break unspoken rules that could shut down the store and the diner for good. "You sure about this, Frank?"

"More sure than I've ever been of anything in my life."

"What's in Memphis?" Tiny says.

"As long as I'm with her, it doesn't matter."

·Chapter Ten·

Early Thursday morning, Claire arrives in Charleston. She parks the Plymouth on King Street and walks two blocks to the address on Pinckney Street. She tries to feel confident in her best dress. She needs this job. She looks down at the gray plaid fabric and knows it's out of season and long since out of style. She'd made it just before she found out she was expecting Jonathan, and after giving birth to three boys, she was surprised it fit at all.

She stops short of the cream-colored stucco law offices of Barkley, Barkley, and Jameson and takes a deep breath. Even the tall, ornately carved door is intimidating. She takes another breath, opens the door, and then almost turns around and walks out.

A long settee covered in fine red satin brocade is flanked by a half dozen intricately carved mahogany chairs, three on one side, three on the other. The floors are so highly polished, they look wet, the rugs so lavish, she has to fight the urge to take her dusty, worn shoes off. She knows the thick silk draperies hanging over the long windows overlooking the street cost more than she will ever make in her lifetime. And if the pretty redhead on the telephone at the reception desk hadn't motioned for her to come in, she probably would have turned and left.

Claire feels like she is going to throw up; she doesn't belong here, and, to be honest, she doesn't belong at the Sheridan mansion, either. She is a mother of three boys who is handy with a needle and thread. Nothing more. Nothing less. From somewhere down the long hallway of offices, someone clears their throat, reminding her of Mr. Stanley and the boardinghouse. Claire doesn't have a choice. She has to be more—if not for herself, for her boys.

The woman ends her call and smiles at Claire. "May I help you?"

"I'm responding to the newspaper ad for a housekeeper—in Round O. Has the position been filled yet?"

"No, dear," the woman says. "The ad has run for some time. Mr. Jameson has had trouble finding a suitable applicant. I'm sure he'll want to see you, but he's very busy. You may have to wait for quite a while."

"That's fine." Claire is sure this is a waste of time. What was she thinking?

The woman picks up the phone and speaks with Mr. Jameson, the friendly tenor of her voice changes, and it's clear this woman is intimidated. "Yes, sir. No, sir. Certainly, sir." She ends the call and smiles wanly at Claire. "Go ahead and get your references out, so you'll be ready."

But Claire has no references, no experience. Nothing. She nods and rummages through her purse and pulls out three papers. They are references in a way, pictures the boys drew for her a few weeks ago, for Mother's Day. Jonathan's is mostly colorful scrib-

ble; Peter tried to capture the mimosa tree in full bloom, with
Claire perched on one of the crates the bachelors sit on. Across
the bottom of the page, "World's Greatest Mama" is written in
waxy black letters.

She looks at Daniel's drawing next. It's good, much more re-
fined than his brothers'. In the picture, he and Claire are standing
in front of the boardinghouse, only Claire is much smaller than
him, almost childlike, and Daniel is big. Is this how he feels, like
he's the grown-up, the protector? References or not, she must get
this job.

Three hours later, the woman's phone buzzes. She answers it, posture ramrod straight. "Yes, sir. I'll send her back now, sir." She
ends the call. "Mr. Jameson will see you, Miss Greeley." She leads
Claire down a long paneled hallway to an office; the pocket doors
are closed. The woman sucks in her breath and opens one of the
doors. "Mr. Jameson, this is Claire Greeley."

"Come on in, Miss Greeley." The dapper old man doesn't look
up from the papers scattered across his desk. "Have a seat, I'll be
right with you." He jots some notes down, and then looks at her.
No smile, almost irritated. "May I see your references?"

Claire sits on the edge of the leather wingback. "I don't have
any, sir, but I assure you I am qualified for the job." As long as
there is no cooking involved.

"I've interviewed many people for the position; all of them fell
short." He leans back in his chair, the springs creaking under his
weight. "Tell me, Miss Greeley, what makes you uniquely qualified for the job?"

"I live in Round O and know the Sheridan place well, sir." A
stretch: She's seen enough of the huge redbrick mansion from the

outside to know it's been deserted for a long time. She'd peered in the windows once, seen the furniture hiding under white drop cloths. "And I'm organized, hardworking, and dedicated."

"Well, to be honest, Miss Greeley, you put the best qualification first. You live there. I've had a hard time finding someone who is, of course, capable and willing to commute, even from Walterboro. And it's not like the crossroads has a newspaper to advertise the job locally."

"Sir, I also have three boys. I really need this job."

"And what does your husband think of you taking a job that will most certainly take time away from him and your children?"

She tries to hold her head up, to meet his gaze, but she can't look at him and say the words. Not that she expects any pity from this man. She despises that first instant of recognition from everyone that she is alone, a widow. "My husband died in the war, sir." There is no apology, just a long silence. He waits like she's on the witness stand trying to finish her difficult testimony. She looks up at him, tilts her chin up, shoulders back. If she can make it through these last two years without Bobby, she can do anything. "And you needn't worry about my abilities. What I lack in experience, I'll make up with diligence and devotion."

"Well, you've certainly got spunk, I'll give you that." He lowers his glasses and peers at her across the tops of the thick black frames. "Miss Greeley, I find it highly doubtful you'll get this job. With no references or résumé to speak of, I know I wouldn't hire you. But I'm impressed by your attitude and you do live right there in Round O, so I'll do you a courtesy and wire Mr. Sheridan in Europe and ask him what he would like to do."

"Thank you, Mr. Jameson. You won't regret this."

"I wouldn't get too excited if I were you. My office will contact you next Friday, or sooner, with the verdict."

Claire doesn't focus on Mr. Jameson's concerns about her lack of experience. She can't. Instead, she holds on to his stingy compliments and the hope that Reginald Sheridan will give her the job. For the first time since the war ended and she thought her husband was coming home, she feels like a girl again. Not a mother, not a widow, more like a teenager who squeals and swoons over the smallest things, but back in Miss Mamie's house, she must do this silently.

She rushes upstairs and into her room, where Vada is keeping the children. Vada jumps up, hugging her, rocking from side to side. Crying. The rush of fear gushes into Claire's happiness, filling her with dread, reminding her that precious little has gone well since Bobby died.

"You're crying." Claire swipes under Vada's eyes with her thumbs. "What happened?"

Lying on the bed, with his thumb in his mouth, Jonathan hears her voice and lets out an ear-piercing scream. Claire's heart races. She snatches him up and holds him close as he buries his little head into the crook of her neck. His brothers look penitent, Vada is pale, almost lifeless-looking, eyes full of tears.

"I'm so sorry, Claire," Vada can barely get the words out. "I was reading with the boys. Jonathan was playing on the floor—"

Claire runs her hands over Jonathan's head, his back, his arms, examining, expecting to feel something broken. She wants to scream at Vada, at Daniel and Peter. *You were supposed to watch him. All of you were supposed to watch him.* But she knows what an escape artist Jonathan is, how one minute he can be playing quietly on the floor and the next he can be stealthily sliding down the stairs on his bottom to see what kind of trouble he can get into.

Between sniffles, Vada tells the story. Her feet had barely

touched the stairs as she ran toward the sound of Jonathan sobbing. She'd burst into the kitchen to find Miss Mamie standing
over him with a long green switch that had been stripped bare, so
it would sting like a leather whip.

Dozens of angry red welts cover his little legs. Claire's heart bursts
as she gently touches the pink slashing marks that cover her baby's
calves and the tops of his thighs. She holds him closer. "*Shhhhh.
It's okay. Mama's got you.*"

"I wanted a cookie," he sobs; his tiny, stubby fingers frame her
face, heartbreaking blue eyes looking into hers. "She made me
pick a switch for her to use on me—and then she—hurt me." He
buries his head into the crook of her neck again.

"You know the rules, Mrs. Greeley. The children are not
allowed in the kitchen," the old witch snaps. Everyone was so
caught up in the moment, no one had heard Miss Mamie haul
herself up the steps. "Make sure your little brats follow them, or
I'll throw the lot of you out."

"*Miss Mamie,*" Claire can't afford that tone; she has no place
else to go, and this abhorrent woman knows it. "I will watch
Jonathan more closely. Should this happen again, which I'm sure
it won't, all you need to do is call one of us, and we'll gladly come
get him."

"Next time, I'll pull his little pants down and tan his behind.
That's what you should be doing right now; that's what he needs,"
she huffs and limps toward the stairs.

Just the sight of the woman, let alone her tone, has Jonathan
wailing so hard, he can barely breathe. Vada is sandwiched between Peter and Daniel, their arms wrapped around her middle.
As Miss Mamie disappears down the steps, they run to Claire,

and she pulls them into her. Peter's crying now, too, and Daniel just clings to her, full of worry and looking so much like Bobby, her heart breaks a little more.

It's bad enough the boys lost their father and Claire was forced to take a room at the boardinghouse, but she has never wanted them to know how tenuous their situation is. She is their mother, for God's sake, their protector, and yet she's failing them and there is nothing she can do about it except pray that job comes through next week. And if it doesn't, she will do the unthinkable and marry Mr. Stanley.

There's a hurricane somewhere in the Atlantic, maybe as far away as Africa, that's blowing the hot, humid air toward the center of the state, making the tail end of Saturday afternoon almost pleasant. Miss Mamie yanks open the door and glares at Frank. "I've come calling for Vada." He stands a little taller, so that he's looking down on her.

"After church Wednesday night, I'm surprised you have the nerve to show your face anywhere." She waits for a reaction, but Frank won't give her one. "You think you're gonna lead another poor woman astray, Frank *Darling*? I'll not have anybody in my house cavorting with the likes of you."

"Miss Mamie." He looks the devil straight in the eyes. "I know I'm a good man. And you know I'm a good man. Now I'm going to ask Vada if she wants to go for a walk, and regardless of what you heard in church, I'm guessing she's going to say yes."

"Frank." Vada is coming down the stairs. "How lovely to see you again." She brushes past Miss Mamie like she's not even there.

The old woman looks like she's about to pop with anger, and

suddenly Frank feels a little remorseful. What if Vada gets kicked out of the boardinghouse on account of him? She'd lose her job. There'd be nothing to keep her here. He spins around to see the old bat trying to stare a hole in them. "I'll have her back before dark, Miss Mamie."

When they are out of earshot, Vada scolds him for being nice to the old woman. "I know all about the Golden Rule, Frank, but really. She's so horrible to everyone, I seriously doubt it applies to her. She actually beat poor little Jonathan with a switch yesterday. You should see his legs."

"I'm sorry to hear that, but I riled her, even enjoyed it a little bit, until I realized she looked mad enough to throw both of us off of her property."

"Well, she rails like a storm cloud, but she can't toss me out like she threatens all the time, and not Claire and the boys, either. Miss Mamie's got money troubles. No matter what that horrible woman says, she can't afford to lose me."

He threads his fingers between hers, loving the way her soft hand feels against his rough skin, and they walk toward Myers Creek in silence. It's been so hot and so long since it's rained, for all Frank knows, he may be taking her to see a glorified ditch.

Thankfully, there is a trickle of water running through the creek bed. Vada begins to unlace the ribbons of her sandals, midway up her slender calves. Her long, painted fingernails loosen the ties, unwrapping her legs so slowly, Frank has to turn away. "You can look, Frank," she laughs. "They're just shoes." But he can't turn around right now. It's the most sensuous thing he's ever seen in his life.

She squeals. He's sure an old cottonmouth has gotten her good. But when he whips around, her face is gleeful, her mouth drawn up into an O. She wades farther into the clear ankle-deep water. With the water so shallow, she doesn't need to hike her dress up, but she does, revealing more leg than he has a right to see at this point in their courtship. But he can't turn away. She's looking down at the current swirling around her feet, smiling at her toes pushing into the sandy bottom.

"How can the water be so cold when it's so hot out?" Frank knows why, but he can't answer her. All he can do is stand here and watch her marvel over the creek. "Come on, Frank. Take your shoes off."

He takes them off even faster than he would have if she'd asked him to strip naked, and wades out toward her. She laughs and links both of her hands in his, and the connection feels complete. Fluid energy passes between them, and he wonders how he lived without her before, if he really lived at all. Then Vada Hadley came into his diner, his life, his heart, and everything inside him shifted. Changed.

He doesn't know how he can stand in the water that comes from an icy underground spring. He's never been able to hold his fist in it for more than thirty seconds. But he loves this woman, her laugh, her smile, the way she wonders over every little thing. She bends down and fingers the current before scooping up some water and flicking it at him. "You're awful quiet, Frank Darling."

He's afraid to move, afraid to let go of her. Ever. Maybe he can't move; the creek is so cold, he can't feel his feet. "Can I kiss you?"

She nods, and he moves closer to her. She smells intoxicating, like roses and yellow jasmine, citrus. As his mouth covers hers, she puts her arms around his neck, pulling herself up onto him and out of the water. He wraps his arms around her waist to hold her, suspended in the air. His breathing is fast; the kiss is long and dreamlike.

"Vada." He scoops her into his arms; she lays her head against his chest, listening to his heart beating for her. He wades back onto the creek bank and sets her down. She looks up at him and touches his face before she pulls his head down to kiss her again.

"I like you very much, Frank, *darling*." She's said the words the way he'd dreamed she would, and he is mesmerized. He should say something, but he can't. If he does, he'll tell her he loves her, and he's afraid she'll run, because it's too soon. Even worse, what if she doesn't believe him? What if she doesn't believe in love at first sight? Hell, he didn't until she walked into the diner. She might think he's crazy, and not just about her. So he kisses her again, slowly, like he's savoring something delicious, and hopes she knows that he more than likes her.

My breathing is fast, too fast, and my body responds to Frank's. Are these the feelings Mother, and even Rosa Lee, cautioned against? Is this what my mother told me I would eventually feel for Justin? *And* I told Frank how much I like him, and he said nothing back. Well, that's not true, he kissed me like I've never been kissed by anyone, like he was trying to show me instead of tell me.

I push away, and he obediently sets my feet on the creek bank. He brushes his lips against my cheeks in a cordial kiss and looks at the horizon. "We'd better head back now."

I sit to put my shoes back on, and he kneels and slips one of the sandals onto my foot. He holds the long white satin, looking adorable and completely confused. I take his hands and guide them until the ribbons are in place. He does the other sandal by himself and lingers a moment over the tie. I can feel that he wants more from me. Until now, I've never thought of giving myself to anyone, but the idea is exciting and terrifying.

"Thank you, Frank." He helps me up, and we stroll back to

the boardinghouse, arm in arm, for the whole crossroads to see. He tells me when Tiny will pick me up and that I should tell everyone, including Claire, that I'm going home for the holiday. The word *home* gives me pause and makes me wonder why Frank hasn't really pressed me about the place I'm from. He walks me to the front steps and kisses me on the cheek, in front of Miss Mamie, who is standing guard at the screen door.

"Cavorter," she hisses and disappears.

"Don't let her give you any grief." Frank smiles and pushes a wispy blond tress away from my face. I shake my head and wish for another one of his kisses that make me weak-kneed.

"I'll miss you," the words come out in one breath. Four days is forever.

"I'll see you soon." He kisses the back of my hand tenderly, sending little shivers down my thighs, making me want more kisses. More than just kisses. "Good night."

Sunday morning Claire is waiting at the bottom of the stairs, and I know all is forgiven. Even though she kept telling me she blamed Jonathan's sweet tooth and Miss Mamie for what happened, I'm not sure I believed her until now. I haven't pressed her about the job interview or her plans, although I'm dying to know if she'll get the job. She'd said the interview went well, and she was waiting to hear back from the attorney, with the verdict, as he'd called it. How sad that it will indeed be a verdict, because with her boys huddled around her that night Miss Mamie threatened Claire, it was plain to see that she was going to do whatever she had to do to get them out of this dreadful place. And I couldn't blame her.

But this morning, Claire's face is hopeful, like if I tell her how sweet Frank's kisses were, she'll be able to taste them, too. "After we eat breakfast, I want to hear all about your walk last night," she whispers as we hurry into the dining room. After a blessing— more or less a heavenward growl—Miss Mamie nods and we start filling our plates. Yesterday's biscuits, overcooked grits, and sausages boiled down to shoe leather make me think perhaps Miss Mamie isn't well. Only the fresh sliced tomatoes are worth eating.

The old bat doesn't believe a word when I declare I'm going *home*, and, to be honest, I don't think Claire does, either. It's bad enough that I'm living a lie just by moving to Round O, but I can't help myself. I window-dress my announcement with the kind of Fourth of July celebration I've wanted my parents to give me since I was a little girl. The bachelors are oblivious, talking about some ridiculous baseball game, and the boys are concentrating on eating and not misbehaving in any possible way.

"Maybe you should give me your parents' phone number." Miss Mamie eyes me hard enough to break me in two.

"I have a surprise," Claire blurts out. Mr. Stanley stops arguing over who is the best whatever in baseball and leers at her. My God, I think he's drooling. "Or I hope to have some news when you come back, Vada."

"Good news?" Methuselah says hopefully. The other two bachelors punch each other and smile while I shudder at the thought of Claire desperate enough to marry Mr. Stanley.

I recross my legs and give him a good swift kick. "Oh, so sorry." He winces and rubs his leg under the table.

"Do tell, Claire." Miss Mamie is glaring at Claire. She must know about Mr. Stanley's intentions; no doubt it would hurt her to lose two boarders.

Claire shrugs and looks down at her plate, her smile fading. "I don't want to jinx it."

"You, of all people, should know there are no jinxes," Miss Mamie snaps. "Just rock-hard luck and plenty of it."

"We'll see about that," Claire says quietly.

I feel a tug on my sleeve. "Miss Vada? How will you get to your house? In an Army truck?" little Jonathan asks, substituting his *r*'s for *w*'s. "I like Army trucks."

"No, sweet boy. I'm taking the bus. Miss Medford is going to give me a lift to the station."

Miss Mamie eyes me suspiciously. "I have to go to Walterboro tomorrow. I'll take you to the bus station. See that you get on the bus. The right bus."

"Oh, that won't be necessary. Miss Medford is glad to do it. Did I tell you all that we're going to churn ice cream?" I hear the words come out of my mouth, and my belly tightens with guilt. "Mother loves to make it for me. We'll make *two* churns. Banana and strawberry, my favorites." My face feels as red as an overripe peach. "And Father's such a jovial man; he loves to tell jokes, and even dances a jig on occasions."

"And your homecoming will certainly have him dancing." Whether Claire sees straight through my story or believes me, she seems genuinely excited. Please, God, let her get the job at the Sheridan place.

"Will you see fireworks, Miss Vada?" Daniel asks hopefully.

"Yes, Daniel, I believe I will," I say, and for the first time throughout my very detailed fabrication, I'm not blushing.

After breakfast, I watch from my window as Frank loads his car with fishing gear and bags of groceries. A minnow bucket slips out of his hand and rolls away from him. When he bends to pick it up, he glances up at my window and then looks away quickly to maintain the ruse. A car pulls up in a cloud of dust, and a young woman gets out and says something to him. He nods, and she follows him to the steps of the store.

I can't tell much about her other than she is petite, with short dark hair, and she is wearing a white cotton shirt and a pair of very short shorts. The thought of Frank alone with the woman, opening the store for her on the spur of the moment, and on the Sabbath, is alarming. And it seems like they've been in there an awfully long time.

I walk to the front porch and plop down onto the glider, waiting for them to come out. Finally the woman appears with two grocery bags. She yells something at Frank over her shoulder that makes him smile, and then gets in her car and drives off. Who is she? Is she just a customer trying to catch him before he goes on vacation? And what did she say to make him smile like that? He climbs into his car, glances at me, and waves good-bye. I don't wave back, but the bachelors do, in unison.

Of course, I will see him in three days. I know his leaving is just a ruse. I know Frank's feelings for me remain deep and true. Still, my heart lurches as he pulls onto the highway that dissects Round O. If I stand here watching his car disappear down the long, straight road, I will cry, and I'm supposed to be playing the part of the girl who is giddy about going home for the holiday.

The children are a good distraction. They lie on their stomachs, playing under the shade of the mimosa tree, away from the bachelors and the cigarette and cigar butts. Claire picked through Miss Mamie's trash last night until she found three jar lids. She washed them and gave them to the children this morning to play with. She pokes her head out the screen door to check on the boys.

"Hi, Vada. Was that Frank I saw leaving?"

"Yes, he's going fishing for the week. Looks like the boys are having fun. What are the jar lids for?"

"Didn't you ever have a roly-poly circus growing up?" I laugh at the very idea in my stuffy home. "Those little bugs will keep the boys entertained for hours, and Daniel is quite good when he does his ringmaster imitation."

On cue, Daniel sprinkles a few of the hard-shelled little bugs into each of the three miniature circus rings. At first, they roll around like BBs before they open and start crawling around the shiny silver jar lids.

"Step right up, ladies and gentlemen," Daniel huffs. "And see the greatest show on earth!" He puts a pine needle in his jar lid, and the little bugs crawl over it. "See nine lions leap across pine barrels."

"Mine are beautiful brown horses. See them jump the obstacles?" Peter shouts.

"Mine are elephants," Jonathan shouts. He gives the jar lid a little shake and squeals with delight as the bugs unfold and start crawling in all directions.

I pull Claire away, out of earshot of the children and the bachelors. "Please, Claire, tell me you're not still considering marrying that horrible old man."

The sadness returns. "I have to get the boys out of here, Vada. I just have to."

Surely she can't be serious about Mr. Stanley's proposal. "Tell me you don't believe in jinxes." Tell me you won't marry him. "The job will come through, Claire, I know it will." It has to.

One of the bugs crawls over the side of the lid, and Jonathan squeals and takes off while the boys pretend to chase him round and round the fat tree trunk. Daniel catches his baby brother and wraps his arms around him while Peter tickles the little boy's fat white belly.

Claire hurries toward them, arms crossed, making sure she has their full attention. "Not so loud, boys." She tries to look stern but can't help but smile at their adoring faces.

I whisper a short prayer to God for a handsome young prince and beg Him to be quick about it. She hugs the boys and sends them back to their play. "Oh, Claire, you are so very lucky. They're so precious."

She smiles proudly and squeezes my hand. "Now tell me about last night."

"We just walked down to the creek. Have you been there?" She nods her head and looks sad for a moment.

"Isn't the water *cold?* I bet the boys love it," I say. She shakes her head just enough to let me know that she's been there with her husband and not the boys.

"Was it romantic?" Claire whispers with a shy smile. "Did you kiss?"

"Yes. It was wonderful."

"What will you do with yourself?" She looks at me smiling, concerned. "Without Frank for a whole week?"

"He's coming back the day after the Fourth; I should be back then, too. But I'm more interested in your surprise, Claire. I do hope it's the new job."

·Chapter Eleven·

If taking Vada on this trip unchaperoned is a sin, four days of not touching her, not hearing her laugh, not seeing her eyes light up when she sees him has been enough punishment. All Frank has been able to think about is Vada, seeing her again, and going on this trip to Memphis because he'd go anywhere for her. Even hooking a huge bass before he quit fishing last night was nothing to him. The thing must have weighed close to twenty pounds, maybe more, and took a good fifteen minutes to land.

When he pulled her in, she was beautiful, heaving to breathe out of the water, her gills flapping, revealing her raspberry innards. She would have made a right good supper, but he was just fishing to pass the time until the girl he really wants arrives. Hell, he must be love-sick, because he unhooked that fish, ran his finger over her fat belly full of roe that would have fried up nice, and let her go. He ate cold pork and beans out of the can for supper. Attempted to sleep.

But that was different, too. Usually, he's a log after his head hits the pillow. Last night, when he closed his eyes, he saw Vada, her hair, her beautiful face, those soft, full lips. Seems like he stays hard over the woman constantly, and, while he knows it's natural, something about it almost makes him feel guilty, lecherous. He doesn't want to mess this up. He wants to go about it the right way. He doesn't want Vada to be the schoolteacher who got knocked up. He wants to court her, marry her, and spend the rest of his life making love to her.

That last thought gets him going again, so that he has to straighten up the place with a hard-on, which isn't really comfortable. But there hasn't been much to do since he stowed the tackle box and fishing gear in the car last night. He sees Tiny's red Ford pickup coming down the long, straight drive and wills himself soft again, because he knows Tiny Medford would say something for sure. Vada has her elbow propped out the window, long fingers trailing in the wind as the truck makes its way to the cabin.

The truck barely stops and Vada is out, gliding toward him. He stands in the doorway of the cabin, gaping at her, unable to believe how lucky he is. She hurries the last few steps but doesn't throw her arms around him, just rocks back and forth from the balls of her feet to her heels, like she's anxiously waiting for something. Frank hopes this something is his arms around her.

"The place looks good, Frank," Tiny says, lighting a cigarette. She blows the smoke heavenward, and then looks at him. He can read the lecture on her face. *Don't screw this up. Don't screw Vada up. Don't screw period.* He wants to tell Tiny it's not what she thinks, but she wouldn't believe him.

She raises her eyebrows at the bulge in his dungarees. Shit. He's grateful Vada's looking at the lake and commenting on a family of Canadian geese that should have long since gone home to Canada to avoid the hot summer.

"I hear they mate for life," Tiny says, looking at Frank. "The gander chooses up a gal, and then that's it. Forever."

While Vada goes on about how sweet and romantic that is, Tiny's staring at him stone-faced. He shakes his head at her words of warning. He knows what he's doing, and if he has anything to say about him and Vada, they will be for life. "It's the way they're made," Frank says. "Couldn't change it even if they wanted."

Tiny shrugs, snubs out her half-smoked cigarette on the porch rail, and puts it back in the pack. "Y'all have a real good time."

"Thanks again, Miss Medford, for the ride." Vada hugs Tiny, and the surprise on her weathered old face is priceless. She pats Vada's back awkwardly and looks glad when Vada turns her loose. "I'll see you Friday."

"You're welcome, honey," Tiny says, ruffled from Vada's gratitude, "but maybe you ought to rethink this trip. Nothing about what you told me seems right."

What is Tiny Medford doing? Was she trying to mess things up? But the fire she usually has in her eyes has been replaced with concern, like a mother's. "We'll be fine, Tiny. Don't worry one bit. I'll have her back in one piece in no time. Scouts honor."

She throws her head back and laughs that deep, throaty laugh that comes from years of hard living. "That don't mean nothing, shug. You ain't never been a Boy Scout in your life."

As soon as Tiny's truck disappears down the road, Vada is in his arms. "I missed you," she says in one long breath.

"I missed you, too." He bends down to kiss her, but she pulls away. He feels her indecision and wants to put her at ease. "Sometimes I think I can read you, but I want to make damn sure I get this right. What do you want, Vada?"

She blushes hard. "I want to go to Memphis."

The sign says they're ten miles from Augusta and almost in Georgia, but, other than commenting on how pretty the Broad River is, Vada has hardly said two words. What's she thinking? Is she worried about the Plymouth getting her where she wants to go on time? Has she realized how absurd her plan is to pay off this Wentworth woman? Is she worried about sleeping arrangements once they get there? And what are the sleeping arrangements? Because she hasn't said.

"We'll stop in Augusta and grab a bite to eat," Frank says.

The car rolls down the main drag, called Broad Street, and Frank can see why. It's three times as wide as Walterboro's Washington Street and has shops and plenty of restaurants as far as he can see. He pulls in front of a place with a JUST OPENED banner out front, figuring they could use the business.

"Luigi's," Vada reads the sign and nods.

"You like Italian?"

"Oh, I *love* everything Italian," she gushes.

Frank can't help but laugh, because what else is there besides food?

The place looks nice; it's a good-size building, about twice the size of the diner, and it smells great. Like their relationship, everything is shiny and new, and he feels pretty good about his choice. Frank orders spaghetti and meatballs because the waiter says it's the best thing on the menu. He's a short, round guy with slick black hair and a neck that disappears when he looks down to write on his order pad.

"*Bella Donna?*" he says, eyeing Frank's girl, and she launches into a conversation he doesn't understand, laughing and talking with this guy like they're on a street corner in another country.

"*Grazie tanto!*" he says and toddles off toward the kitchen. He shouts something to a man behind the lunch counter, who gives Vada a big smile, kisses the tips of his fingers, and tosses them Vada's way.

"What was that all about?"

She blushes. "Oh, I took a little Italian in college."

"Wow. You got all that out of one class? You sound like it's your native language."

She reaches for Frank's hand. "Thank you for taking me on this trip, Frank. I know I haven't said much, but I do appreciate it. I'm just worried I won't get to see Darby. Ever."

Maybe Vada is coming to her senses and has realized this Wentworth dame is a first-degree shyster. And who knows? People change. Maybe this Darby character is in on what Frank is sure is a scam.

"What did Darby do to get run out of town?" Franks asks.

"She fell in love."

"Okay, now you've lost me."

"I was away at college when it happened. Darby worked for a very wealthy man, a married man. She fell in love with him, and I believe he loved her, too. His wife found out about the affair and wanted to hurt Darby back. She demanded that Darby's mother send her own daughter packing or she'd lose her seamstress business. Darby's mother was shamed into running her own daughter off, forced to, really. So she left, and the woman ruined Darby's mother's business anyway."

"And you think what happened to your friend is somehow your fault?"

"Darby wrote me and told me about the affair; I knew she was going to get hurt, but I didn't know how to counsel her, so I asked my mother. She put two and two together and told the man's wife, so, you see, it is my fault." She looks at him with the saddest blue eyes and then pulls away.

"How is paying off this woman in Memphis going to change anything?"

"I can tell by your face you think my plan is stupid, don't you? You think I'm stupid."

"God, Vada, no. But you're not responsible for your mother breaking your confidence, or for the choices your friend made. It just sounds like Darby's taking care of herself. She got out of a bad relationship, landed in Memphis, and then had the good sense to get away from this Wentworth woman. What scares me is, you're running right to her with open arms." *And an open wallet.* "If this Wentworth woman can find Darby like she claims, if she has the power to put her in jail, why does she have to get the money from you?"

"Because Darby doesn't have that kind of money."

"And you do?" Her face blushes hard. She nods slowly and Frank tells his brain to shut the hell up, but it won't. Fresh out of college, how the hell does Vada have that kind of money, and why is she so eager to give it away? He's afraid if he obliges these questions, the road trip will end, and he'd like nothing better than to ride across the good old USA for the rest of his life with his arm draped over his girl. *Better let it lie, for now.* He'll handle this Miss Wentworth when they get to Memphis, and she might be surprised to find that she's the one rotting in jail.

"You're sure about this, Vada? That's two or three months' pay."

"Darby and I swore we'd always be there for each other forever."

"When you were kids?" She nods and looks like she's going to cry. Frank tries not to react, but two hundred and fifteen dollars is a lot of money, and children make grown-up promises they can't possibly keep. "This isn't a good idea."

"I failed Darby, Frank. I won't do that again."

The hurt from Frank's objections is evident. God, she's so beautiful, so young and unacquainted with the ways of the world. He'll go along, or at least let her think that, until they get to Memphis and he sizes this shyster up.

Their plates arrive, and every Italian man in the joint has stopped what he's doing to see Vada's face when she tries the food. A surge of jealousy pulses through Frank as she closes her eyes and lets out a deep, satisfied sigh. *"Delizioso! Eccellente!"* They all applaud and slap each other on the back like every single one of them has just proposed and she's accepted.

Between bites, Vada gushes about this Darby character. Frank looks at the three huge meatballs staring at him and affirms his decision to keep his trap shut. From the look on her face, Frank couldn't stop Vada even if he tried. And if trying meant he'd lose her, he sure as hell doesn't want that.

He forks a meatball and takes a bite of it. He doesn't know Italian, but it must sound enough like English that delicious and excellent sound the same. Vada's right about the food; it really is good. Maybe she's right about this plan and maybe she isn't, but Frank is going to do his damnedest to keep his reservations to himself as long as she wants him along for the ride.

·Chapter Twelve·

Frank leans against the gas pump as the attendants service the car. He looks regretful he agreed to take me on this trip, and I understand his reservations, really I do. But who in their right mind wouldn't want to save their best friend? Especially when they have a second chance to make up for failing her like I failed Darby. Of course I didn't mean to hurt Darby when I went away to school, but I should have seen through her veiled pleas, stayed home, and gone to the College of Charleston. If I hadn't left, maybe Darby wouldn't have fallen for Mrs. McCrady's charming husband. But if I had stayed any longer, I probably wouldn't have finished college and I would already be married to Justin.

Frank gets back into the car, and we head northward. The edge of Rosa Lee's pouch, with my grandmother's necklace, peers out of my brassiere. It's worth more to me than any price that can be put on sapphires and perfect diamonds, but not worth more than Darby.

I rearrange the pouch between my bosom. Perhaps I should sell the necklace in Memphis. But that would be impossible to do without Frank knowing. His knowing would lead to questions about who I am and where I come from, and I'm not ready to tell him that yet. I may never tell him. It would change everything between us. I know it would. I'll just trade the necklace and pray Miss Wentworth accepts it. Otherwise, this whole trip will be for naught.

I want to make him see that I need this trip and hope that he wants to be a part of the bright future I've planned for myself. But the silence is killing me. I have to know what he's thinking. "Pull over. Now, Frank. Pull over."

"Jesus, Vada." The car limps onto the shoulder, and he shoves it into park. "Are you all right? What's wrong?"

I slide all the way across the bench seat and wrap my arms around him. He holds me tight, kissing the top of my head, swearing whatever is wrong, he'll make right. His strong hands cup my face, and his thumbs dab at my tears. "I know you think this is crazy, Frank." I'm trying to choose my words, but they're coming too fast. "I want this to work. More than anything, I want this to work with you, but I need to know that you take me seriously. For me, it's the starting place to know if we can have something together. And I want to have that something with you."

The car is stuffy and still. I think I can hear his heart beating wildly out of control, or maybe it's my own. I feel like I've just said "I love you" and he hasn't said it back. Oh God, why didn't I just keep it to myself and take the bus?

"Vada, I've got to say something before we go any farther. It's something you ought to know."

I'm bracing for him to let me down easy, because Frank's the kind of man who would care enough to do that. I can't look at him. I press my face against his chest. Everything I've hoped for is going to end, here, in Georgia, of all places.

"The truth is, I love you, and have from the moment I saw you. I never believed in that kind of thing until you walked through the door of the diner, but, by God, I do love you. I don't expect you to love me back right now, but whatever you ask me to, I'll do it or die trying."

He kisses me differently than before, like we're sharing the same breath, and I believe every word he's said. His hands are tentative, like he wants more, but he's afraid to go too fast. I'm not even sure what that means, but I want them everywhere. When we come up for air, I press my forehead against his cheek. Three cars zoom past in quick succession, making a haze of dust swirl around the car.

I want to tell Frank I love him, but I've never said the words to a man before, and when I do, I want it to be at the perfect time, in a special place, something I'll remember forever. I stay wrapped around him, hoping he knows the words on my heart, and he must, because he pulls back onto the highway headed for Tennessee.

The car slows, and I stir as it comes to a stop in front of a Sinclair gas pump. It's unbearably hot. My hair is wet and stuck to Frank's chest. He raises my chin tenderly and kisses me wide-awake. "You must have been tired. You slept through Atlanta."

I stretch and yawn. "Where are we?"

"Almost to the Alabama state line; I think we're over halfway there, give or take. Why don't you get us a couple of Cokes?" He presses a dime into my hand, and his fingers linger on it for just a second before he gives my sweaty forehead a peck.

A team of men in sparkling white uniforms rushes to the car. "Fill it up with high-test," Frank says.

"Restrooms on the right side of the building," one of them shouts after me.

Surprisingly, the powder room is shiny and clean. The mirror is small, but I take account of myself. I'm not the least bit ashamed or guilty about making this trip with Frank, and I think it shows. There's a woman in the mirror looking back at me where a bubbleheaded blonde was just a few days ago, only she was dressed for her own wedding. I smooth my hair back into a long ponytail, intent on finding the Coke machine and cooling off.

Before I went to college and was around, well, normal people, I didn't know that a Coke was a treat reserved for special occasions and road trips. I always had Coca-Cola whenever I wanted it; Desmond bought it by the case from the grocer, and for a long time, I thought they were for me, because he and Rosa Lee told me so. But they were really for my father, on mornings after he'd over-imbibed at a party or a stuffy dinner.

The dime clanks into the coin receptacle, and the machine spits out a nickel and a Coke. I shove the nickel back into the machine while I toast to my newfound independence, and then I hand Frank his drink. He turns the bottle up, downs all six and a half ounces in a matter of seconds, and with a brazen smile, turns his head, to burp I'm sure, and to make me laugh.

Back in the car, the engine strains as it climbs across the foothills, like it would rather be back on the flat of the Lowcountry. The drought that has made Myers Creek an ankle-deep trickle has been stingy with rain here, too; only brown weeds and broomstraw line the red clay roadside. The pines here are different, their needles twice as long as the coastal pines. There are hardwoods I don't recognize, and tall slender oaks that look like they can't possibly be kin to the fat round angel oaks back home. All of the treetops are beginning to turn brown, and some are even changing color like it's October instead of July.

The temperature is a little cooler now, which may have more to do with the billowy masses of clouds hiding the sun than the altitude. If we stay on schedule, we'll be in Memphis by eleven.

It was nice of Miss Wentworth to offer us a place to stay. She said something about being closed for the week of the Fourth, which was puzzling, because she said Darby worked for her in her home. Maybe Miss Wentworth has some kind of home business, something for me to consider should things with Frank progress and we have a family. I'd want to stay home with my children, that much I am sure of, and the extra income would be nice.

I'm excited about my new job, about having my own money that isn't tied to a trust fund I have to do tricks for like a little dog. And if a home business isn't possible after I have children, I see no reason why I couldn't continue teaching. I'd have the summers off to spend with the children; I wonder how Frank would feel about that.

"We've got about six more hours to go," he smiles, "and I want to know everything about you."

"Like what?" I unwrap his arm from around my shoulder and sit up straight.

"I don't know. I have this picture of what you were like growing up. Blond. Precocious. Adorable."

Oh, dear. Frank's been so forthright with me, and I want to share myself with him. But there's so much I can't tell him.

"Did you have a happy childhood?" He prods me toward the beginning.

"Yes." It's true, but as much as I love Rosa Lee and Desmond, it was difficult not feeling loved by my parents, feeling more like a fixture, or a much-needed accessory to make the right impression. "And no."

His eyes are sad at the last part of my answer. He threads his fingers in mine and kisses the back of my hand. "You don't have to talk about it if you don't want to."

I want to give him something, so I fast-forward to the last four years of my life. "I liked college. I met a lot of nice people. I loved my professors. One of them recommended me for the teaching position. She was from a very wealthy family in Boston; she married a Southern boy she met at Oxford one summer."

He nods seriously. "Mississippi."

"Oh, no, England. After they married, her family promptly disowned her."

"Why?"

"Because they thought he wasn't good enough for her. But they couldn't have been more wrong. Even in their sixties, they still stroll the campus, holding hands, so in love."

Frank nods his head like he understands that kind of love. "You appreciate something more when you have to fight for it."

He's right. I am so grateful for my newfound freedom, and I know from Frank's words, from the certainty in his eyes, he would fight for me. I smile to myself, surprised that I've done the same for him, standing up to Miss Mamie, ignoring the horrible reverend and his mindless zealots.

"You've thought of something good?" he asks. "Wanna tell me?"

I nod and wrap my arms around his middle again. "It's hard to think about the past when everything about the here and now is so exciting and wonderful. I'm starting anew."

He takes his eyes off the road and studies my face. "With me?"

"With you, Frank, darling."

Twelve hours after leaving Round O, Frank catches a glimpse of the sign that says they're almost to Memphis. Vada is asleep again, against his chest; God, he wants to wake up with her like this to-morrow, but he knows that won't happen. And, to be honest, it shouldn't happen, not with a girl like Vada. Vada's the kind of girl you honor and cherish. Hell, the kind you treasure and marry. But the want that he has for her now is so big, it swallows up his good intentions.

A car whizzes past, going the other way. She stirs, wipes her mouth with the back of her hand, and smiles at Frank before she stretches to kiss him on the cheek. "What time is it?"

"Past midnight."

"We didn't make very good time."

"No, we didn't." And it probably had a lot to do with Frank going slow while she slept, to savor the smell of her hair, her breath against his chest.

"Where are we?"

He's right where he wants to be. "City limits. Do you know where this place is?"

"I have directions." As crazy as Vada's plan is, she sounds giddy. "What if Darby's come back? What if she's waiting there for me?"

He hears the excitement in her voice and wants to hurry up and get her there, but he's loved having Vada all to himself.

"Turn right on Adams Street up ahead," she says.

Holy shit. This looks more high-dollar than Charleston. Frank gawks at the big houses, and Vada barks at him to watch out for a car parked on the street. "Are you sure this is the right place? Somebody who lives here wouldn't miss a couple hundred dollars, maybe a couple thousand."

"You'd be surprised at what lengths the wealthy go to, to hang on to their money." Vada points to a monstrous house and whispers "French Victorian" like the words are holy. "Stop here." She waves toward a home that isn't quite as grand as the fancy French one.

Frank parks the car. By the thin light cast off by the holy house next door, this place looks small and gaudy. A pair of shiny gold lawn jockeys welcomes them. The landscaping has cracked the walkway around it into concrete puzzle pieces. Vada's pace slows like she's come to her senses and is as unsure of her plan as Frank is. But the minute she hears the yipping of a little dog from inside the house, she makes a dash for the front porch and rings the doorbell.

Frank takes off after her and trips over a root that has pushed its way up through the concrete, landing on all fours. Before he can get up, the front door opens and a harlot is standing there with the tiniest black dog he's ever seen in his life.

"Miss Wentworth? I'm sorry we're so late; I hope we haven't kept you up." Vada gushes. The woman nods and eyes Frank as he gawks at her. "I'm Vada Hadley and this," she looks surprised to see him on the ground, "is my boyfriend, Frank Darling."

Frank should be ecstatic or, at the very least, dazed that Vada has called him her boyfriend, but the sight of that woman looking down on him like he's her last meal holds him in place. Her scarlet lips part, and she runs her tongue over them. She says something to Vada, still looking at Frank and making no pretense about the way she's dressed. Vada blushes and looks away from the woman in the black lace negligee, which leaves absolutely nothing to the imagination. The black ball of fluff in the woman's arms is yipping for Vada like it knows her.

"Have you found Darby?" Vada scratches the little mutt behind the ears. "Is she here?"

"No," she snaps, and then she catches herself. "Where are my manners? I'm sure you're tired from your trip. I have many rooms, all of them made up and ready for guests. Why don't you get a good night's sleep and we'll talk business tomorrow?" The little dog struggles to get to Vada, who looks like she might cry from disappointment. The woman sizes Vada up quickly, taking note of her weakness for wayward friends and poodles, and hands the dog, no bigger than the palm of Frank's hand, over to her.

"I'm sure we can find a hotel," Vada says, like she really hadn't thought of that until now.

"Nonsense, my dear. I won't hear of it. You'll be my guests."

"That's so kind of you," Vada says, glancing at the negligee and then looking away quickly. The dog bathes her face in kisses. "And I'm so sorry to have gotten you out of bed."

"Oh, I wasn't in bed. Yet." She winks at Frank.

Frank gets to his feet; he isn't sure if Vada realizes this place is a cathouse, but there's no way he's going to let Vada sleep here. He brushes off his hands. "We'll find a place in town. We're not staying here."

"You can try, but with the Fourth of July holiday tomorrow, the hotels are probably full. And I assure you, Frank, my place is as grand as the Peabody and has some amenities they don't. Besides, I'm sure your girl needs her rest."

"I know what my girl needs." Frank reaches for Vada's hand. "We'll see you in the morning."

Vada looks at him, irritated, and pulls away. He wants to throw her over his shoulder and take her away from this place, but that's a bad idea. The harlot's breathy little laugh says she's enjoying the standoff. He looks at the place again, and then at

Vada. Does he really want to have their first fight here, in front of a high-dollar cathouse? But can he let his girl sleep in some whore's bed?

"Stay, Vada," the woman coos seductively, "you can sleep in Darby's room. It's a servant's room, but it's nice enough."

That settles it. Vada doesn't say anything to Frank, turns on her heels, and heads into the house.

Miss Wentworth stands too close to him in the dark entryway, like an animal taking in the scent of its prey.

He reaches for the light switch beside the door, so this woman can look at him and see his heart belongs to Vada Hadley, but nothing happens. He works it back and forth a couple of times, praying it sputters on. "You've got a bad switch." Frank's voice sounds nervous.

"Yes, it seems I'm having a little trouble tonight, but I bet you could make it work, Frank Darling." She draws out his last name, her lips close to his ear. She smells like hard liquor and cheap perfume. She lights a candle on the foyer table, then her long silver cigarette holder, and blows out the smoke so it billows down over his head. She laughs, because she knows he refuses to look at her dressed like she is. "Are you handy like that?"

"Maybe I could take a look at it tomorrow," Frank says and bolts toward the woman he loves, in the parlor.

The woman grabs his arm, her long fingernails digging into his skin, stopping him in his tracks. "The electricity goes out from time to time in these old houses, but no one ever complains. It's nothing that can't be fixed. And I'm counting on you to fix it quite well, Frank."

The room is lit by three cheap lamps, the kind Frank sells at the store. Oh, God, everything about this place looks wrong. There's a long mahogany bar in the living room, and a dozen settees line the walls, making the place look more like a dance hall than a home.

"Oh, Miss Wentworth, your little dog is adorable. Thank you for having us in your lovely home. I hope we're not putting you out."

"Of course not. My girls are gone for the holiday. They work fifty weeks out of the year, so it's a well-deserved respite, and I happened to have empty rooms."

"How delightful and progressive. I'll be working myself in a few weeks."

"How delightful indeed," the harlot coos.

The little dog bathes Vada's face with its bright pink tongue. She laughs that musical laugh, and doesn't seem to see what Frank sees. He wants to reveal Wentworth as the scoundrel she is, but Vada's made it clear she's not leaving here, and Frank's not about to leave without her.

He spies several large trophies on the mantel over the white marble fireplace. They sit gleaming and gaudy. He runs his finger over one of them marked BEST IN SHOW. "Keep your damn mouth shut, Frank," he whispers under his breath. "At least until morning."

"You like my trophies, Frank Darling?" With her back to Vada and her hand on Frank's shoulder, it must look like the woman is proud of her hardware, but her breasts are pressed against the back of Frank's arm.

"I don't see you or your trophies; I only see Vada," he says, clearing his throat and sidestepping away from Wentworth.

She takes a long draw off of her cigarette holder and blows the smoke away from her prize. Her fingers trail down her neck, and Frank looks away to avoid where they are leading.

"So you're ready for bed, then." Wentworth picks up the puppy, turns off the oil lamps, except for one, and leads Frank and Vada up the long staircase. The higher they go, the mustier the air gets. The baby-powder scent is odd for a brothel, but it's strong enough to make a baby smell good. There is a more dominant scent, some kind of overpowering perfume, a trick Smudge's wife used after they'd had sex, so the reverend wouldn't suspect anything. Vada threads her fingers through Frank's and smiles warily, like maybe she's seen the blood-red walls, the portraits of naked women. Maybe she does know what this place is.

"Vada, this is one of my finest boudoirs. You're welcome to stay here instead of Darby's room." Wentworth opens the door to a grand room. The oil lamp casts long shadows against a pretentious four-poster bed, similar to a rice bed back home, and a matching chifforobe overflowing with garish costumes. "There's a basin if you want to wash up. The bathroom is down the hall, on the left."

"Thank you, Miss Wentworth," Vada whispers, like she's actually considering sleeping here. Her gaze settles on a fanciful-looking chair with a long seat and stirrup-looking things on each side. "What an unusual piece."

"Yes." Wentworth's smile is wicked and proud. "I liked the design so much, there's one in every bedroom."

"What's it called?" Vada asks of what can only be described as a sex chair.

"Why, it's a chair, my dear, and those appendages on the side can be quite handy for many things."

"Like—like—putting on stockings." Vada nods slowly.

"Precisely. Seams are always straight as an arrow. If you like, I could give you the name of my carpenter. You could commission one for yourself."

"Does Darby have one of these—chairs—for putting on stockings?"

"No. Darby was very handy with a needle and thread, and an

excellent help to the cook. I treated her as well as any of my girls and yet she took off without so much as a thank-you."

"I'm sorry, Miss Wentworth, and I'm grateful for your hospitality, but if it's all the same to you, I'd rather sleep in Darby's room."

The harlot opens the door to a tiny room where Vada's friend spent the last three years of her life. It seems more like an afterthought than a bedroom. Wallpaper peels off the walls, and heavy draperies look like someone started hanging them but gave up before the job was done. There is no sex chair—just a cot no better than the one at the cabin, a bedside table with a lamp, and no basin. If this was Darby's room, no wonder she left.

The harlot lights the lamp on the bedside table. "My dear, your face is tearstained." How could Frank not have noticed?

Vada swipes at her cheeks. "Happy tears. Mostly. I haven't been this close to Darby in a long time," she says sadly, reaching out and scratching the puppy behind the ears. "When I was a little girl, I was so lonely, sometimes I'd cry myself to sleep, and then I met Darby." She waves her hand in front of her face like she can shoo away the tears. The little dog yips at her, like it's trying to distract Vada from her sadness.

"Perhaps you should have Franceline tonight. She'll sleep on your pillow and guard your dreams." She holds the puppy out to Vada, and it leaps into her arms.

She turns to leave, but Frank stays put, hoping Vada will come to her senses. He's more than ready to get the hell out of this place. All Vada has to do is say the word. "Frank," the harlot draws out his name. "Are you coming?" Vada is entranced by her sadness, and she barely looks at him to say good night.

"Will you be okay?" he asks.

"Yes, of course. I'll be fine. Thank you for bringing me here."

Her words surprise him, reminding him that he's responsible for Vada being here in the first place. But he knows how much Vada loves Darby and understands the regrets she has about what happened between them. Frank has lost friends before, a few during the war. But he also knows what it's like to want to undo things, to make them right, and the truth is, Vada wants that so much, she would have come with or without him. Good thing he came along to protect her from this Wentworth dame. "Good night, Vada."

He follows the woman to the opposite end of the hallway. She opens the door to another opulent chamber, and he steps inside. "Your room, Frank."

Wentworth moves in, and Frank moves away from her, until she has him pinned against the wall. Her lips move toward his. He turns his head. His heart beats so fast, he can barely breathe. There's no way to get this woman off of him without knocking her on her lacy chiffon ass.

"There's a big, comfortable bed and one of those lovely chairs your girlfriend found so interesting." The black strap of her gown slithers off of her shoulder on cue. "And my room is directly across the hall."

·Chapter Thirteen·

A soft knock at my door makes the tiny black ball of fluff yip. I whip on my robe and hold the little one on my shoulder. "Come in."

Frank looks like he didn't sleep a wink, but still he's devastatingly handsome, even though he's not smiling. "Good morning," he says from a gentlemanly distance.

"Good morning, yourself. I was just getting ready to take the dog outside. Care to join me?"

I step into my slippers and start down the stairs with Frank trailing behind me. The house smells funny, like perfume trying to mask something earthy and musky. The whole place is garish and not at all as grand as the neighboring homes.

"Did you sleep well?" Frank asks, opening the French doors that lead out to the backyard and a fabulous garden with hedges so high, the rooftops of the neighboring mansions are barely visible. There is a pedestal that almost looks like a throne, with one of those curious chairs in the center, all made of marble and encircled by rows of crescent-shaped benches.

"Not at first. How about you?"

"Not a wink." He hesitates, searching my face. "You know what this place is, don't you?"

If the overabundance of seating, lack of accent pieces, and, of all things, a bar in the living room didn't give it away, Miss Wentworth and her stirruped chairs did. "I'm not stupid, Frank. But nothing is going to keep me from finding Darby, not even a night in a brothel."

"I didn't mean to imply anything of the sort. I just don't like you being here." His tone is apologetic. He rubs his hands up and down my arms, making me weak. "All I want to do is keep you safe. Take you home. But I know how important Darby is to you."

The puppy noses around one of the crescent benches, makes a perfect little pile, and runs back to be scooped up and nuzzled.

Frank smiles and scratches her behind the ears. "You like this dog?"

"Yes." It's like Miss Wentworth knew the one thing I'd always wanted but never had. "But I didn't come here for the dog."

"So you're still going through with this?"

"Yes, of course. Why shouldn't I?"

"I'm not so sure this Miss Wentworth is on the up-and-up. There's no evidence Darby was ever here, as far as I can tell."

"But she was here. I found a stack of letters she'd sent her mother, in her bureau; they'd all been returned, unopened. Even if I never see Darby again, Frank, after all she did for me, I owe her this."

"She was a childhood friend, Vada. It seems to me what this

woman is demanding goes above and beyond obligation. Darby
chose to live here, and she chose to leave. If there's a price to pay,
it seems like Darby's the one who should be responsible."

"She changed my life, Frank. Before I met her, I was a miser-
able, lonely little girl. She changed all of that, but when she needed
me, I was away at college, home for a few weeks during the summer. I discarded her. I hurt her. And when she needed me most, I
destroyed her."

"Vada, you had no idea your mother would break your trust.
You don't have a hurtful bone in your body."

"That doesn't matter, Frank. Even if Darby never knows what
I did for her here, even if I never see her again, I can make things
right now."

"From what I've seen, Vada, you give as much as you take.
Isn't that what loving someone is about?"

I'm not sure if Frank is talking about me and Darby or me and
him. I rub my cheek against the puppy's soft black curls. There
was a time when I wanted a dog more than anything. To be honest, there is a small part of me that melts over this little one, like
I'm six again, in my bedroom on Legare Street that looks more
like a queen's room than a child's. Only this time, instead of wak-
ing up to the disappointment of a stuffed dog beside my bed, this
precious little girl is in my arms.

Frank comes close, smiling at me with those jade-green eyes
that say he loves me. The puppy leaps out of my hands, and he
catches her. He rubs her tiny face against his, studying me with a
thin smile. I know he can see how much I want to help Darby,
how much I love her.

"I want to give you everything," he says in one breath, wrapping his arm around us. The puppy nestles between us. "We'll
sort this thing with your friend out. Hell, maybe we'll even get us

a dog when we get home." He cups the puppy in the palm of his hand and pulls me close, lavishing me with a long, wet kiss.

Frank tries to place the feeling he gets when he holds Vada in his arms. It seems comforting and familiar, yet utterly foreign. The tightness in his chest. The way his heart beats so fast, the way every inch of him is anxious, yet he is as content as he has ever been in his life.

"Well, aren't you all just a picture." The light of day sharpens the angles of the harlot's face, and the sheer negligee does little to hide her nakedness. He keeps his eyes on Vada.

"Thank you for your hospitality, Miss Wentworth." Vada presses the pup against her cheek and then puts her down. She runs to the small, older poodle trailing after her mistress and tries to nurse but is rebuffed with a deep growl.

"Just can't stay away from the teats." She bends over so that the bodice of her gown falls away from her breasts, and then picks up the mama dog, making the little one beg.

Frank looks away quickly, and Vada is looking anywhere but at the harlot. "Thank you, uh, for letting Franceline stay with me. She really is a lovely little dog, but can we talk about Darby now? I'd like to get on with our transaction."

"As much as I'd like that, I'm a creature of the night and make it a policy never to do business at such a wretched hour. We'll continue our transaction at a more decent time. Say, three o'clock?"

"Of course. We don't want to disrupt your schedule, Miss Wentworth," Vada says tentatively. "We'll entertain ourselves until you're fresh and ready."

"Would you like to see what Memphis has to offer, Frank?" The harlot twirls a set of pearls around and then lets them drop on her cleavage, which is inhumanly high and makes her tits look like they're resting on a shelf. "*The Velvet Touch* is showing. I could tell you how to get there."

"I didn't come here for that," Frank says. The quicker he and Vada start looking for Darby, the quicker they can leave, and maybe get out of paying this woman off. But Frank's not about to tell either woman that. "Rather go see the sights. Just me and Vada."

"There's definitely plenty to see." She rattles off several local attractions and gives general directions to a park Vada acts like she's interested in. "It was the city's oldest cemetery, and they've turned it into a fabulous park, so the newspaper says. I'm sure Franceline would love to tag along."

"Thank you, Miss Wentworth." Vada scoops up the puppy. "We'll return promptly at three."

Vada takes Frank's breath away in the blue dress that matches her eyes. The little dog is so small, it fits in her handbag. "Do you want to grab a bite to eat?" he asks as he opens the car door for her.

Vada shakes her head and gets in. "I want to find Darby, but I don't know the city and haven't the slightest idea where to look."

"If she's still in Memphis, she'd need a job. Wentworth said she kept house and sewed. We could ask around the grocery stores, places that sell fabric." Franceline barks in agreement. "You're sure you want to take the dog?"

Vada nods. "Let's get started."

Every shopkeeper who claims to know nothing about Darby seems to take Vada's spirits down a notch, until she is so low, neither

Frank nor the puppy can perk her up. After three hours of searching, Vada sits down on a bench, nuzzling the dog, and Frank ducks into a Woolworths to grab some sandwiches at the lunch counter.

"I'm sorry we haven't found her." Frank tucks the sack under one arm and wraps the other around Vada.

"Thank you. I don't know why I dragged you around to look for her. Darby's not here. I can feel it. I'm never going to find her."

"I've got to tell you, Vada, if I was Darby and I'd finally gotten away from that Wentworth woman, I'd go as far away as I could get."

"You don't have to run far to run away," she says absently and shrugs. "But you're right. I'll do what I came to do, settle Darby's debt and go home."

She looks at Frank with a sad smile. "Look, I know you're disappointed, but we still have some time to kill. Let's head over to the park. The guy at the lunch counter says it is really something. We'll have a nice picnic and be on the road home before suppertime."

The park is as crowded as the World's Fair and looks like the back lot of a movie set. Young mothers are flocked together, completely enthralled with one another, while their children run wild on the cemetery playground outlined in small American flags for the holiday. Men dressed in church clothes, carrying golf sticks, move in groups of four toward a caddie stand and a sign that promises championship golf.

The way Vada is rubbernecking, Frank can tell she likes the liveliness of the place, but she won't set the dog down until she can get away from the commotion. A rise under a large spotted oak gives them a good view of the place, away from the frenzy. They stop short of getting run down by a group on horseback headed from the stables to the trails. Vada presses herself against him, breathing hard, her cheeks flush with excitement.

Frank grew up with Labs, black and yellow, but after his daddy passed and Buck died of a broken heart, he swore he'd never own another dog. As much as Frank hates to admit it, this little dog is cute as hell. She's as prissy as Vada is, not in the annoying way some girls are. The pair of them is beautiful, delicate. The pup piddles in the sand, and Vada acts like it's won a prize.

"You like this? Us. Together." She nods, spreading out the sandwiches from the sack, and gives the pup little bits of turkey. "Me or the dog?"

She grins and punches his arm. He throws the food back in the sack and pulls her on top of him, so she is draped across his chest. She rests her head against him, sighing, content. He likes not asking for permission to kiss her but loves the invitation when she tilts her face toward his and closes her eyes. Their lips touch, and the dog starts yipping. Frank tries to kiss her longer, deeper, but she starts laughing, scoops the little thing up, and nestles it between them.

"I'm not sure how I feel about that." Frank breathes out the words slowly, making lazy circles on Vada's back. "To be honest, I'm jealous." She laughs, and the dog wiggles out from between them and yips like it's Rin Tin Tin, trying to say something. Judging from her expression and dainty growl, she's telling him to take a hike.

Frank can feel Vada smiling against his chest. She runs her fingers over the soft black curls, and the little dog stops. "You have nothing to be jealous of, Frank. I loved you first."

She squeals when Frank flips her over onto her back, and she can hardly catch her breath. "Oh really? I bring you all the way to Memphis. I'm expecting more than first, Vada Hadley." He covers her neck in breathy kisses so that it makes her giggle, and she makes a lame attempt to fight him off. "Say you love me best. Say it." He drives her crazy, until she pushes him away just enough so Frank can see her face all flush, and beautiful. And happy.

"I love you best."

"If you people are going to behave such as this, you can pack up and move on." They bolt upright. Vada fixes her dress while the cop smacks his billy club against the palm of his hand like they're hardened criminals. He's a mountain of a man, with a funny accent, Irish maybe, and looks like he'd like to give them a whack. "Only decent people here. And children. Straighten up."

"Yes, sir." Frank starts to pick some grass out of Vada's hair but thinks better of it. "Just came here for a picnic. That's all."

"Well, see to it that it is all," he says, casting a long shadow over them as he walks away.

Frank eats his sandwich and watches her with the fluff ball. As much as he wants Vada to himself, he can't help but think what a great mother she'll be to their little towheads someday. Sometimes, it feels like they're close enough to forever to reach out and touch it. But what will happen when they go back to Round O and there's no dilemma, or even a little dog, to bring them together? What happens after Vada settles this thing with Wentworth and goes back to the boardinghouse? When she starts her job? His stomach tightens. The words shoot out of him like fireworks, explosive and beautiful. "Marry me."

She sucks in her breath like he's shot her through the heart. There's a hint of a smile, but she looks terrified. "Marry you?"

"Yes." He uses the dog as a shield because, for the love of Pete, he can't read this woman just now. "I know it's just been a few days, but I can't imagine my life without you, and if I could, well, I don't want to. I want you, Vada."

Children squeal. Women laugh. Chains clank against playground equipment, but she says nothing. God, why didn't he just keep his mouth shut and eat his sandwich? But the pig is out of the poke. "I know you're thinking we barely know each other and it's too soon, but it's not. I love you, Vada."

·Chapter Fourteen·

Frank's proposal has me paralyzed. As much as I want to be with him, the thought of running from one groom into the arms of another is more than enough to give me pause. I've had a taste of independence, and I love making my own decisions. I don't know if Frank is the kind of guy who would want to take that away from me. If he's the kind who's fool enough to try.

"I'm sorry." He's embarrassed. "I thought—"

"Frank, I do love you. I love the way I feel when we're together, and when we're apart, I'm counting the minutes until I see you again. And your proposal—"

"Look, I know this is spur of the moment, but I knew the moment I saw you that I wanted to spend forever with you." He presses my hand between his hands and kisses my fingertips. "Vada, for as long as I can remember, I've wanted something else out of life. I thought I'd find it going off to war, but that didn't happen. Now I know that it's you; you're what I've been waiting for all along, and all I want to do is make you mine."

Frank's been so open and honest with me, it would be wrong not to tell him how I really feel. "I am yours, Frank. But for the first time in my life, I'm mine, too. I don't want to give anything up right now, not you. Not my freedom."

He's desperate to read my face. The corners of my mouth turn up to reassure him, but I can't stop thinking about the girls I knew during college who married soldiers they had only known a few hours. It seemed wildly romantic at the time, them being swept off their feet after a few dances, giving themselves to men who were going into battle. Surely they regretted getting caught up in the moment.

My roommate, Halley, was one of those girls. She always begged me to go to the dance hall with her, so I could be one, too, but I never went. A handful of us stayed in the dormitory and congratulated ourselves for not falling for some soldier's ploy to deflower us. We all swore we'd never disgrace our families by marrying out of our social circle, or, an even worse fate, ending up pregnant and alone.

At the time, I thought I was afraid of what my father would say, what he might do if I became pregnant or married a lowly private. But now I know I was terrified of marrying a man I didn't love. Of worrying myself sick over his safety and knowing I'd be expected to learn to love him if he came back.

"Vada, I don't want you to give up anything for me. Especially your freedom. But you love me and I love you. Getting married would make us free to be together all the time." I tilt my face up toward his, asking him to kiss me. Convince me. And for a moment, there is nothing but our lips touching, our breath. "We'll settle the thing with Darby. Hell, I'll buy you this dog, if you want, but I want to marry you the minute you say so."

His face is so beautiful, his eyes so true. He cups my face in his hands and dabs at my tears with his thumbs, waiting for my answer. I've never known the kind of happiness I feel when I'm with Frank; it's like being on the edge of forever with untried wings and all I have to do is keep my eyes on his and take the leap. He presses a kiss on my forehead, and I know I'm as precious to him as he is to me. I close my eyes and spread my wings.

"Yes."

He smiles against my lips. "To me or the dog?"

"Yes, to everything."

Vada has Frank on his knees, but she's on her knees, too, pressed against him, her heart beating against his; with his. He kisses her, breathing her into his soul forever, and nothing exists except her.

"All right, that's it." The cop is back, glaring down at us. "Get your things and go or I'll arrest you on the spot for indecent behavior."

Vada ends the kiss and looks at Frank with a smile as glorious as the most beautiful summer day. "She said yes," Frank says to the cop, his eyes still on Vada's. She laughs and scoops up the pup. Their pup.

"I don't much care what she said. You people need to move on."

He stands there as they pack up. They glance at each other with matching grins that say they're getting married. Someday. Maybe soon. She points to their pup, who looks like a picture, passed out on a little tuft of clover. Vada picks her up so carefully, she doesn't wake, and cradles her like a newborn on her shoulder. She mouths,

"Thank you" to the cop, who seems a little disappointed that Frank and Vada are so compliant.

In the car Vada ticks off her plan. They'll go back to Wentworth's to get their things together, Vada will give her the money, and they'll leave. Frank hopes the harlot will be in such a good mood, she'll sell him the dog for a song, but if she doesn't, Frank will get Vada a puppy as soon as they get home. Maybe a Lab.

He doesn't like Vada knuckling under to what is essentially blackmail, but he's not saying a word. His girl has agreed to marry him and soon they'll have a ready-made family with a little dog, until they have kids. They haven't talked about this kind of thing, how many Vada will want, or when, but Frank would be happy with a dozen Vada Hadleys.

They pull up in front of the cathouse, and Frank shoves the car in park and kills the engine. "Don't worry. I'll handle Miss Wentworth." Vada's head snaps back, and she's not laughing anymore. He's not sure what her slight smile means. "Or you can."

"Yes. I will." Vada's beaming again, but Frank doesn't trust the harlot any further than he can spit a rat.

The front door is unlocked, and no one seems to be home. Frank throws the clothes he wore yesterday in his satchel and walks down the musty hallway to Vada's room. The tiny dog is perched at the head of the bed, on a pillow, watching as Vada scurries about getting her things together. Frank doesn't hear the harlot, but he can feel her standing behind him. He waits for Vada to see her, but she's too busy trying to stuff that pouffy dress she wore yesterday into her suitcase.

"Going so soon?" The harlot breathes out the words.

"Oh." Vada's face is flushed. "Miss Wentworth. Yes, we were just packing. May I speak with you privately?" Vada looks at Frank, but he won't budge. "Frank, would you please excuse us?"

Hell no. But Vada and the harlot are looking at him impatiently. He remembers Tiny's warning not to screw things up, nods, and closes the door behind him.

I take the roll of money out of my handbag and hand it to the woman. "This is all the cash I have."

Miss Wentworth rifles through the bills with blinding speed. "A little less than half is never enough."

"I'm proposing a trade."

"I can't possibly imagine what you would have of value that I'd want."

As the necklace pours out of the pouch, Miss Wentworth sucks in her breath. I splay it out across my fingers so she can see the impressive design. Twenty-seven perfect diamonds call to her like glistening sirens wrapped in gold, surrounded by sapphires. "It's worth far more than the money Darby owes you."

"And you would trade this?" She takes it from me, inspecting it closely.

"I'll keep the cash. You keep the necklace, and Darby's debt is paid. Forever." I thought it would be hard giving up my grandmother's necklace, but I feel relieved, happy that the last vestige of my old life will help Darby. "Under one condition."

Miss Wentworth flings the necklace at me. "It's obviously a fake. Otherwise, you would have sold it yourself and simply paid me the money that little tramp owes me." She's trying to sound terse, but I can hear the wanting in her voice.

I pick the necklace up off of the floor and place it around her neck. "I assure you, Miss Wentworth, it's genuine." She's trying to pretend she's indifferent, but her fingers trail adoringly over the stones. "When you first called me, you said you could find Darby.

Promise me you'll keep trying, and when you do, ask her to please call or write and let me know she's okay." She's entranced by her image and says nothing. "Do we have a deal?"

"Yes," she whispers, drawing out the word. "I'll find her, and soon."

I thank her and give her a piece of paper with my address and phone number. "And, Miss Wentworth, please don't say anything to Frank. I don't want him to know about the necklace."

·Chapter Fifteen·

Frank presses his ear against the door, but can't make out anything Vada is saying. And to make matters worse, she sent him out of the room like a child. He understands that Vada's independence is important to her, but what will it cost her? Besides, there's no telling what that woman is getting out of her, and his presence on the wrong side of the door makes him a willing accomplice.

Vada and Wentworth look awfully friendly when they come out of the room. Frank takes the suitcases and starts down the stairs after them. In the foyer, Vada thanks, and actually hugs, the harlot, who stiffens and, for the first time since he stumbled up the walkway, wishes them a good ride back home, without undressing Frank with her eyes. What happened upstairs to make these two so chummy? This doesn't smell right at all.

"Frank, Miss Wentworth has graciously agreed to find Darby for me," Vada gushes. "She's promised I'll have a postcard or a letter, maybe even a phone call, in no time."

Frank harrumphs. What the hell? He's leaving, there's no need to play nice with the harlot anymore. "At what price?"

"Frank, dear," Vada says. "I've handled everything to my satisfaction. It's really none of your concern."

"We're getting married. It is my concern."

"Married?" Miss Wentworth draws out the word. "How lovely. Let me be the first to congratulate you."

"Stop pretending. You don't care about Vada any more than you cared about Darby. You're nothing more than a shyster—"

"You've insulted me, Frank. Why I'm tempted to call the whole thing off. Darby can rot in jail—"

"No. Miss Wentworth," Vada gasps. "Please."

"You're the one who should rot in jail," Frank shouts.

Vada looks at him sharply, and he knows to just shut the hell up, but honest to Pete, Vada's no match for this woman. She probably sold her soul to the devil woman. The harlot somehow got Vada's name after Darby moved on, and then made the whole scam up. Who knows? Maybe Darby's in on this, too.

"I said I'd handled it, Frank. It's done now, let's go."

"Let me give you some advice, dear," Wentworth coos. "I know men, especially the likes of him. They love nothing better than to change you. Bend you to their will and ruin you."

Vada swallows hard. "With all due respect, Miss Wentworth, Frank loves me. I hardly think he will ruin me."

Frank has never wanted to hit a woman in his life, but he's glaring at Wentworth as she rakes her long, spiky, red nails across her necklace, and his fists are balled up by his side. "Give Vada back whatever you took from her. We're leaving. End of story."

"Frank," Vada snaps.

"I know men like you, Frank. You think women like Vada are little puppets." The harlot glares at him. "You wouldn't know what to do with a woman who can think for herself. You like them mousy, dependent. That makes you feel like a real big man, doesn't it, Frank?"

"Lady, you don't know anything about me. All you know is you need a good distraction so Vada won't see what a mistake she's making."

"You have no idea what Vada wants or what she's willing to do to get it." She runs her fingers across the gaudy trophy around her neck. "If Vada didn't want to settle the debt, she would never have traded her grandmother's jewels for Darby's freedom."

"What the hell?" Frank stares at the stones. They look real, and must be, if they satisfied the harlot.

"She's right." Vada steps in between Frank and the harlot, who is glaring triumphantly at him. "This is what I wanted."

"Vada, that necklace looks like it's worth way more than two hundred dollars. And it belonged to your grandmother? This is crazy."

"There's probably a lot you don't know about *your girl*, Frank. Obviously, she doesn't trust you enough to tell you, and I can't say I blame her," Wentworth snaps.

"Let it go, Frank. Making things right for Darby means that much to me. Miss Wentworth has graciously agreed to find Darby for me and have her contact me. Even a simple postcard from Darby is worth more than any necklace, more than anything; it's what I want most."

He tries to sound reasonable, less confrontational. "Can't you see this woman is using your love for Darby to con you?"

"If I'm not mistaken," the harlot laughs, "you barely know this bright young woman, and you're treating her like a shackled bride. Who's conning whom, Frank Darling?"

"That's it. We're leaving, Vada. Now." Frank grabs her hand, and she jerks it away. Her body stiffens, and her face looks like she's balancing on a tightrope wire. "Vada, is this some kind of test? Do I love you enough to stand by and watch this woman fleece you?"

"Why? Why would you try to stop me, Frank?"

"I won't just try, damn it."

"Is it the necklace, because it's worth a lot? Is this just about money?"

"No, Vada, it's not about money. Well, maybe it is a little. I don't know. This whole thing is ridiculous."

"Ridiculous." Vada's nostrils are flaring. "I'll tell you what's ridiculous, Frank." How in the hell did this fiasco get turned around on him? "You thinking you can make me do what *you* think is right. That's ridiculous." She wheels to face the harlot, who looks like the cat who swallowed the cream. "I am leaving now, Miss Wentworth, but I expect you to honor the agreement we've made." Tears stream down Vada's face as she spits out the last word.

She has obviously lost her mind, but Frank will be damned if he'll lose her forever by saying another word. He'll just keep his damn mouth shut. He refuses to go to jail for strangling this Wentworth woman. But someone ought to.

"Well played, Frank," the harlot goads him, barely loud enough for him to hear.

"Miss Wentworth." Vada swipes at her tears. "Would you be so kind as to direct me to the bus station?"

"Of course, dear. Let me call you a cab."

"Vada. No."

"I think it would be best, Frank, if I went back to South Carolina alone."

"Alone? Please tell me what the hell just happened, because

one minute we're getting married, and the next you want to take a slow bus back home without me."

"I need some time to think."

Vada's posture is more erect than when she spars with Miss Mamie. Is that where he ranks now? Oh, hell, if this can be fixed, he's got to fix it now. "I don't want you on some bus." He rakes his hand over his face and takes a deep breath in hopes that he can sound sincere and not riled anymore, but he is angry at Vada. Angry that she'd let this woman con her. Angry that she'd let what they have slip away so easily. "Vada. Honey. I'll take you back to Round O, and I promise you don't have to say a word if you don't want to. Please. Let me take you home."

·Chapter Sixteen·

Home. The word stings almost as much as Frank's assessment of me. Can Miss Wentworth be right about him? I want to believe that his intentions are good, but if he doesn't trust me enough to let me make my own decisions . . .

"I can have a car here in no time." Miss Wentworth grabs the telephone receiver and asks the operator to ring Yellow Cab. Frank searches my face. I steel myself from looking into his beautiful eyes. I don't care how reckless he thinks I am, or how very angry I am at him for trying to control me, I do love him.

"That won't be necessary, Miss Wentworth. Frank and I are leaving."

"Thank God." Franks reaches for me, but I turn away.

"You look distraught, dear, and completely undone," Miss Wentworth says. "Perhaps it would be better if you stayed over. At this hour, you'll be driving through the night and well into the morning."

"No. Thank you. I have to go now."

The car is suffocating, stuffed with so many things that need to be said. But Frank is true to his word. He doesn't say anything until the car is nearly out of gas. We pull into a truck stop just outside of Birmingham, on the never-ending Route 78 that ends squarely in Charleston. Two attendants saunter out, and Frank tells them to fill up the car and check under the hood.

"Vada," Frank says softly. "Would you like to get a bite to eat?" I nod and look away from him. "Good. I'm starved." His tone sounds less guarded.

He laughs at a joke one of the attendants makes about how hot the weather is and pays the man. Frank doesn't know these men from Adam, yet they seem to have some sort of rapport, a regard between the three of them that reminds me of the stuffy men my father and Justin sip brandy and smoke cigars with. The quiet attendant raps on the hood of the car to signal he's done. They all nod at each other respectfully, and Frank pulls the car in front of the restaurant.

"Come on, I'll buy you some dinner," Frank says.

I'm out of the car before he can put it in park. He sits in the booth, across from me, smiling, trying to make me smile back at him. "We've got seven hours to go, Vada. Are you going to make me talk to myself the whole way?"

"Maybe."

"Come on, Vada. Don't be mad." He takes my hand and weakens me considerably with his smile and those emerald-green eyes. "I know I said some things I shouldn't have, and I'm sorry. You told me how important your independence is to you, and I—I messed up. I admit I should have butted out. But it's been five hours since I heard you laugh, since you said—"

"You want forgiveness, Frank, and I want you to look at me the way you did those attendants a few minutes ago."

He runs his hand through his hair. "Okay. Now you've lost me, because I could never look at you the same way I looked at those grease monkeys."

"I don't mean romantically," I snap. His smile fades. "They tell you the car needs oil. You nod, they nod, and it gets done. You don't question them. You don't try to analyze their motives."

"Well, honey, if a car needs oil, it needs oil. It's as simple as that."

"No," I groan. "What I'm saying is, you respect their knowledge, their opinion. That's what I want from you."

"But you have my respect."

We suspend our argument while a waitress takes our order. I order tea and white toast, because as upset as I am, I'm sure it would be a mistake to eat.

"You should eat something more, Vada." He reaches across the table and pushes a wispy tendril from my face. "Look, I'm not going to fight with you anymore, and I'll do whatever I have to, to get us back to the point where you were ready to marry me."

"Anything?"

"Anything."

In truth, I am starved. I call the waitress back over and order the Hungry Man blue-plate special with pie. Frank seems thrilled and is doing most of the talking through dinner.

"God, your lips are beautiful." He dabs at the corner of my mouth, and then licks a dab of blackberry pie filling off of his thumb.

Our waitress puts the check on the table and my hand is on it a second before Frank's. "Vada, what are you doing?"

"I'm buying dinner."

"Oh no you're not. Let go of the check."

"Frank, you've paid for everything on this trip; it's only right."

"A woman doesn't buy a man dinner." His face is red, but his voice is low. "That just doesn't happen. Besides, I wanted to do this for you."

"And I want to do this for you."

"So you're going to march up there and pay that gal at the register for our dinner? Just like that?"

"There is nothing to be embarrassed about, Frank, but no, I'm going to leave the cash on the table."

"So now we're all square?"

The realization of what I really want from Frank is so big, I pause a moment to let it sink in before I say the words out loud. "Now we are equals."

I leave five dollars for a three-dollar tab, and Frank starts to say something about leaving such a big tip but thinks better of it. The moment he gets in the car, his mouth is on mine, kissing me like it's been weeks instead of hours. I hesitate, but not for long. I moan into his mouth, and he pulls away. "God, Vada. What you do to me." The whole truck stop is watching us. He cranks up the car and starts down the highway.

Frank feels like he's worked two shifts at the diner, three, if there was such a thing. He doesn't know why he's so tired. He hasn't done anything all day, just propose to Vada and then nearly lose her. Forever. But she's asleep in his arms again, and that's all that matters. Another car passes by in the opposite direction, and the light is barely generous enough for Frank to glance down at her. God, she's beautiful.

He knows she's still smarting over him doubting her and trying to butt into her arrangement with the harlot. But Frank did what any man worth his salt would have done. And then she made him pay for it with that ridiculous talk about wanting to be equal? Women aren't equal to men, and men certainly aren't equal to women. They can't possibly be. They're as different as chalk and cheese, and Vada paying a tab won't really change anything. But if it does in her mind, then it was worth it.

A billboard says there's a motel twenty miles down the road. A hot shower and a soft bed would feel real good right now. But what should he do? If he suggests a motel, she'll think he's being presumptuous, and he's already on thin ice as it is.

"Are you tired, Frank?" She lets out a long sigh he feels dead center of his chest.

He kisses the top of her head and breathes her in. "A little. How about you?"

"Yes." She doesn't look up at him. "I saw a sign for a hotel."

There's a world of difference between a hotel and a motel, but Frank doesn't bother to correct her. "We can stop if you want. See if they have a couple of rooms."

"I'd like that."

He glances at the speedometer and slows down. She unwraps herself from his middle and digs through her pocketbook until she finds a brush. She runs it through her hair, arching her back slightly and purring as the bristles scrape across her scalp and then down the length of her silky blond locks, almost making Frank miss the motel parking lot. The car comes to an abrupt stop, announcing its presence to the desk clerk of The Rainbow Motel, who glares at them for a few seconds before going back to his business.

"Is everything all right, Frank?" She throws that damn brush in her pocketbook, looks at him, and smiles sweetly, the smile of a good girl who's going straight to bed. By herself.

"Everything's fine. I'll be right back." Frank reaches for the screen door of the office. Arthur Godfrey's "Too Fat Polka" is wailing on the radio. The attendant has the newspaper splayed out, working a crossword puzzle. He's tapping the fat red eraser on the end of his pencil against the long, narrow counter, keeping time to the beat. "Frank," Vada calls after him, and he swears he'll lose his good sense if she tells him she wants to pay for their rooms. "Just one room."

The guy behind the counter must have been at this job for a while, because he never looks up from his puzzle. He points to the register for Frank to sign, shoves a room key across the counter, and holds his hand out for the five spot.

Frank hurries back to the car and eases toward the back of the lot, which is dotted with a dozen or so tiny stand-alone rooms that look dingy gray in the headlights. The doors are painted the different colors of the rainbow. Theirs is red. Number Three. The other rooms are dark and quiet except for the one on the end. An old woman pokes her head out the door, with her hands on her hips, and eyes them suspiciously. Frank gives her a slight wave, but she just shakes her head and closes her door.

The place is so bad, it makes sleeping in the Mayflower seem like a good idea. It smells like spoiled beef stew and cigarette smoke. There's one twin bed in the middle of the room, a dinette standing cockeyed, like it's missing one leg, and a ratty blue couch covered in nubby fabric. Two fat roaches, as long as playing cards, scurry across the concrete floor and under the bed and confirm this is no sane woman's idea of romantic.

Frank isn't sure if Vada saw the vermin, but she looks horrified and not at all like the girl who cooed "Just one room" a few minutes ago.

"I can see if they have another room, but I doubt it will be any better than this one." She sits down on the couch, draws her feet up to her chest, and tucks the wide skirt of her dress under her so she looks beautiful but legless. "Or we could turn the key in and drive to Atlanta; we'd get there around two, if we're lucky, maybe closer to three. At that hour, I'm not sure if we'd find a place any better than this one."

She nods and takes another look around. "It's fine. Really."

"You're sure?" She nods. "Okay. I'm going to jump in the shower, unless you want to go first."

"Go ahead. I prefer a tub bath." She looks like she's judging the tub by the room, and then shakes her head. "I'll wait until I get back to the boardinghouse."

"Okay. I won't be long." Frank isn't sure what to expect. Will Vada be in bed, waiting for him, when he gets out of the bathroom? Should he sleep in the raw, like he usually does, or wear his Skivvies? He turns the water on, grateful that it's good and hot. He yanks his shirt over his head, painfully aware of how hard he is when he slips off his pants. He presses his palms against the tile and the water beats against the back of his neck, dissolving the tension from a day's worth of fighting and making up.

He keeps thinking about Vada, in bed. About her scent that's like some kind of fancy perfume mixed with sensible lemon. Her blue eyes. Rose-petal-soft skin. Long, slender legs parting. His private nods his head at Frank, and while he likes its thinking, Frank isn't sure how Vada would feel about these thoughts he's having. She suggested getting one room, but was she thinking what Frank was thinking? He turns the hot water off and wills himself to stay under the icy spray.

With his Skivvies on, he opens the door and stops in his tracks. The room is barely lit from the full moon and the streetlight beside the office. The bed is turned down. Vada is sound asleep, curled up on her side, on the couch, in some sort of white gown as thin as cheesecloth, or at least that's what the sleeve of it looks like. The rest of her is covered with a blanket too heavy for such a warm summer night, tucked tight around the outline of her body. Frank takes the better of the two pillows and slides it under her head. Her eyelids barely flutter; she smiles. "Thank you."

"Good night, Vada." The room is suddenly oppressively hot. Frank whips off his T-shirt and stands over her, watching her sleep, wanting to wake her up. He presses a kiss against her temple and lingers on the tiny pulse beat. "I love you."

·Chapter Seventeen·

In the dim early-morning light, the room is even more dreadful than it was last night. My skin crawls at the memory of the pair of huge palmetto bugs that scurried under the bed. Just the thought of those awful things and all their relatives prowling the night away makes me shudder. I rake my hands through my hair desperately, quickly raise the blanket up to make sure they didn't invade my cocoon during the night, and tuck it back around me.

Frank looks so beautiful. Peaceful. His breath is slow and steady, and his cheeks are flushed from the room that is already hot. My good sense is still at war with my body, and I'm certain this familiar stirring is one of the ambiguous warnings Rosa Lee and Mother used to go on about. But like most admonitions that come from parents, they're hard to take seriously when no one will explain exactly why something is wrong. Especially when it seems undeniably right.

I feel things about Frank I don't understand. I want to touch

him, and I want him to touch me and not stop at common bound-
aries. Even the fragments of my anger are no match for his charm,
his patience, his easy way. Of course, he knows exactly what he's
doing, using kisses, that smile, and his kindness to try to make me
forget what he did yesterday.

No matter how good his intentions were, it wasn't his place to
intrude into my arrangement with Miss Wentworth. Granted the
woman, and what was obviously a brothel, did give me pause, but
that's not the point. Frank's protests made me all the more determined to do what I wanted. I'm concerned his behavior was a
window into our future, a glimpse of what my life will be like
after I say, "I do." Is that what he thinks a marriage is, him deciding everything, simply because he's a man?

But in a way, I'm glad Frank did chisel in, because it made me
stand up to someone I love, for what I want. I've only done that
once before in my life and that was the night after I graduated
college, after three glasses of sherry. Maybe I should have kept up
my protest about marrying Justin, instead of stealing away like a
thief in the night. I should have put my foot down and refused my
parents. But if things hadn't happened the way they did, I would
never have met Frank.

His challenge opened my eyes to what is possible, not just in
my life but in life itself. Otherwise, I'm sure the notion of being
any man's equal would have never occurred to me. Of course, my
father would make fish eyes and keel over at the very idea of a
woman and a man as equal partners in anything, much less a
marriage, but I think that's what a real marriage is. Or at least
what it should be. But was Frank simply trying to appease me? Is
he even capable of seeing me as his equal? Would any man be? He
stirs a bit and turns onto his side, so his broad back is facing me.
Is that a sign?

"Vada." He sighs out the word, and I'm not sure if he's awake or if he's dreaming. "Are you up?"

"Yes, Frank. I've been up for some time."

He rolls over, and his smile is glorious. His mussed hair and the stubble on his chin make him even more desirable. "Did you sleep well?" My heart races, and I can't help but squirm at the thought of what is under his opaque cotton sheet.

"Yes, thank you."

I know about the birds and the bees, about going all the way, but technically, I'm not sure what going all the way is. Girls at college threw that term around when they were in love, like the words themselves were dangerous and fun. He raises up on one elbow and looks at me like he's contemplating asking me to join him. I want to, but I don't have the slightest idea what I'd do. I imagine there would be hours of delicious wet kisses that would make me think I'd like to go all the way with him.

He pulls the sheet over his bare shoulder. "You okay? You look a little scared."

"I've never been alone with a man before—in a hotel room."

"Relax, Vada. You're safe with me. Why don't you get dressed?" He laughs softly and flops onto his back, his hands covering his beautiful eyes.

As charming as Frank is, I'm not laughing, and the silence is awkward, but what am I supposed to do? It wouldn't be wise to give in to these feral urges, not until I'm sure Frank Darling is the man I think he is, the man I want him to be.

She crawls off the couch and bends over her suitcase, pulling out a few pieces of clothing and a lone shoe. Her round bottom is staring at Frank through her paper-thin nightgown; she looks to see if he's peeking through his fingers and seems satisfied that he's not. She rummages for the other shoe, stands, and digs her fists into her slim hips as she considers where the mate might be. Frank can see her breasts, full and beautiful, the outline of her nipples.

She turns her back to him and gets down on her hands and knees. Good God. He'll be hard the rest of the day. He raises up just a bit to see her hesitate before she reaches under the couch. She jerks out the prodigal slipper with a little squeal, tossing it about like a hot potato, and then checks the shoe to make sure the roaches haven't moved in.

Frank can't help but laugh. "Are you all right?"

"Yes. And no peeking." She looks over her shoulder as she rushes into the bathroom and seems sure that Frank hasn't seen a thing. She tries four or five times, but the door is warped and won't stay closed.

"It's okay, Vada. I can't see through the door."

Her laugh sounds nervous; she turns on the faucet in the sink. There's not enough water pressure to cover her dreamy sigh. Frank imagines her naked, bathing with the same rough terry-cloth rag he used last night. Water dripping down her breasts. The rag moving over her flat white belly, between her legs. She turns the water off.

Frank eyes the sliver of a crack where the door doesn't close. Glimpses of bare skin make him even harder. He lies on his back, not making a sound, barely breathing. But his silence takes him someplace he doesn't want to go, memories of the preacher's wife achingly sad and then so happy to see him. Lila always rode him in a desperate way, like she was trying to outrun the darkness that always seemed to dog her. When they came, she held her hand over his mouth and bit her lips together, for fear they would be heard, before they were dressed and pretending nothing had happened. Before her sadness returned.

Vada's hand is wrapped around the edge of the door, ready to open it. "Are you presentable, Frank?"

"Just a minute." He pulls on his dungarees and starts to button them. "All clear."

She comes out of the bathroom and stops short, blushing hard at his bare chest, and for the life of him, all he can do is stand there with his shirt in his hand. He wants to make her sigh, make her moan. Maybe her face is flushed because she wants him, too, or maybe she's just embarrassed that Frank is half-naked. She's transfixed, like she wants what he wants, or, at the very least, is considering it. Then she looks away. He takes the hint and dresses quickly.

"Hungry?" Jesus, Frank. Can't you think of anything to do for this woman besides make love to her and feed her? "Want to get some breakfast?"

She nods hesitantly, and it feels like they've backtracked to the tenuous moments when she slammed the car door in Memphis and didn't say a word for three hundred miles. She kneels on the floor, snaps her suitcase shut, then abruptly opens it again and shuffles through it to make sure she doesn't take home any six-legged souvenirs.

"Ready," she says softly.

"Vada?" She doesn't look at him. "Honey, what's wrong?"

"This. Us. It's going too fast for me."

Frank knows what she means, this pull that draws them together is so powerful, he accepted it the moment he saw her. But what is welcoming to him might be terrifying to a young woman like Vada. "You want to go slow?" He wraps his arms around her and rests his chin on her head. He holds her like a timid animal until he feels her body relax a little. "Then we will."

Two meals and four hundred miles later, she's still not talking. From time to time, she looks at Frank and smiles, almost apologetically, like she's going to break off what they have going as soon as she gets back to Round O. He almost wishes she'd do it while she's captive in this car. At least she'd be forced to listen while he tried to talk her out of it.

"We're not far from Walterboro. I'll call Tiny to come pick you up at the bus station."

"Thank you, but I'll call Tiny." She nods and smiles wanly. "She gave me her phone number."

The silence is killing him. "Vada? Can I ask you something?"

"Of course."

"I know we had a fight, and I thought we'd made up. But what happened back at the hotel to change your mind? Did I do something wrong?"

He holds his breath and hopes to God she doesn't say yes.

"No, Frank. You were a perfect gentleman." She pauses, looking at him far less adoringly than usual.

"It's just that you seem different, Vada. I've had a lot of miles to guess exactly why that is, and I've told myself it's nothing. But that's not true. You're unsure about me. About us."

Her beautiful face makes Frank want to kick himself for not keeping his damn mouth shut back in Memphis. At this moment, if she wanted to sell her soul to the harlot, he wouldn't say a word.

"It's just that I've never been swept off my feet, Frank. I've never even been in love before. And while being with you has been wildly romantic, and then, of course, your proposal—I just want to go slow and make sure that what we have is what we'll have fifty years from now."

Frank wants to pull off the road and convince her there's no reason to doubt him or their love. But the way her jaw is set, her eyes refuse to smile, and her lips are pulled into that tight line— all tell him that would set them back more than it would move Vada closer to the forever with him.

"Nothing good stays the same, Vada. It only gets better, and it's no different with love." She kisses the back of his hand, and he swears to God it feels like good-bye. "I love you."

He's sure she can smell his desperation, but she doesn't answer him, just trails her hand out the window, her fingers sifting through the wind.

They pull into the tiny Greyhound station parking lot, and there's not a soul in sight, no buses, just the heat rising from the asphalt. Not so much as a car passing disturbs the silence, until the Mayflower's engine makes a pinging sound as it cools. She eyes the pay phone by the ticket stand.

Frank's heart stops when she pushes the car door open. "I'll wait with you until Tiny comes." He sounds desperate. He is desperate.

"That won't be necessary, Frank, but thank you for driving me."

"It feels like we flew back, like we didn't get enough time to talk." She looks at him like he's a liar, and she's right. They just didn't talk. "Besides, it would be wrong to leave you here all alone."

"I need to think, Frank, before I get back to Round O." She attempts a smile. "If Tiny doesn't come soon after I call, I'll walk over to the Dairy Queen and sit at one of the picnic tables and wait for her. I'll be fine."

"But what if it rains?" He gets out of the car, or at least partially, and leans over the roof that is doing less to separate the two of them than Vada is. She thanks Frank again and walks toward the pay phone. "God, Vada, if you won't tell me what you're thinking, at least tell me what you want, right here. Right now."

"I already told you, Frank. I want to go slow."

·Chapter Eighteen·

It's Saturday night and nearly dark, but the boys are finally asleep. From the lace curtains, Claire watches Vada get out of Tiny Medford's truck, which isn't unusual. Claire's been doing that a lot lately, living through little bits and pieces of Vada's romance with Frank.

Most of the time, it feels like she's browsing a store, running her hand over fine fabrics she knows she'll make into Sunday clothes for someone else and never have herself. It hurts on those days, to see the blush on Vada's face, the way her eyes light up and her breath quickens when she talks about Frank. But the worst is watching Vada remember Claire's heart is irreparably broken. She always cuts her stories short, leaving out the most intimate details, because she feels sorry for Claire, making the pill all the more bitter to swallow.

Claire didn't buy the story Vada told at the supper table a few days ago any more than Miss Mamie did, and she'd bet this and next month's rent it was a cover for a romantic rendezvous with Frank. Claire lets the lace curtains fall back into place and smiles at her boys draped across each other like latticework on a sweet pie. It's been a long time since she's had any news that was good news. Her life has been the same since Bobby was killed, never moving forward, and, thankfully, not moving backward into the darkness that enveloped her after his death. She couldn't afford that, not with three boys. They saved her from dying of a broken heart, and for that she is grateful.

The front door opens and closes. Claire knows everyone in the house by their footsteps, knows Vada is padding up the stairs in her expensive shoes.

There's a soft knock at Claire's door, but she doesn't answer. Even though she's only known Vada a few short weeks, she loves her like a sister, because it's impossible to know Vada Hadley and not love her. Part of Claire wants to fling open the door and squeal and shout that luck has finally nodded Claire's way. But as good as the news that she and the boys are moving is, she'll wait until tomorrow, at the breakfast table, to make the announcement, just to keep a bit of something wonderful for herself.

For years, getting out of bed at four thirty in the morning has been automatic. Frank's eyes would open, his brain would already be ticking off the to-do list of things to get ready for the breakfast crowd. Lots of days, trucks roll through in the middle of the night. Sometimes, there are as many as a dozen parked in the seashell gravel between his house and the diner, their drivers catching a little shut-eye before they eat. On good mornings, Frank takes the coffeepot out there to give them a hit of go-juice to get their morning started, talk about the weather, listen to their stories. But he doesn't have to open his front door to know there are no trucks in the parking lot, because he was up all night trying to figure out how his life got back to where it was before he met Vada Hadley.

The clock in his body tells him to get the hell up soon or Tiny Medford will be banging on his door to see if he's dead or broken-hearted. The moment his feet hit the floor, he is back to hating the sameness in his life. He dresses. Using a comb seems like too much effort, so he runs his hands through his hair and sighs like an old man. He passes the mirror without looking at himself, which isn't unusual. This morning, he can't. He doesn't want to see the face of the man who was stupid enough to lose the perfect girl.

The screen door slams behind him as he starts across the parking lot, which needs to be scraped again. The big divots from a gully washer say it rained while he and Vada were gone. It must have been some storm; he bets the creek is high and beautiful. A note sticks out of the screen door that connects the general store and post office. His heart sinks. It's probably from Vada, thanking him for opening her eyes to the fact that he is a huge asshole.

He breathes a sigh of relief when he recognizes Miss Oda Johnson's scrawl. Miss Oda lives about two miles past the creek road and is the nicest person Frank has ever known. Except Vada. Miss Oda is one of those people who always passes out compliments, but they're never phony, and, even to a crusty bastard like Frank, they're always appreciated.

Dear Frank,

I woke up this Independence Day with your store on my mind. With so many youngins leaving Round O after they're grown, I am so grateful that you cared enough to stay and keep this place open. I know you wanted to go into the ser-

vice and the government didn't have the good sense to take
you. But I wanted you to know that you do us a great service
by being faithful to our community six days a week. And I
wouldn't worry one bit about Reverend Smudge. Bitsey, the
little gal who keeps house for me, told me what he did to you,
and I don't mind telling you it made me grateful that I'm
unchurched. Bitsey was so mad at Smudge, she put one of
those Gullah voodoo spells on him good and proper. With a
dead chicken to boot. So please know that your service to
our community is highly appreciated.

With a grateful heart,
Oda Mae Johnson

Frank almost smiles, then shoves the note in his pocket. He
goes around back to the kitchen and unlocks the door. The key is
jiggling in the lock when he hears a low growl. Ben Ferguson's
bird dog is out by the trash pile, nosing around in the ashes like
there's something there. Frank almost laughs at the sight of him,
muscles twitching in excitement, tail so straight, you could use it
as a level. "There's nothing there, Coot. Go on home now." But
the dog claws at the trash, whining with excitement at the pros-
pect of finding a mouse or some poor animal to torment.

"Go on home." Just as Frank pushes the door open, the dog
yanks a long, fat black snake out from the bottom of the pile.

"Damn it, Coot, don't you kill that thing." Frank runs and
grabs the water hose, but it doesn't come close to reaching Coot,
so he ratchets his thumb over the end and turns it on full blast to
try to shoo the dog away. The poor snake is coiled up. Frank's
pretty sure it's the same one that's been keeping the field mice and
rats away from the diner for over a year now. The snake is shak-

ing the end of his tail, pretending to be a rattler, striking at the dog, but the dog knows the snake's about as vicious as he is. "Go do your job, Coot, and let the snake do his. Go on now." The dog looks at Frank for a split second, and Frank blasts him good with the hose. Before Coot can shake the water off, the black racer lives up to his name and slithers under the pump house.

The dog noses around the pile desperately, growling. He follows the scent to the pump house and starts digging. Frank gives him another squirt, and Coot decides to go on about his day, just like Frank.

The biscuits are just out of the oven when Tiny saunters through the door with a sly grin like she's hung the moon all by herself this morning. "When's the wedding?"

"Coffee's ready."

Her face drops because she knows Frank well enough to know the moon has fallen out of the sky altogether. "Frank, I know you don't talk about things such as this, so just shut up and listen. I'm real sorry. You're a good man, and if she can't see that, I'll spit in her eye."

The bell on the front door jangles, and a couple of truckers lumber in. "Hey, y'all." Tiny puts her waitress face back on. "Coffee?" They nod and settle into the booth toward the back of the restaurant, closest to the store.

Tiny puts the first orders up and Frank gets busy. The kitchen racket and commotion are salve as the diner begins to fill up. Much like Coot, Frank's body seems to know what to do. Everything is instinctual, moving about, snatching orders off the wheel, barking at Tiny. It feels really good until he looks down at the next ticket. Crab cakes and grits. He shoves the ticket back across the counter at Tiny as she makes a pass to refill the coffee cups.

"No crab cakes."

She looks at Frank like he just shot the dog out back. "What do you mean no crab cakes? We got the blue crab. I saw it myself in the refrigerator." She puts the ticket back on the wheel and gives it a defiant whirl. "You've lost your mind. I've been working here thirty years and there hasn't been a day gone by that there weren't any."

He's lost much more than his mind. "I said no crab cakes, damn it."

"Today? Or ever?" Her hands are on her hips, her jaw jutted out. If she had a butcher knife in her hand, she'd be dangerous. Hell, she might be dangerous without one, but Frank refuses to answer her.

She hustles back to the offending customer, a stranger who won't know that the world has ended, for Frank anyway. He'll just think the diner is out of blue crab. Tiny tells him his coffee is on the house. "We got salmon croquettes. The sausage is real good, and the bacon is smoked out back twice a year with oak and hickory."

Frank nods as Tiny puts the order back on the wheel with a good hard look that says he'd better snap out of this right now. "Special with grits." He shoves a plate of liver pudding and grits through the window at Tiny and stops for just a second. The look on her face says she's about to light into him to make him change things back the way they were, and he'd give anything if he could.

There's enough diner noise to cover what he has to say. "Just shut the hell up, Tiny, and let me be." He means for the words to come out gruff, but they sound more like a prayer.

"Do all you can, shug, and let the rough end drag." She nods at him, gets a piece of paper off of the tablet she keeps beside the register, and makes a sign that she scotch-tapes to the outside of the screen door. NO CRAB CAKES.

She still looks as bowed up as a Halloween cat. It's clear she's demanding Frank get himself right again, and soon. He nods at her and cracks a pair of eggs, without breaking the yolks. Most everybody in the diner is a stranger. The regulars have seen the sign on the door and turned around and gone home. But it's a good crowd, so good Frank has to bake biscuits twice.

Frank plops a half dozen sausage patties on the griddle and nods at Hank Bodette as he makes his way to the lunch counter. The old man's steps are small, like he's afraid to move any faster, for fear his brittle body will turn to dust. Eventually, he gets to the counter and shoves his mug Tiny's way for free coffee. "With the post office closed for the holiday last week, there'll be a fair amount of mail today. Reckon I'll be right busy." Hank blushes when Tiny smiles at him. "You're looking mighty pretty today, young lady."

Frank laughs out loud at the idea of anybody calling Tiny Medford young. Her head snaps around at him, and he laughs again because Hank has actually made her blush.

"Thanks, handsome," she says to Hank. "You're not so bad yourself."

Hank shuffles back to the store with his coffee and the compliment he was fishing for.

Just after ten, the last customers leave the diner, and Frank wants to go with them. Tiny has wiped down the lunch counter a million times, biding her time until they are alone, with the exception of Hank, who can't hear them from all the way in the back of the store. The parking lot is empty. She throws the slop towel on the counter and wheels around. "Franklin James Darling, you are the best man I know. Hell, that I've ever known—"

"I'm not talking about this to you or to anybody, Tiny. Besides, there's no point in beating a dead horse."

She puts her hand on his shoulder. "But it can't hurt, either. I haven't seen you this low since—" He was rejected by every possible branch of the military. "What happened, Frank?"

He turns his back, refusing to answer her. He digs the scraper across the griddle until it glows with a dull black sheen. If Coot isn't still out by the trash pile, Frank will walk through the peanut patch behind the diner until he gets to the woods and leave the scraps for Coot there. The dog will find them eventually, or he'll find the other animals that do. Maybe they'll keep Coot busy, so he won't bother the snake. Makes more sense than calling Ben Ferguson; he won't keep that dog penned up like he ought to.

Setting out across the field, the slop bucket seems heavier than usual, but Frank knows it's not. His good sense tells him this probably won't work, that it's an awful lot of trouble to go to, to save a black snake. Maybe. But even a snake deserves some peace.

·Chapter Nineteen·

I hear the clatter coming from the kitchen and know I've missed breakfast. Miss Mamie is probably stomping around, adding that to my long list of tribulations. But I couldn't eat even if I wanted to.

"Vada." Jonathan's stubby little legs race toward me, his arms outstretched. He wraps himself around the skirt of my dress. "Missed you."

I pick him up and breathe in the scent of his neck, making him giggle. "I missed you, too, sweet boy." The swinging door flies open, and Daniel comes out carrying two full plates. His face turns bright red, but his smile is brilliant and welcoming.

"Good morning, Daniel. What's all this?"

"Isn't it wonderful! Miss Mamie's sister is in the hospital, on death's door, because she broke her tailbone." He whispers the last part so that Jonathan won't hear, but the little guy squeals out loud.

"Miss Mamie's a monkey, too. Her sister's got a tail," Jonathan sings.

The door swings open, and Claire is standing there with Miss Mamie's apron on, wagging her finger hard. "Jonathan Carl Greeley. You stop that kind of talk this instant."

"But Mama, I want her to be a monkey. Peter says she's a witch, and witches are scary." By the time he finishes his sentence, he's almost in tears.

"Mama," Peter shouts from the kitchen. "The biscuits look done."

I scoop the gangly baby up and hold him close again, shooing Claire back to the kitchen. She gives me a grateful look, and the door swings shut behind her.

"Don't you dare try to take those biscuits out, Peter. You'll burn yourself good," Claire fusses from the kitchen. "Give me those oven rags this instant."

Jonathan shifts around and lays his sweaty head on my shoulder, sucking his thumb for all he's worth. Jealousy is etched in hard lines across Daniel's young face. "Daniel, would you be a dear and do something for me?" He nods, still looking at his toddler brother like a predator. "Please, get the bachelors up if they're not, and tell them breakfast is ready."

In no time, we're all seated at the table, without the pall of Miss Mamie hanging over us. The bachelors don't seem to notice her absence. Mr. Stanley is wearing a new but horribly ugly bow tie and leering at Claire as she takes her place at the table. Jonathan is in my lap, kicking Miss Mamie's chair like it's as soothing as sucking his thumb. He wouldn't dare do that if she were here.

Peter is so hungry, when Claire asks him to bless the food, he says the prayer like it's one word, followed by "Ouch." I open my eyes slightly to see him pouting at his mother, who has just pinched him. "But I'm hungry," he whines.

"Amen," Claire says reverently, and everyone starts eating.

"How was your trip, Vada?"

"Very good, Claire." My face is redder than the piping on my dress. "These grits are wonderful."

She gives me a sly look and then mortifies Daniel by dabbing at some blackberry jelly at the corner of his mouth.

"Mama, are you going to tell her?" Peter whispers.

"Tell me what?"

"Oh." Claire finishes chewing her food and nods. "Yes. Miss Mamie will most likely be gone all of this week, and possibly the next."

"The surprise," the boy whispers again. Claire gives him a stern look, and he falls back into line.

"Of course." As much as I'm trying to sound cheerful, I can't. Mr. Stanley is seated beside Claire at the head of the table, with his new bow tie that enhances the lecherous beam on his face. "You had some news you wanted to share when I returned. I do hope it's wonderful news. Well-thought-out news. Something that's really good." And not horrible.

Claire shrugs and takes a sip of coffee. "I was going to wait until Miss Mamie gets back, but I suppose now is as good a time as any. I'm getting—" She looks down at her plate and smiles, because she's out of her mind. She must be if she's agreed to marry Mr. Stanley.

Mr. Stanley reaches for her hand and accidently knocks over his coffee cup. He's so excited, he doesn't even have the good sense to apologize. Peter jumps up and dashes into the kitchen without being told. Having knocked over his fair share of glasses at the dining table, he returns dutifully with two clean dishcloths for his mother.

"It's all right," Claire says to the doe-eyed old fart as she sops up the mess. "It'll all come out in the wash."

"As I was saying." Please, Claire, let it be the job.

"Oh, look," I say. "Jonathan has a new tooth, Claire. I do hope it came in easily this time. It's so awful when those old things are slow. Painfully slow, and ugly." I think I've offended her. "Of course, I didn't mean to imply Jonathan's teeth are ugly, because they're certainly not. They're beautiful. Young teeth. Very young. Like pearls."

"Mama's got a job," Daniel shouts triumphantly.

Mr. Stanley's coffee cup slips from his hand and crashes onto his plate. All during breakfast he's been looking at Claire like she was bare naked. The disbelief and blighted hope on his face is delightful.

"It's true." She's gushing like a schoolgirl. "I got the job at the Sheridan place. Reginald Sheridan is returning from Europe to reopen the plantation house soon, and I've been hired to handle the unpacking and keep house for him."

I push back from the table and rush to hug her. Maybe a little too tightly. "Oh, Claire, I'm so relieved—I'm so happy for you." I take my place at the table again. "What is he like? Is he handsome? Is he married?"

"To be honest, I haven't met him yet, but his attorney, Mr. Jameson, told me he was quite happy to find someone who already lives in Round O."

"That place has been closed for over twenty-five years." Mr. Stanley seems to suddenly have enough of his wits about him to plead his case. "It's probably a ramshackle mess. Full of squirrels and other vermin."

"Actually, no." She's positively glowing. "I've already been over there to look around. It's really quite grand, and it's over a hundred years old."

"The Yankees missed that one." Mr. Clip nods. "But they

scorched a path clean to the Middleton plantation. My pappy and his pappy told me that much. Goddamn Yankees."

"Mr. Clip!" Claire snaps. "The boys."

"Sorry, ma'am."

"But the best news is that there are servants' quarters on the property. Mr. Jameson said they're not in the best of shape, but with a little work, the boys and I will be able to live there. He even gave me fifty dollars cash to get started."

"Claire, this is wonderful news." Mr. Stanley gives me an icy stare. "For you and the boys."

"It is wonderful." Peter is nearly breathless, ticking off all of the good things he thinks will come of this. "And . . ." He makes a grand gesture with his spoon, like a boy king making his first decree. "No more playing in the street."

Everyone, except for the bachelors, cheers wildly. I'm so happy for Claire I could burst. We finish breakfast, and Claire declines my offer to help clean the dishes. With a beautiful smile on her face, she asks me to watch the boys and retreats to the kitchen.

They are every bit as happy as she is, no doubt because they haven't seen her like this since before their father's death. We go out on the front walkway, and Peter takes a piece of coal out of the winter stash to make a hopscotch board on Miss Mamie's sidewalk.

"That might be a little too permanent." I take the lump out of his hand and toss it aside. "Here, we can make a place to play in the dirt." I draw out several squares with a stick. The boys gather stones, a part of the game they added to test their skill. Peter calls the number eight and tries to toss the stone into the eighth square, but it lands on twelve.

He hops on one foot to the stone, picks it up easily, and looks at his older brother, daring him to do the same. The game continues, and it's decided that I should play with Jonathan on my hip, but there's no way I can hop on one foot and pick up my stone with the baby. I fall into the boys, and they catch me so that we end up in one big hug. We're laughing so hard, Claire has to tap me on my shoulder to get my attention.

"I forgot to give you this. It came for you while you were gone. They forgot to use your post-office box." She holds out the envelope.

"Who's it from?" Peter giggles.

My thumb brushes over the Charleston postmark, hoping for good news from home.

My Dearest Vada,

Desmond told me about your job, and I'm so proud of you and know you will be a wonderful teacher for those children. I miss you more than I thought I could ever miss anybody. I love you so much and want you to have the life you want for yourself. Every day, I pray that God will watch over you, but I'm worried. I've worked for your daddy for over thirty years, and I've never seen him so worked up as he is about your leaving. He sent Justin to bring you back; you and I both know that man don't know enough about you to have the first idea of where to look. I'm not worried Mr. Justin's gonna find you, but I am very worried about what your daddy will do when he comes back empty-handed. It breaks my heart to say this, but maybe you ought to leave South Carolina for good.

Whatever you do, my precious child, keep yourself safe.

Love always,
Rosa Lee

My face is wet with tears. I reread the words *"leave South Carolina for good."* My knees almost buckle at the thought of leaving this place, the Lowcountry, Claire and the boys. Frank.

Peter pulls on the skirt of my dress to get my attention. "Miss Vada, are you crying?"

"Leave her alone." Daniel pushes his brother aside. "Someone's died."

I shake my head, and should reassure the boys that everything's all right, but I can't.

Claire watches as Vada slides her finger slowly across the opening and flinches when the paper cuts her. She pulls a fine linen handkerchief out of the pocket of her fancy skirt and dabs at the blood. She opens the pages. Her posture drops; her head is down. Peter asks her if she's crying and she shakes her head, but it's apparent she is.

Claire feels guilty, standing here doing nothing while Vada wilts as she reads the letter. Claire wonders how Vada has gotten mail so quickly, but guesses that whoever sent it is the same dark figure who brought her here. For the most part, personal letters are supposed to make people happy, not that Claire would know. She doesn't have any family to speak of, but she knows what it's like to hold an envelope that certainly holds bad news. To feel your heart crumble as your finger slides along the opening.

She had begged herself not to unfold it. She knew Bobby was already gone, but reading the words would make it certain. This letter of Vada's seems different, more troubling than disastrous. At least that's how Claire looks at it; Vada's so cheery all the time, it's hard to tell what's real with her. But not now; she is sad, almost frightened.

Claire wraps her arms around herself, shivering. Remembering the words, "The Army Department regrets to inform you . . ." As much as she loves Vada, she can't go to her just now.

"Boys." Claire's voice comes out hoarse and not at all like she means for it to. Her oldest hears the tone and picks up his baby brother, who looks so much like Bobby sometimes, it slices Claire to bits. They file upstairs quietly, like little soldiers, and lie across their mother's bed, making a place for her in the middle. Jonathan crawls onto her chest.

No one speaks. They'll lie here with Claire, quietly loving her through the reality that she has to push out of her mind every day of her life, so that she can put one foot in front of the other, so that she can live for her boys.

Even with everything good that has happened, the sadness is still a powerful drug, lulling her off to sleep. The baby is already there, breathing softly against Claire's neck. Down the hall, Vada is crying, and Claire feels sorry for her, because she is alone. Claire clings to the boys because they are all she has, and maybe that's the way it's supposed to be. She knows Daniel and Peter won't drift off, not because they just woke up a few hours ago. Because they are her sentries, guarding her while she sleeps.

When Claire wakes up, Daniel will pretend this never happened. Peter will look at her hopefully, silently asking her to promise this is the last time she will fall apart. He'll dog her all day, waiting for the promise she wishes she could give him. The baby will be fussy and clingy the rest of the day, a sweet distraction from her sadness.

·Chapter Twenty·

It's been a week since Frank has seen Vada. He's called on her twice, and while he's not grateful Miss Mamie's sister is on death's door, it was a lot easier hearing from Claire that Vada isn't accepting callers than it would have been from the old battle-ax.

But not seeing Vada has him parched for her and worried sick that he's already lost her because this doesn't feel like taking it slow. He and Vada have come to a screeching halt and are racing backward. But Frank is counting on his third visit being the charm.

It's still ninety-two paces to her front door; he prays that's the only thing that hasn't changed. He stands on the stoop, afraid to knock. The boys are playing chase in the front yard. The littlest one pretends he's a big boy, too, but he falls down more than he keeps up with the others. The oldest is good with him. He picks him up and reminds him if he wants to play, he can't cry. The bachelors are talking among themselves, looking at Frank, standing here like a coward. Mr. Clip says something to them, and they all look at him with their sly, know-it-all smiles.

"Are you here for Vada?" The bigger kid eyes Frank suspiciously and spits on the ground. "Again?"

"What's your name, boy?"

He straightens as tall as his small frame will go and cranes his face up at Frank's, reminding him that the boy's daddy was a short, wiry man. "Daniel."

Frank almost laughs at what's meant to be an intimidating glare, but he gets it. "Oh." He nods. "You like her, too."

Daniel's face turns as red as a beetroot and the defiance has gushed out of him. He's as limp and lifeless as Frank is without her, but the kid doesn't know how good he's got it, living under the same roof with Vada, seeing her every morning and before he goes to bed at night. Frank sits down on the stoop and nods for Daniel to do the same. "I've got it bad for her, too. I can't imagine what it must be like for you."

He looks horrified. "You won't tell her. Please don't."

"Oh." Frank laughs, not mockingly, just man-to-man. "She knows. Women know everything."

"They do?"

The middle boy runs from around the corner of the house proudly, with the youngest in Miss Mamie's wheelbarrow, holding on for all he's worth and laughing so hard, he can barely breathe. Daniel knows as well as Frank does that the old bat would skin these children alive if she caught them.

"Look, Daniel! It's fun. Jonathan is too little to push me. I want a turn. Come play so I can have a ride."

The boy shakes his head and moves a little closer, to say what's on his mind. "Do you think she likes me?"

"Now that's where the problem begins for the both of us.

There's not a man alive who can really know what a woman's thinking, and certainly not Vada." The muscles around his mouth twitch like that simple truth is enough to make him cry. "But my guess is, and it's only a guess, mind you, she likes you a lot."

Daniel's face drops into his hands, which are big for a short kid like him, more like a man's hands. Being the oldest, he'll be expected to be a man a lot sooner than a boy ought to be. "But I *love* her."

"I know you do, and there's no point in telling you to love somebody your own age or to love somebody else. When Vada Hadley gets under your skin, it's forever." The poor kid looks like he's going to throw up. "When are you going to tell her how you feel?"

"When I buy the Sheridan place." He's got some spunk again, a little defiance meant to ward Frank off.

"You have that kind of money?"

"No, but I went over there with my mother. It's fancy and beautiful, just like her. Except it's a big mansion. When I grow up, I'm going to buy it for her."

Frank's hands go up in surrender. "No way I can compete with that, Daniel. But a girl like Vada may not be around that long; I'd bet a three-legged cat that she'll be married by then."

He nods, his face grim. "And you have a three-legged cat."

"No, son." Frank tousles his hair, and the boy automatically smooths it back into place. "I don't, and I can't give her a mansion, either. But since you appear to have the upper hand here, I'm going to ask you, man-to-man, to let her go." Daniel looks at Frank like he's just shot Ben Ferguson's dog and fed him to the black snake. "It'll hurt like hell. Trust me, I know, but I promise I'll take good care of her. Make her happy."

"She's been so sad lately," Daniel says to himself, and then cocks his head to the side. "You can do that? Make her happy?"

"I'll do my damnedest or die trying."

He doesn't say a word, just leaves Frank sitting on the porch by himself. There's an extra crate turned up where the bachelors have sat for as long as he can remember. At the rate Frank's going, it will probably be his one day.

A door slams inside, and footsteps rush down the staircase, bringing Frank to his feet. "Hurry, Vada," Daniel says.

She doesn't even see Frank standing right in front of her as she bursts through the screen door. She stops on the stoop, breathless, and scans the yard. "Jonathan? Peter?" The middle boy comes running around the corner again with the wheelbarrow. He and his little brother are red-faced, giggling. "Boys, are you all right?" They look at her like she's crazy for asking such a thing, and then she sees Frank.

Just as Daniel is slipping away, she nabs him by the arm. "You said the boys were hurt. Bleeding." With that tone, she'll make a really good teacher.

Daniel stands up extra straight and tall, shakes loose, and walks away.

"Really. Frank." Still with the teacher voice.

"Hey, it wasn't my idea, but I'm glad he did it. I've missed you so damn bad, I can hardly stand it." There's a moment in the movies when the star looks into the camera for a close-up and you suck in your breath because she's so beautiful. That's what every moment is like looking at Vada Hadley. No wonder the boy has it so bad. "You said you wanted to go slow, but it feels like you want to stop. Is that what you want?"

She shakes her head. "I've been busy, preoccupied with a personal matter, and with Miss Mamie gone, I've been helping out around the house. Claire has a job now."

"Really?" Frank hopes he looks like he believes every word she says, but he doesn't. She's been avoiding him all right. "That's great."

"She's readying the Sheridan house for the owner's return. I've been watching the boys, and both of us have been sharing the cooking and the wash."

"Reggie Sheridan's coming back to Round O? And you're cooking?"

"Horribly, and Claire's not much better. If she wasn't their mother, and if Daniel and Peter weren't head over heels in love with me, all three of them would mutiny. Especially on the nights I cook. And then there's—" She bites the thought in half, refusing to share the other half with Frank.

"The personal matter." He finishes her sentence, but she won't look at him. Her arms are wrapped around herself like she's bitterly cold; her eyes are slightly puffy. She's either tired or, more likely, she's been crying. "I check the mail every day myself to see if there's anything from the Wentworth woman." He hopes she knows what a huge peace offering this is for him to say the woman's name without spitting on the ground. "I know you're waiting to hear from her about Darby."

Darby's name startles her, like Vada's almost forgotten about her. "Thank you." The words are barely out, and she bursts into a chest-heaving sob. In one swift motion, Frank scoops her up and hurries to the porch swing. His aim is bad, and he ends up on the left side, making the thing sit lopsided and the chains groan, but he doesn't care. He holds her against him with a want he's never known before, a primal feeling that screams at him to protect her at all costs from whatever it is that is crushing her. But what if it's him?

"*Shhh.*" He kisses her face. "Talk to me, Vada. Tell me what's wrong, we'll work it out. Together." She shakes her head. Her fingers fist his shirt. Frank tells himself she's clinging to him, but he knows she's just hurting. So he sits, intent on holding her until she's all cried out.

The bachelors are looking disgustedly at Frank, spitting on the ground more than usual, craning their withered necks his way like they think he made her cry. Daniel is frozen in front of Vada, along with the middle kid, the baby brother in the wheelbarrow, even the cicadas. The whole world has stopped because it can't bear knowing Vada Hadley's heart is broken.

"She's all right, boys," Frank says. "I've got her."

"Frank?" It took longer than he thought, but she's calmed. Her body quakes a little with each sniffle.

He kisses her on the head and holds her a little tighter. "I'm right here. I'm not going anywhere."

Tears still pool in her eyes, making the irises look like glistening blue jewels. "It's my night to cook dinner." Her voice trails like that's enough to set her off again. "I've got to go."

She pulls herself away from Frank to sit beside him in the swing, her legs tucked off to the side, an unspoken reminder about the going-slow business. He can do slow. He can do anything as long as Vada is the prize, but he can't help but push a little, just enough to make sure they're still moving toward forever. "What are you making for dinner?"

"Claire left some liver mush out to thaw."

"Not again," the middle child whines and shoves his hands disgustedly into the pockets of his dungarees. "Come on, Daniel, let's play while we can."

"I've got some chicken in the cooler," Frank says. "Denny Fox brought in some fresh vegetables this morning. I'll take Daniel with

me to the diner; we'll be right back." The boys are cheering, but as
much as Vada loves Frank's fried chicken, she looks a little leery.
"If that's okay with you. If it's not, I understand. Completely."

"All right." To lay down her cross as easily as that, the poor
woman must be starving. "But I want you to teach me. How to
cook. So I can do it myself."

Frank smiles immediately, a good mask to hide the questions
he has as to exactly what that means. Does it mean doing it
without him? For good?

Daniel falls in beside Frank as they start over to the diner. He's
as happy as Frank is to see that Vada's not crying anymore, but
both of them are smart enough to know that doesn't mean she's
not hurting still. He jogs alongside to keep up with Frank's long
legs that want to break into a run. But he's going slow. Slow.
Sloooow. Whatever Vada wants. Just the way she wants it.

Daniel's a good kid, as eager to please Vada as he is. Frank
loads up paper sacks full of things he'll need and takes a dozen
pieces of chicken out of the buttermilk they've been swimming in
since early this morning. The boy asks a lot of questions and says
"yes, sir" or "no, sir" every time Frank answers. As automatic as
that is for a boy his age, hell, even a man Frank's age, it makes
him feel old, and he refuses to take his place under that mimosa
tree with the bachelors anytime soon. Hopefully, never.

He's looking for the coffee can he has his secret spice mix in
when he notices the boy standing by the counter in front of the
cake plates, looking longingly at the red velvet. "Can we have
dessert, too?" Miss Mamie might be a mean old bitch, but she
does make desserts almost as good as Frank's.

He sets three other domed plates alongside the red velvet. The
boy is practically drooling. Hummingbird cake, the Coca-Cola
cake Vada loves, and a whole pecan pie. "You pick," Frank says.

Daniel runs his fingers across the glass tops long enough for Frank to see his nails are bitten down to the quick. "Or, I got some peaches in just this morning. We could make a cobbler, churn some vanilla ice cream." The boy claps his hands, and that settles it. "Get those two aluminum pails by the sink in the kitchen and fill them both up as much as you can with ice."

The boy approaches the humming ice machine warily. Frank opens the lid to show him there's nothing to fear. "It does that all by itself? Makes ice?"

"Yep. No trays to fill. Pretty neat, huh?"

He fills the buckets with the giant scoop. "I'd rather have a TV," he says, trying not to sound impressed.

"Well, that would be something. Nobody around these parts has a TV, that I know of."

"There's one at the mansion. I saw it. Sort of. It's still in the box." The door of the ice machine bangs shut.

They don't have enough hands to carry everything and the churn, so they load up the Plymouth. The promise of warm peach cobbler and homemade vanilla ice cream is enough to distract the boy from his feelings for Vada. Frank glances in the backseat at the paper sacks holding the makings for dinner and hopes they have the right ingredients to win Vada back.

She's rocking the youngest in the porch swing when they pull up. His head is resting on the swell of her breast, his chubby hand in her shirt pocket. The little guy's cheeks are red from the heat. Vada's smiling down at him, drawing lazy circles on his back. She looks as exhausted as he is, but she's never been more beautiful. Daniel and Frank shuttle things from the car, and the screen door bangs shut, but the little guy doesn't stir.

"Can I take him upstairs for you?" Frank whispers.

"I don't want to wake him. He's so tired."

"I'll be gentle." She leans slightly forward, and he flops gently into Frank's arms. The little one cries out, and the muscles in his forehead are trying to do the heavy lifting, but his eyes are too tired to open. He settles onto Frank's shoulder, and Vada takes Frank's right hand and puts it on the child's back, just below his neck.

"Just bounce him a little if he stirs." She nods toward the screen door and lets Frank in. "It's too hot upstairs, I have his pallet on the floor in the living room." In the few steps to the boy's bed, Frank can feel Vada sizing him up. God, he hopes he's doing this right.

He lays the child, who looks too old to go down for a nap every day, on the well-worn quilts, but he doesn't question Vada. And it wouldn't be right to question Claire. Frank imagines she treats him like a baby because she wants him to stay that way, and Frank can't say that if he were in Claire's shoes, he wouldn't do the same. The child takes in a deep breath that stutters out before he goes down for the count. Frank and Vada stand there for a moment, looking down at his cherubic face as if he belongs to them. She reaches for Frank's hand and leads him into the kitchen.

·Chapter Twenty-One·

Frank feeds me a slice of the ripe peaches we peeled for the cobbler. His slender finger lingers in my mouth. Instinctively, I suck the sweetness off, then turn away, wiping my mouth with a dishcloth. Slow. I remind myself, I'm going slow. Under the circumstances, it wouldn't be fair to Frank not to. But his easy way is like his cooking, and I can't help but want more.

"Good?" I can feel his determination not to push; he's smiling, so at home in the kitchen. He pours a little lemon juice over the peaches and puts them in the refrigerator. "Let's get started on the rest of the meal."

He shares his secrets—how he gets the fried okra so good, the boys are picking at the platter like it's filled with cookies; what makes his mashed potatoes so delicious, I can hardly remember Rosa Lee's. He instructs me and watches me carefully, not in a seductive way. But when we touch or I taste something that is good down to my core, I feel drawn to him in such a way that it's easy to forget the boys and the bachelors are waiting on their dinner.

"So what's in this little container?" I ask. I open the coffee can, take in a deep breath, and inspect the contents. I see salt and black pepper. "Garlic?"

"Powder," he says.

"But there's something else. Basil?"

"Oregano."

"And the red stuff?"

"Cayenne pepper and paprika."

"It's that simple?"

He nods. "Put a couple of tablespoons in the flour and dredge the chicken. Give each piece a little shake to get the buttermilk off, but not completely." The meal smells so good, I can't believe I've done everything except peel the peaches, with Frank's instruction of course. I know it wasn't easy for him, but he held back and let me do this myself. "Be careful." He hands me the tongs, and I flip the chicken pieces.

"We have so much going." The sweat is beading down my face, trickling down my neck and back. "I don't know how you do it."

"Timing. It's all about timing."

"There are so many pieces in the pan. I'm afraid the crust will fall off if I don't hurry. Can you help me get them up?"

"This is your meal. You can do it."

I pick up the pace, and everything looks wonderful. Nobody around here has had a decent meal in so long, we set the table an hour early. The ice-cream mixture is in the refrigerator, ready to be churned. The boys squeal and run to Claire as she walks through the door. She picks Jonathan up off of the pallet, takes a big whiff, and looks warily at me.

"Come see, Mama," Peter says. "Come see," Daniel echoes.

She looks amazed and ferociously hungry. "Frank, you're such a dear to do this for us."

"All this is Vada's doing," he beams.

Frank wouldn't lift a finger in the kitchen, but he insists on cleaning up after dinner while Claire gives Jonathan a bath and I supervise the boys with the ice cream. They take turns between working the crank and sitting on a towel on top of the churn. Mr. Clip pitches in while Daniel hurries back to the diner for another pail of ice. He's so good with the boys, except when he swears—never at them, of course.

While the boys argue over whose turn it is to work the crank, the ice cream is getting hard, and their determination wears thin. They seem grateful when Frank takes over. Peter plays with the icy saltwater pouring out of the drain while Daniel perches stoically atop the churn. When it's too hard for even Frank to turn, the boys cheer.

"Sorry, but it's not ready yet." Frank pours on extra ice and shrouds it with the towel. "It needs to harden."

"But it's taking too long," Peter whines. "Can't we have it now?"

"Some things are worth waiting for," Frank says, looking at me. "But I promise you, it won't be long."

"Don't worry, boys, Frank and I will go put the cobbler in the oven. As soon as it's ready, we'll have our ice cream, too."

I take the peaches I peeled out of the refrigerator and stand there, looking at the ingredients Frank's laid out. An almost-melted stick of butter on a saucer, flour, sugar, a little cup with salt and baking powder, another with cinnamon, brown sugar, and nuts. Some milk and a lone egg, so they would be at room temperature. "Dry ingredients in the bowl first," he says softly.

I make the mistake of looking into his eyes. "Show me?"

He moves behind me so that I feel the heat from his body before he wraps his arms around my waist. Knowing I'm too sated to protest, he breathes me in. I add the ingredients, arching into him like it's the most natural thing I know. The soft flour floats into the bowl, then the warm melted butter. "Is this slow enough for you?" he asks. I nod, adding the rest of the ingredients, watching our hands on the wooden spoon, stirring the sweet batter. "Want to go slower?"

My intention was to say yes, but I'm shaking my head, nuzzling it against his chest. I can feel he wants me, and he has something to say, but he doesn't want to mess this up. So we mix the batter together, like a slow dance, until I'm nearly breathless.

The fruit spills over the bottom of the dish in its rich, sweet juice. "Okay, now pour the batter over the top." He holds the bowl, and I guide the thick concoction over the ripened peaches. He sets the bowl down, and his hand slides slowly down my arm, giving me chills, a stark contrast to my body heat. He guides my hand to the little bowl of brown sugar, cinnamon, and pecans, and we sprinkle them across the cobbler.

The sweet crystals sticking to my fingers are my undoing. He puts my finger in his mouth. "See how good it already is, Vada. How it will soon be even better." He turns me so that I am facing him and takes another finger into his mouth, licking and sucking so slowly, until I feel like I'm going to explode.

Footsteps rush up the front steps. The screen door slams. The sound of the boys' voices pulls us apart.

"Is it ready?" Peter asks breathlessly. "Please say it's time."

They look at the unbaked cobbler, and their faces fall. "*Aww.* How much longer?"

I pop the cobbler in the oven and can't look at Frank, not in front of the children. "It won't be long now."

·Chapter Twenty-Two·

Early Monday morning, Claire takes in a deep breath, ready for anything. "How do I look?"

Vada motions for her to turn around and nods. "You look beautiful, Claire. It's a smart uniform, really. The navy blue brings out your eyes. Are you going to wear your hair down?"

Claire's hands are shaking so badly, she can't even make the same simple bun she's made every day of her life since she was a young girl. "Can you put it up for me?" She's such a wreck, but after a week of preparing for Reginald Sheridan's arrival, the fact that today might very well be the day he arrives has her as nervous as a first date.

"I bet he's handsome." Vada wraps her hair into a tight bump. The bobby pins scrape across her scalp. "This could be an answer to a prayer."

Claire can't help but laugh. "Not my prayers. I'm just grateful to have a job and a chance for the boys to have a real home."

"But what if he is breathtakingly handsome? And kind? What if he falls in love with you and you love him back?" Vada pushes a few stray hairs into place and looks at Claire's reflection in the cheval mirror. "I'm sorry, Claire. I don't mean to push. I just want you to be happy."

It had been a week since Vada opened the letter that had shredded her. It seemed wrong to let Vada Hadley carry her burden alone, but each time Claire broached the subject, Vada played it off and said she was fine. Claire knew that trick and didn't believe her for a second. Vada was better, for certain. Frank Darling had a lot to do with that. But something was still hanging over her.

"And I want the same for you, Vada."

"This is going to be a magical day for you, Claire. I just know it."

Vada's young and beautiful and head over heels in love with Frank Darling. It's no surprise she looks at the world like it's a place where everyone lives happily ever after. Chasing after the boys and sewing and mending for people has made it easy for Claire to become dowdy. Frumpy. She wants to look professional for Mr. Sheridan, so that he has no doubts about her qualifications and her commitment to be the best housekeeper he has ever known. But she is definitely not looking for love.

"Thank you, Vada." Claire stands extra tall and smooths the bodice of her uniform. "But I am happy." She knows that's so hard for Vada to understand. Since Vada moved here, so much of her happiness has been tied up in Frank. Claire was the same way with Bobby. But she's had to find a way to be happy, to show her boys that she's okay. So they will be okay, too.

"I hope this job is everything you want it to be." Vada hugs Claire and lingers a little, like she needs this almost as much as Claire does.

"There's so much yet to be done, I almost hope he doesn't come today. But I am anxious to meet him. The attorney didn't give me a clue as to what he's like. Judging from the things I've unpacked, I'd say he's very particular. He has a fine appreciation for beautiful things, or whoever furnished the house did."

"Daniel says it's quite beautiful."

"He hasn't seen the third floor. It's a mess, jam-packed with crates and boxes. All of them from Europe. It will take weeks to finish putting it together; I do hope Mr. Sheridan doesn't hold that against me."

"Oh, Claire, don't give it another thought. He'll love you. I'm sure of it. But if you'd like some help, when it's time for Jonathan's nap, I can bring him over, and we can put him on a pallet and work while he sleeps."

"He does sleep through anything. Oh, would you? That would be wonderful."

The sight of all of Mr. Sheridan's chattel dampens Claire's enthusiasm considerably. She shakes her head, pulls a pasteboard box down from one of the stacks, and slits it open. As well-organized as the contents of the other boxes have been, this one is a jumbled mess of photographs. There's been precious little time to pause over Mr. Sheridan's belongings, but the face of the boy in the pictures calls to Claire.

Most of the dates and particulars are scrawled on the backs in a broken, primitive-looking handwriting, maybe by a servant like Claire. Precious few are captioned, in letters so precise, they'd put a printing press to shame. Those pictures show a stoic little boy with a beautiful woman. The tall man beside them is holding his pocket watch as if to say he doesn't have time for such things. His expression couldn't look more disinterested.

"Hello?" Vada's voice pulls Claire from her distraction.

Claire told herself she'd look just for a few minutes, but to her horror, she's been sitting down on the job for hours and is surrounded by the photographs of an adorable little boy who grew up to be a stunningly beautiful man. She wants to linger over the photos and doesn't understand the kinship she feels with Reginald Sheridan. Maybe it's the vulnerability etched in the photographs of him as a young man, the sadness in his beautiful eyes. She shrugs off the thought, repacks the box. What could she possibly have in common with a man of his means?

"Up here, Vada."

She hears Vada talking to Jonathan, and stopping on her way up, most likely to look at the view out the arched window that looks over the gardens. While the view itself is beautiful, the gardens are not. Weeds have run wild, completely covering the cobbled walkway in all but a few spots. Seedlings have turned to trees that have pushed the brick pavers out of the sandy soil altogether. As good as Claire is with a needle and thread, with the exception of her boys, Claire is horrible with anything that grows. She prays her job doesn't depend on sorting out that briar-filled mess as well.

"Oh, Claire. It's a lovely house." Vada's words sound sincere, but there's something in her tone that Claire doesn't understand. She imagines it's a longing for this kind of grandeur. Envy. But Vada's face is passive, almost sad.

Claire dusts off her hands, proud of all her hard work putting the house together. "I can't understand why anyone would ever want to leave such a beautiful place and why it would take them twenty-five years to come back." Vada nods her head absently and runs her hand across a stack of crates marked FRAGILE. "I think those are more paintings. Honestly, Vada, I don't know how one man can have so much stuff."

Claire spreads the quilt she brought from home in a corner, and Vada lays Jonathan down. His eyes are so heavy, his little brow creases as he fights to keep them open.

"And he'll sleep through this?" Vada says, opening a box of fine linens.

"Sleeping in the bed with two brothers has trained him to sleep through anything." Claire drops a large book from waist high; it makes a thunderous noise, but the baby doesn't stir. "See what I mean?"

Vada is a huge help, and the work is easier with some company. Claire knows she'll only have her for a couple of hours at the most, so she works as fast as she can and gently encourages Vada not to stop and admire Mr. Sheridan's pretty things.

They've opened so many boxes, the air is thick with dust, and the afternoon sun beating down on the room has made their work stifling hot. The baby's cheeks are redder than when he had roseola. Claire picks him up. She knows he's not a baby anymore and doesn't know how long she can hang on to him like this. Mr. Clip says he's like the runt of a litter and will always act like a baby as long as he's the youngest. But he's getting so big, making it even harder to pretend he's a baby.

His head rolls around his little jelly neck until it settles onto Claire's shoulder. "It's too hot for him up here. You'd better take him home."

Vada takes Claire's precious baby into her arms. He wakes suddenly and reaches for his mother. "Vada's got you, sweet boy. I'll be home soon."

"No, Vada," he says, still reaching. "I want Mama."

His legs dangle near Vada's knees. It breaks her heart that Bobby almost escaped going to war in the first place, that he didn't make it back from the war to see Jonathan. But no matter how badly Claire wants to, she can't make Jonathan stay little forever. Something else that won't wait for Bobby.

She takes the boy in her arms and kisses the top of his head. The baby smell she'd hoped he could miraculously maintain is gone. "You have to go with Vada now. I'll be home soon."

"*Nooo*," he whines pitifully. "No. Vada."

"Be a big boy." Claire barely gets the words out. She turns her back and slits open a new box. "Please, Vada. Take him home."

I know Jonathan has heard his brothers say that a million times, but he seems startled by his mother's words. He grips my hand tightly and follows me down the stairs, taking some of them like a toddler does, using the same foot to descend each step, and some mirroring my steps. He looks up at me like he's unsure about everything. "You are a big boy," I say. "You can play hopscotch with your brothers when we get back."

"And you won't hold me?" He grins warily. I shake my head and smile back.

At the bottom of the stairs, the sound of a key jiggling in the lock stops both of us in our tracks. "The door is open," I yell. Jonathan dashes behind my skirt and glues himself to my leg. "Claire," I call up the stairs, "I think Mr. Sheridan is here."

The person on the other side of the door laughs and jiggles the doorknob. "It seems so, but for the life of me, it won't open." Claire is rushing down the steps, and just when she gets to the bottom, something hard hits the door, and it flings open, landing a very tall, very handsome man at her feet, who is laughing so hard, he can't get up.

"Oh, dear. Mr. Sheridan, this is so embarrassing. You are Mr. Sheridan, aren't you?" Claire looks at his finery from head to boot. "Yes, of course you are. I'm so sorry—the door sticks. I've asked the handyman to fix it. I really thought he had."

His laughter dissolves into a happy sigh, and he sits back on his heels and surveys what he can see of his house. Claire is holding her breath and looks like she's waiting for him to fire her.

He rises to his feet in a single graceful movement and is even taller than Frank. He has a face that would stop the most indifferent woman in her tracks, an impish smile that emanates from sparkling blue eyes. Thank you, God, he's exactly what I ordered for Claire.

"Madam." He extends his hand to Claire, who is too flustered to notice, so I place her hand in his, and she suddenly stops apologizing. She is dumbstruck by his beauty. Oh, I couldn't be happier. "Reginald Sheridan." She says nothing and is probably incapable, at the moment, of coherent thought.

"Claire Greeley," I croon, giving their clasped hands a good shake, "and she's so pleased to meet you, Mr. Sheridan. Aren't you, Claire?"

"Please, call me Reggie." He seems very kind. And he is rich and extremely beautiful. Why, I couldn't have answered my prayer for Claire any better myself. Say something, Claire, something striking, so that when he toasts your wedding anniversary for years to come, this is the moment that will come to mind. When your eyes met, when your lips parted . . .

"Mr. Sheridan—"

Something for the ages.

"Reggie," he says, still holding her hand.

"The toilet in your bedroom isn't working, either. Please don't use it."

He throws his head back and laughs, letting go of her hand. Oh, Claire, couldn't you have thought of something more romantic to say?

"Claire has worked so hard, Mr. Sheridan—" He raises his eyebrows so that he doesn't have to ask for the third time. "Reggie. Really, she has. You'll not find a more diligent woman, caring, beautiful—" Claire gives me a good stiff elbow to the ribs and is the color of a freshly cooked lobster.

"And you are?" He extends his hand toward me, and I shake it curtly.

"Vada."

"And do you have a surname Vada?"

"Hadley," Claire blurts out.

"Really?" Reggie rocks back on his heels a little and looks like he's sorting through acquaintances in his mind. "Of the Charleston Hadleys? Your father wouldn't by any chance be Matthew Hadley, would he? You do favor—"

"No." I'm trying to remain calm, but I'm every bit as red as Claire. "Not those Hadleys."

"*Hmm.* Maybe not."

"Of course not."

"You do favor Katherine, her nose, I think."

I peel Jonathan from behind me, and he is miffed that he is back on my hip again.

"Put me down. I'm a big boy." His words break Claire's heart. Oh, this isn't going the way I thought it would at all. "Put me down."

"I have to go, get the baby home."

"I'm a big boy." He's kicking so hard, I have to throw him over my shoulder.

"Yes, it appears that you are a big boy." He shakes one of Jonathan's flailing hands, but the boy is impervious to Reggie's charm and squirms even harder.

"But rest assured, Mr. Sher—Reggie—that Claire Greeley is the best woman who will ever come into your life." It's clear he's enjoying Jonathan's show and my exasperation as I fight with the doorknob. Finally, the door flings open, and I start down the palatial staircase. "And I," I say, as Jonathan is still kicking and proclaiming his independence for all he is worth, "am a descendant of the poor Hadleys, the very, very poor Hadleys, who are most certainly *not* from Charleston."

·Chapter Twenty-Three·

The last time Reggie left this place, he was running away from everything it represented. But standing in the foyer, he feels strangely at home, something he never felt growing up here, something he had found with Lesley in Florence.

He likes what the widow woman has done to the place. She hadn't known to rehang the heavy tapestries along the staircase. Instead, she'd uncrated some of the watercolors he'd bought from a fellow artist of Lesley's and hung them where the depressing relics from the Middle Ages once were. His father had called the gaudy dark weavings great works of art, but their depictions of savage wars, complete with beheadings, had terrified him as a child.

From where he stood, she'd also gotten the Persian rugs all wrong, laying the dark and heavy ones in rooms where the windows accentuated their colors and the lighter ones in the mahogany-paneled rooms to brighten them up. Even dead, he was sure his mother was exasperated with the touches Claire had put on the place, but he was quite pleased.

"I know you asked me not to uncrate your paintings," Claire says, her voice barely above a whisper, "but a few of the crates came open during shipping, and these," she waves at the watercolors, "were so beautiful. I thought they'd look nice on the stairway. Brighten the place up a bit. I hope that's all right."

"It's beautiful, really, Claire—do you mind if I call you Claire?"

"No. Of course not. Would you like to see the rest of your house?" She's quite lovely, especially when she blushes. "Except for the third floor. There are still a lot of boxes and crates. But I'm working on it."

"You've done a fine job." From what he can see, but he can't move just now. With his family long since dead, it would hurt too much to wander the same rooms he had as a lonely child. And now, with Lesley gone . . . This was a bad idea, coming home. And is this really home? It had never felt like it. He was twenty, barely a man, when he'd left for Europe. Twenty-five years later, part of him feels like he is still running. But from what?

"I wasn't sure about the rugs," she says nervously.

"They are perfect."

"I'd be happy to give you a tour." As nervous as she is, Reggie can tell that she's proud of her hard work, as well she should be. He has no idea of what the place looked like before he instructed it be prepared for his arrival, but it's positively gleaming now.

"Maybe tomorrow." He hopes she can see he's not ready for this now, but she's obviously hurt. He looks away from her, ashamed. He can't accept this place, this life, without Lesley. But the shock of seeing the wooden boxcars he'd played with as a child on his mother's gaudy Louis XV chest unhinges his feet. One of the servants, Charles, had been teaching him how to make these in the woodshop when his mother caught him and tanned his hide for fraternizing with the help. Charles had felt so bad about it, he made Reggie a whole train set, and, like so many things, Reggie had concealed it from his mother for fear of her reaction.

"I hope you don't mind. Daniel, my oldest, was helping me and found these. It's a fine set, he said so himself, and he tries very hard not to be impressed by anything."

"No. Of course, I don't mind at all."

"Peter, my middle son, thinks they're wonderful, too. But I haven't let Jonathan—"

"The vocal one?"

She nods and is really quite beautiful when she smiles. "Jonathan's just a baby, he's too little to play with them."

"Really?" He likes her. She's a warm, wonderful mother. He can tell just by the way her voice changes when she speaks of her boys. He picks up the cars that are linked together by little metal hooks and spins the wheels on the first secret he learned to keep. "He looks like precisely the right age, Mrs. Greeley—Claire." She looks away like he's admonished her, but he understands her wanting to hang on to her little one like that. At least he thinks he does. "When I was growing up, this was a dreary, awful house."

"I hardly believe that. It's the most beautiful place I've ever seen. I couldn't have imagined anything more grand."

"My parents made sure it was always as quiet as a grave, which was horribly difficult as a child. To be honest, I'm not even sure I can live here again. Certainly not like that. So please, the boys are welcome here anytime and, by all means, let them play with anything they can find."

"That's quite generous of you."

There's nothing generous about me, he thought. I'm incredibly selfish; Lesley reminded him of that playfully but often. Having the boys here might serve as insurance against the solitude, and perhaps make this place a home, a real home. "You've done a fine job, Claire. I'm sure the rest of the house is stellar."

"I really would love to show it to you."

He hesitates before he offers her his arm. "May I?" She blushes again, obviously unaccustomed to such pleasantries.

He stifles his laughter at the way she's put the downstairs together, the way she's taken the heavy, austere richness of the place and turned it inside out to make it look—well, he's not sure what to call it, actually. Cheery? If his parents were here, they would fire the woman on the spot, or perhaps have her arrested for high crimes against gaudy ostentation.

They start up the same grand staircase that near-royalty once ascended, remarkably without falling on their faces. Or, who knows, maybe with their haughty noses so high, they did, and his parents conveniently edited that part of history. The same way they'd edited his story, even to their graves.

Claire runs her hand across the base of a frame of one of the impressive watercolors he'd offered the artist a fortune for, but the artist had refused because the gift was meant for both him and Lesley, and Lesley was dear to him, too.

"Really, sir—"

"Reggie."

"Yes, of course. You have some of the most beautiful things I've ever seen. This job has been a true pleasure, and I'm sure with some care everything will be back to the way it was before you left."

He watches the patterns the sunshine makes on the second-floor landing and hopes Claire is wrong. His father stood in that spot so often, his footprints are permanently indented on the runner. He loved to survey his kingdom from here, especially the gardens. Reggie feels a pang of guilt that he let the weeds take over his mother's gardens, that he just had the caretaker watch over the house.

"Thank you, Claire. That's very kind of you to say."

Before Reggie had left for good, Charles had made him a little pouch with a handful of sandy rich soil from one of the fields. He spoke a few Gullah words over it and told Reggie to wear it around his neck to keep him safe, to remember where he came from. But like the prodigal that he was, Reggie had wanted to forget everything about this place and had thrown it in the Arno River the first chance he got, not giving it another thought until Lesley was gone and he was lost and alone again.

Why had he come back home? To make peace with this place or to fill up another pouch and leave? From the center of the garden below the giant crape myrtle tree he'd climbed on as a boy waves at him. It is split down the middle from a lightning strike, a sign from God that coming back was a huge mistake. Yet both sides are alive with delicate bunches of fuchsia-colored blossoms.

·Chapter Twenty-Four·

"Order up." Frank shoves the first plate of the day in the window.

Tiny looks down at the crab cakes sitting alongside buttered grits and gives him that know-it-all smirk of hers. "I know who put the good on your candy this morning."

Frank smiles before he catches himself. "If you don't get that plate out, I'm gonna be looking for another waitress."

"Save yourself the trouble, Frank. You won't find one as good as me." She yanks the plate onto her forearm like it's not hot and grabs the coffeepot to avoid making two trips.

"One that actually works, that's not a smart-mouth."

"Better watch whose weeds you're pissing in, Frank Darling. You might just get your wish, and then you'd be riding this gravy train on biscuit wheels." She turns to scurry back with orders from two tables of truckers who were sleeping in the parking lot before Frank opened up.

"Sweet-potato biscuits," Frank says with a full-on grin when she returns to the window.

"Lord. And it ain't even Christmas." Tiny nods at a wiry little trucker who hollers for more coffee. "I bet if you had half a chance, you'd drink that girl's bathwater."

Frank gives her a one-fingered salute, and she saunters off with the same behind her back.

Hank Bodette starts toward the diner from the back of the store. This place isn't that big, but Frank bets himself he can flip the dozen hoecakes on the griddle and they'll be done before Hank gets to the counter. Tiny is in the middle of listening to one of the trucker's stories, her secret to getting big tips; Hank nods at her, points to the cup he brings from home every day, and beams when Tiny finally slides behind the counter to serve up his coffee.

"Pretty day out, but not half as pretty as you, young lady. How are you this morning?"

"Well, I'm kicking, Hank, but not real high. How about you?"

He pours too much sugar into his coffee and stirs it thoughtfully. "Can't complain. I got a good job. The view is mighty pretty from where I sit, watching you pass by."

"You're slicker than a mess of okra, Hank. And twice as handsome." Tiny shoves her pencil behind her ear. She balances two plates on each arm and holds one in each hand; she'd probably carry one on top of her big head if it were flat. "You boys better be hungry," she calls to the truckers.

Hank watches her prissy butt walk away, sighs like a schoolboy, and looks back at Frank. "Well, I'll be getting back to work, Frank. There's a lot of mail today. The mailman didn't come two days. Truck broke down."

Tiny puts the hard sell on all the truckers about the biscuits, but none of them want to pay extra. In truth, they cost the same as a regular biscuit that comes free with a meal. She's trying to get ten cents apiece for them, and Frank can't help but smile. Big Jim, a Georgia man who stops in the diner at least once a week, is sweet on Tiny but is too shy to flirt with her. He orders a dozen biscuits for the table and tells her to wrap up the rest for him to take along.

"Forgot to tell you something." Hank is back at the counter, looking like he's not at all sure what he remembered. He pats his pockets and the lightbulb goes on when he finds what he was looking for. "You told me to be on the lookout for mail to that pretty gal of yours."

He sets a postcard down in the window, and Frank wipes his hands off on the rag he keeps over his shoulder. The card is just like the ones Hank sells in the post office for two cents. Frank runs his finger over the stamp with Abe Lincoln on it, and then turns it over quick because there's nothing honest about what he's doing. Wentworth's handwriting is as gaudy as she is.

Dear Vada,

Still looking for Darby. May require more resources at some point to keep up an extended search, but confident I'll find her. Perhaps your next postcard will be from Darby herself.

Sincerely,
Kittie Wentworth

Frank can hear the harlot's smirk in the ridiculous words that are meant to fan Vada's hopes of finding her friend. He should toss the postcard on the trash heap where it belongs, but honest Abe is eyeing him, reminding him how thrilled Vada will be when she sees the card, that she'll probably come around every day hoping for another. Above all, Abe Lincoln is screaming at Frank to do the right thing and give it to her. She'll be over the moon for sure, which will play in his favor, and it will buy him more time to make her see what a grifter the harlot is.

The postcard is barely in his shirt pocket when the screen door opens. She glides into the diner.

"Morning, Vada," Tiny hollers from the back of the diner. "Be right with you."

Vada picks the menu up off of the table and pretends to study it, when they both know what she came for. She must feel Frank looking at her. She pinches her lips shut with her teeth and still smiles like she's on the verge of a belly laugh, if a girl like Vada does such a thing.

"What'll you have, shug?" Tiny flips the page on her order pad and licks the end of her dull pencil. Frank can't hear what Vada is saying, but Tiny is nodding, smiling, making small talk, but not too much, before she clips Vada's ticket onto the wheel. "That girl blushes when she orders the crab cakes, like she's sending you a love letter instead of asking for breakfast. Why, the last time I saw her, she was madder than a mashed cat, but it appears all that's done with. No need to look at the ticket. Just the usual."

There's nothing usual about Vada Hadley. Frank gets to work on her order and is glad that breakfast is almost over. The postcard peeks at him as he plates her food, reminding him it's a powerful thing that could go either way. Maybe it will make Vada happy and keep her coming to the diner, or to the store to check her mail six days a week. Or maybe it will break her heart when she realizes the harlot is playing her. Frank can't abide that. He knows it shouldn't be his choice as to whether or not she gets these cards, but it is. He buttons his shirt pocket shut and cleans the griddle, waiting for the diner to clear out.

As the last table of truckers leaves, a spindly, short one, who knows good and well Big Jim is sweet on Tiny, pinches her ass. Tiny's a vocal woman to begin with, but Frank almost feels sorry for the guy, for what's coming.

Quick as a cat, she catches him by the wrist. "Well, lookee here." She gets the laugh she wants and, though he deserves it, the poor guy's face is burnt red. She underlines letters just above his shirt pocket with her long index finger. "Dolphis." She draws out his name like it has seventeen syllables. "Well, Dolphis, you do that again, and you're liable to lose a couple of them dainty fingers."

He finally has the good sense to pull away and rushes out to his truck, and the other truckers follow, ribbing him all the way. The satisfied look on Tiny's face always comes under similar circumstances, usually after the diner has lost a customer for good. But Frank also knows that if Big Jim had done the same, Tiny would have pretended to ignore it. Then, when she thought nobody was looking, she would have wrapped up a couple of those sugar cookies he loves so well and slipped them into his pocket.

"It was a good morning." Tiny reaches for the slop rag from behind the counter. "Good tips."

"Yep, it was. You got somewhere to go before the lunch crowd comes in?" Frank nods at Vada, and Tiny seems to take the hint.

"Well, I do now. See you 'round noon, Casanova."

He buses Vada's table himself and slides into the booth across from her.

"Morning."

"Good morning, Frank. I loved my breakfast, especially the crab cakes."

"Oh, so that's how it is. You just love me for my cakes."

"Well, they're sort of an added bonus."

"But if you had to choose, right here, right now. Which would it be?"

"*Hmm.*" She props her elbows on the table and rests her chin on her clasped hands. "Gosh, that's a hard one. You *or* crab cakes. And you're sure it's an either-or kind of choice?" She barely gets the last word out as Frank leans across the table and takes her smart mouth in a long, wet kiss, leaving her breathless. "I'm just not sure what . . . the attraction would be . . . without the food," she says and returns the favor.

"You know damn well what the attraction is, and it doesn't have anything to do with food."

A loud noise in the back of the store pulls them apart. It could be Hank Bodette finally keeling over, for all Frank knows, but he's staying right here. God, Vada looks beautiful, her eyes full of love, her face flush with want, and all he wants to do is make her happy. "I have something for you."

"More food?" Frank shakes his head. "More kisses?"

"That's for sure." Frank slips the postcard out of his shirt pocket and lays it on the table between them. She looks horrified until he flips it over so she can read it.

In a flash, she's on his side of the booth, pinning him against the wall with a long, deep kiss. "And now what do you think about Miss Kittie Wentworth?" Her lips are pressed against Frank's. He can feel her smiling. "And me."

"Lately, to be on the safe side, I'd say I don't have an opinion. But if a postcard makes you this happy, I'm all for it."

"I'd love to stay here and kiss the day away with you, Frank, but—"

"Why don't you?" Frank pushes my hair off of my shoulder.

"I'll close the diner, give you all the kisses you want. Give you whatever you want."

"Claire will be leaving for work soon, and I have to watch the boys." He feigns brokenhearted-ness as I pull away, but that's what it feels like to tear myself away from him. "Come over after you've closed for lunch?"

"And compete with the boys and the bachelors for your attention? Hell, no. I want you all to myself." I laugh and press a tiny good-bye kiss against his lips.

"Sure you won't change your mind and stay?"

"I have to get some things from the store. I'll see you soon." I can feel him watching me as I leave, and I know he feels the same kind of rubber-band love I do, the kind that stretches between two lovers only to pull them back together again and again.

Sweet old Mr. Bodette stands and smooths his thinning hair when I walk into the store. "Good morning, pretty lady."

"Good morning, Mr. Bodette."

"I sure wish you'd call me Hank."

"I have a small list of things I need, and I'm sure I'll find some things I don't, Hank." The blush on his stubbled old face is adorable. "I hope your Fourth of July was lovely."

"It was. I understand you went out of town for the holiday. Home, somebody said."

I think only about the best parts of our trip to Memphis and smile. "It was a wonderful holiday."

Hank tallies up my purchases on a small paper sack, and his math is off, in my favor. I'm not sure whether he's still flirting or he can't add properly, but I'm guessing he was quite the ladies' man in his day. I pay him and want to hug him for being so adorable. I'm almost out the post-office door when he calls after me. "Miss Vada, did Frank give you your mail?"

"Why, yes, he did." I'm so excited I could fly all the way back to the boardinghouse.

"Here's another for you." He hands the envelope to me, and I shove it into the paper bag.

"Vada?" Claire calls after me as I disappear up the stairs. "I have to go to work now."

I don't answer her. I dash into my bedroom and lock the door.

"Vada, I really have to go. If you're indisposed, Daniel and Mr. Clip will watch Peter and Jonathan," she hollers. "I'll see you tonight. Oh, and by the way, Miss Mamie called to say her sister died and she'll be home next Monday, after the funeral."

I lay the letter beside the postcard in hopes that the good will outweigh the bad. The postmark reads Charleston, and I'm sure it can't be anything but terrible news. I could shove it under the mattress and forget about it, but what if something's wrong with Rosa Lee or my parents? Wouldn't Desmond call instead of write?

His handwriting on the envelope isn't painstakingly perfect like Miss Wentworth's. My fingers tremble as they slide under the opening. The page unfolds like a bad dream.

Dear Miss Vada,

Things are bad here since Mr. Justin come back from looking for you. I've seen that look on your daddy's face enough to know he's gone put the screws to somebody, and I'm afraid that somebody is me and Rosa Lee. She doesn't say anything, but we are old and I know she fears what he might do to us just as much as I do.

You know me and Rosa Lee love you as good as our own, and I can't tell you what to do. But if you don't want to be found, hog-tied, and married, run. 'Cause your daddy won't stop 'til he find you.

Love,
Desmond

·Chapter Twenty-Five·

"Mama," Daniel hollers at the top of his lungs.

"*Daniel Culliver Greeley.*" Claire nabs the boy by the collar. "You act like you're in a house and not a cattle stampede this instant."

She doesn't have to look in the foyer mirror to know she is beet red over this kind of display in front of her employer. She and Reggie were just discussing whether new draperies were in order for some of the rooms downstairs when Daniel burst through the door of the Sheridan house like a maniac.

"But Miss Vada is crying. Loud. I tried to open her door to see if she was okay, but it's locked." The poor boy is crying himself. "You've got to come quick. She's hurt. She may be dying."

Claire takes him in her arms. "I just saw her, Daniel, not even an hour ago. She may be upset about something, a fight with her boyfriend, but I promise you, she's fine."

"*But I love her.* I gave her to Frank because he said he would make her happy. It's all my fault. I just wanted her to be happy."

"Oh, honey, you're not responsible for whatever is going on with Vada." He shakes his head against her shoulder and cries harder.

Reggie pats Daniel on the shoulder and smiles with genuine amusement that the boy is so taken with Vada Hadley. "Really, Claire, this can wait. Go tend to your friend. You can come back later today, or we can continue our discussion tomorrow."

"I'm so sorry about this." Lately, she's been glad Daniel has been less affectionate, because when he is wrapped around her like this, it reminds her how much he is like Bobby and how much Bobby has missed. "Really, it won't happen again."

"They are children who need their mother. Of course it will most definitely happen, until they leave the nest. And it's perfectly fine. As a matter of fact, it's both novel and refreshing to see such a display of unbridled emotion in this house."

"Thank you, Mr. Sheridan."

"Reggie," he corrects her and tousles Daniel's hair. The boy wipes his face on Claire's dress and looks at Reggie for a moment and mouths *sorry.* "Time heals all wounds, son."

Reggie smiles his most convincing smile, but Claire doesn't believe it. She knows that he is smarting, too, over the loss of Lesley, the way every little thing reminds him of his beloved. She suspects his childhood here wasn't as wonderful as an outsider like her believes, and she knows that Lesley was a respite from whatever drove Reggie away from the Sheridan plantation.

"Thank you," she says again, helps her son down the grand imperial staircase, and hurries toward the boardinghouse.

Claire can hear Vada crying before she gets to the front door and tells Daniel to go play with his brothers while she tends to her. If it's something trivial, a lover's spat that happened five minutes ago but feels like forever, as much as Claire loves Vada, it will be hard not to shake her and remind her how lucky she is to have the love of her life just a few paces away.

Hopefully, Claire will mind her temper and won't tell Vada what forever really is, what it feels like deep down in her core, how unbelievable it is that Bobby Greeley will never saunter up beside her and hold her hand or say her name. It would be too cruel.

"Vada? It's me, Claire. Can I come in?" She tries the door, but it won't budge. "Vada, Daniel's so upset that you're crying, I promised him I'd talk to you. Please move the chair away from the door so I can come in."

The chair scrapes against the floor, and Claire turns the knob and opens the door slowly. Vada falls onto her bed, into a crumpled heap. The pain emanating from her makes Claire's insides throb with the certainty that death has robbed Vada of someone dear. For two years she's begged God for her husband's life back, even asked that her cup be passed to someone else. But Bobby can't ever come back, and Vada Hadley doesn't deserve this kind of loss any more than Claire does.

She holds Vada and cries with her until neither of them can cry anymore. The bedroom door opens and closes several times, and Claire knows the boys are worried, especially Daniel.

"Vada?" Claire pulls away and strokes Vada's hair. Her fingers travel over the back of the bodice that is some kind of blend, maybe silk and cotton. She smiles at the gaping neckline where Vada cut the haute tag of her dress out, trying to disguise its worth. "Daniel fetched me—I'm so sorry for your loss."

She looks at Claire, tearstained, beautiful, and puzzled. "I'm sorry—I didn't mean to frighten the children." She flops onto her back and swipes at her tears with one hand, a piece of crumpled paper in the other.

"I just assumed someone was—"

Vada shakes her head. "Oh, Claire, I've made such a mess of things," her breath stutters, "and now . . . it looks like I'll lose Frank . . . my job . . . everything." She breaks down again.

"Nonsense. Frank loves you, and how can you lose your job when you haven't even started it yet? Let me help you sort this out."

Vada shakes her head. "I don't want to get you mixed up in this." She looks away from Claire. "But I can't stay here. I have to leave."

"Why? What have you done that's so terrible?"

"Nothing . . . I—" She tries to collect herself and reaches for Claire's hand. "I ran away from home. I didn't want to marry Justin . . . and now—"

She hands Claire an envelope postmarked Charleston. Claire doesn't recognize the return address, but 32 Legare, she knows that street is fancy, expensive. Claire opens the letter and reads. The words *hog-tied* and *married* make her stiffen. As hard as it's been to watch Vada in love with Frank Darling, the idea of Vada being forced to marry someone she doesn't love is barbaric. Yet she sees the logic, a handful of wealthy families, trying to keep their power and their money in a small circle. Was that why Reggie fled to Europe, to escape his family's expectations of whom he should marry?

"Sit up." Claire's voice has the timbre she uses that snaps the boys to attention, and Vada does the same. "You're a grown woman, Vada. What can your father possibly do to you?"

"You don't understand—" She sucks in her breath. "When he finds me, he'll—"

"Ground you? Send you to bed with no supper?" Claire hates the control this man seems to have over Vada that has her cowering like a child. "You have a life. In a few weeks, you'll have a job.

You have someone who I'm reasonably sure you love, and I know, just from looking at Frank Darling's face the moment he sees you, that he loves you back."

Vada swipes away her tears and reaches for Claire's hand. "I know you're right. He can't make me do anything I don't want to do, but I worry what he'll do to Desmond—and Rosa Lee. They raised me." She breaks down again, barely getting the words out.

Claire nods and understands the scene she witnessed from her bedroom window the night Vada arrived, the beaten-up old truck, her embrace with the old colored man in the full moonlight.

"My father keeps a portion of the servants' money—he says he invests it for them. When he learns they helped me—" She shakes her head.

"Eggs break. Families break. But one thing I know for certain is, Vada, you and I don't. You had the courage to choose a different life for yourself, and you're thriving. This is what growing up is." Claire pushes a strand of silky blond hair away from Vada's tearstained face. "If your father turns Desmond and Rosa Lee out, you'll take them in and somehow you'll make do. And when the time comes, I have no doubt you'll stand up to your father.

"What's this?" Claire says, picking the postcard off of the floor.

Vada takes the card and swipes at her tears. "Some really good news." Her voice catches in her throat.

"So, tell me something good, something wonderful. Right now." Claire's tried-and-true line with the boys, because she wants them to count their blessings so often, it's second nature.

"It's about my friend Darby. We lost touch a few years ago. I paid the woman who sent me the card to find her." She traces her collarbone with her finger. "Not with money, with my grandmother's necklace."

"Darby must be a good friend."

"She's bawdy and Irish and wonderful, and I love her to bits. Frank thinks the idea is crazy, but I hope I can find her, maybe bring her here. It would be a true miracle." She rolls onto her back and looks into Claire's eyes. "Do you believe in miracles?"

"Of course I do," Claire laughs. "Now, get out of this bed and start supper. Thankfully, it's your night to cook."

·Chapter Twenty-Six·

It's been three weeks since Frank gave Vada the postcard from the harlot. She was so happy, all over him with kisses and breathy promises of love. Since then, he's seen a difference in her, and not just because Miss Mamie is back from burying her sister. Vada's in charge, navigating the old bat with a steely attitude that sometimes makes him concerned she might end up homeless. Maybe that wouldn't be such a bad thing, a good reason to marry her sooner.

Most evenings, even if it's raining, they go down to the creek. Miss Mamie barely guards the front door and is more like an old sidewinder who's given up on its prey. There are no warnings or hard looks. She just slithers back to her bedroom, most likely to mourn. But the old bat still won't let the boarders use the phone. So Vada's used his a couple of times to call Miss Wentworth. Frank wasn't the least bit surprised when whoever answered couldn't get the harlot to the phone, but Vada felt bad enough there was no word from her friend Darby, there was no need for Frank to say, *I told you so.*

He shoves the blanket under his arm and smiles about how that would seem so presumptuous of him a few weeks ago. Now it's a necessity for long hours of kissing on the creek bank. He's surprised to see Vada walking across the crossroads to meet him. The skirt of her yellow dress blows about in the hot August breeze. She's so beautiful, for a moment all he can think is that school will be starting next month and he'll have to share her with a bunch of little rug rats. As much as he isn't crazy about the idea, it will be good practice for the life he wants with Vada. They'll have lots of kids. She hasn't said so, but he knows from the way she watches Claire's boys and looks at him, with a shy smile that seems to say *we'll have this one day.*

She meets him halfway and threads her fingers in his, and they start toward the creek. Frank likes that Vada seems to know what she wants, and he's grateful she wants him. But as much as Vada is changing, and for the better, every day she still checks her mail, still asks Hank to double check to see if there's another postcard for her. She tries to hide her disappointment when Hank says no, but it slices Frank to the core to see Vada unhappy, even if it's just for a few seconds.

The creek comes into view, running high thanks to the rain two days ago. Vada spreads the blanket out, slips off her shoes, and sits down, watching the water flow toward the Edisto River. Usually the kissing commences before her bottom touches the blanket, but she's quiet. Frank ignores the thick, sticky air and puts his arms around her, pulling her close.

"You were right," she says, picking up a handful of sand and letting it run through her fingers.

"Was I? Do I get a prize?" He moves in to kiss her, but she turns her head away from him. "Guess not."

"About Kittie Wentworth," she says. Frank crooks his finger under her chin and turns her face toward his, but she won't look at him just now. "I gave her the only thing I had left from my grandmother, when it was obvious Miss Wentworth had no intention of looking for Darby; I feel so stupid."

"Hey. Hey. It's okay. You were just trying to help your friend."

"No, it's not okay, Frank. I should have listened to you and stood up to that woman instead of letting her deceive me. I'll never see my grandmother's necklace again, and I'll never see Darby again, that much I deserve. But I've had enough coercive, manipulative people in my life." She turns to look Frank straight in the eyes. "You love me too much to be either of those things."

She kisses him hard, almost desperately, fisting his shirt. She pulls away from him and starts to unbutton her dress. "Are you sure?" he says. At least he thought he said the words, but maybe he didn't, because his mind is focused on her fingers sliding down the placket of her dress, the swell of her perfect breasts above her lacy white bra.

She nods and pushes her dress off of her shoulders. He is completely lost, fumbling with his shirt. His heart pounds like a big bass drum, and he can feel the blood rushing through each chamber and headed south. He's a little worried he'll scare her when she sees how hard he is for her, but that doesn't stop him. She stops him.

Her eyes are wide. She holds her gaping dress together. "Someone's coming," she whispers and starts putting herself back together. She's already pushing the top button through the loop, but disappointment and months of desire for this woman have him paralyzed. "*Frank. Get dressed.*"

He slips his shirt back on but doesn't bother to button it. It's hot enough out so that whoever it is will think he was just cooling

off. A big coon dog bursts into the clearing and heads straight for
Vada, licking her face. She's cooing to Joe Pike's dog, and Frank
is praying Joe isn't anywhere nearby. But Frank and God have
been on the outs for so long, it's no surprise when Joe wobbles out
of the woods. He calls his dog, who whimpers when he has to tear
himself away from Vada and sit at his master's feet. Frank knows
how the dog feels, but he'll not cower to Joe Pike.

"Has he ruined you yet?" Joe sways on his bowed legs enough
for Frank to know he's a dangerous drunk.

"Go home, Joe," Frank growls. "Sleep it off."

"I asked you a question, girl." The dog lies down, sinking onto
the ground with a pitiful, whining grunt.

"Mr. Pike, Frank has done nothing of the sort."

"I been watching you, stealing away with the likes of him."
Joe hawks and spits on the ground. "He'll ruin you, just like he
ruined her."

"Shut up, Joe." Frank wants to rough the old man up—or, at
the very least, threaten him—but he has better sense than to whale
on a drunken old fool in front of Vada.

"What's he talking about, Frank?" Vada's face is pale. She
pulls away.

"Joe thinks I seduced Lila, before he and the good reverend
shamed her into leaving Round O," Frank says.

"It's your fault, goddamn you."

"He hates me because he's Lila's father."

Joe fists a crumpled piece of paper and throws it at Frank. "I
hate you because she's dead."

"Dead?" Frank picks up the paper and straightens it out. He
runs his thumb across the Atlanta Police Department letterhead.
"We regret to inform you that your daughter, Lila Pike, died July
4, 1947."

Vada's hand is on his shoulder. "Oh, Frank. I'm so sorry."

He nods and rereads the words addressed to the parents of Lila Pike. Smudge would have never given her a divorce, but at least she'd taken her name back and gotten him out of her life.

"Joe, I'm sorry about what happened to Lila." She'd told Frank the only time she was happy was when they were making love. He was just a horny love-struck kid and was flattered, but her tenacity when they coupled scared him. He could never tell anyone. Boys his age would think he was crazy, and if Frank had told his dad, he would have put a stop to it. "She was sick, Joe. Her mind wasn't right, and there wasn't a damn thing anybody could do about it."

"You'll burn in hell for what you did to her," he screams, spittle flying, red-faced, tears streaming down his stubbled face. "And you mark my words, girl, he'll ruin you just like he ruined *her*."

He can't even say his daughter's name, just stumbles back toward the path and disappears. The dog laid his head in Vada's lap, whining, not wanting to leave, but his master was hurting so badly, he didn't have a choice.

Frank sits down on the blanket and stares out at the water. Just on the other side of the creek bank, a fat black water moccasin lounges on an oak branch that stretches out over the water and stares back. Vada starts unlacing her sandals. Any other time, the sight of her long, slender fingers working the ribbons would have been his undoing. The moccasin watches her wade out a few feet into the water, silently, no squeals from the icy spring-fed water, no mouth shaped like a perfect O. The snake plops into the water, most likely to fetch its supper, but it is cause enough for him to warn Vada.

The part of Frank that Lila claimed when he was a child stays silent. He slips his shoes off and wades out into the water, taking her by the hand. It's no big rescue. He can't even see the snake in the amber-tinted water, but still it makes him feel a little better. No matter how hard he tried, he could never save Lila.

They sit down on the blanket. Silent, only the sounds of katy-dids and cicadas practicing their raspy tune for another hot, sticky night intruding. Vada laces her sandals back up and looks at Frank, not smiling, still beautiful. The line between what he felt as a boy, for the preacher's wife, and what he feels as a man with Vada has never been clearer, a small consolation for what did and didn't happen tonight.

They start down the path back toward the crossroads, hand in hand. Frank stops at the trellis over the front gate instead of walk-ing her to the door. He kisses her on the cheek, lingering, breath-ing her in. She doesn't look at him when she asks the question. Since he's known Vada, he's asked her the same question so many times, it's only natural she'd want to know. "What did Lila want?" Vada asks again, barely breathing.

He knows what Lila wanted. She'd said it over and over again. She knew it was impossible, but she'd promised Frank if he could give it to her, she would be happy, and he'd wanted so badly for her to be happy. After the scene with Joe, Vada deserves some answers. A vicious pull, as tenacious as Lila herself, fights to keep the words inside him, but Frank isn't fifteen anymore, and the love he has for Vada wins out.

"She was barren. She wanted a baby."

Reggie watches Claire intervene between Daniel and Peter, who are fighting over the wooden airplane he bought them at the Charleston Market yesterday. He should have bought three of them, but he didn't think about that when he'd paid for the toy and a dozen roses for Claire.

He loves the way she negotiates peace with ease and in no time has the boys playing like friends instead of adversaries. "You amaze me, Claire." Reggie laughs as she blushes. "You're so good with the boys, so good at everything, really."

She sets the teakettle on the trivet alongside the plate of cookies and sits down.

"You're good with them, too."

He loves sharing afternoon tea with her and has every day since he returned to Round O. He knows she doesn't want sugar in her tea, but he suspects she learned to drink it that way thanks to rationing during the war, or maybe poverty. She inspects the imported biscuits that he found at a specialty shop on King Street, chooses one, and nibbles the corner like she's rationing the cookie. Her eyes close as she savors the buttery sweet goodness.

"Allow me," he says and pours. "Lesley desperately wanted children. I nearly gave in, but I was afraid I'd be a horrible father."

"Nonsense." She brushes her hand across his knuckles. "You're patient and kind. You have a wonderful sense of humor, and most of the time when you play with the boys, I have a hard time telling you apart from the children."

He laughs, reveling in her compliment. "I had the final say on whether we had a family; Lesley didn't press the issue. But sometimes, I wish we had."

"I know you miss Lesley every bit as much as I miss Bobby. The boys have helped me with that; maybe they will help you, too," she offers.

"They already have, Claire; I love having them here. They make me feel at home, and that's saying more than I could ever put into words. But more than anything, the time you and I have spent together feels like home."

"I hope you are . . . at home here." She positively glows. "And you're so gracious to let us stay in the servants' quarters. I really never thought I'd see the day when the boys and I would be moving out of the boardinghouse, and for someplace better. Wonderful. And we'll have that in a few more days, thanks to you."

"About your moving," he says, unable to resist teasing her. She looks alarmed that he's paused, like she thinks he might renege on Mr. Jameson's offer to let her live in what were once slave quarters. "I'm not so sure about that anymore."

She stirs her tea, with a thin smile like she's trying to decide if he'd really be so cruel. "Of course. You want us to move into the house with you." She waves her spoon in the air. "What mansion is complete without three little Indians running wild?"

"Claire?" His tone has obviously frightened her, but he wants her to know he is serious. "That's exactly what I want."

"Reggie, you can't be serious."

"But I am."

"This is your home. It's not exactly the kind of place to raise children; it's more of a museum." She looks like she's choking on the idea, but it's quite possibly the best idea Reggie has ever had.

"But it shouldn't be a museum, Claire. It has been like that for the last hundred years; I want it to be full of joy and laughter for the next hundred years. Tell me you'll seriously consider my offer."

She has tears in her eyes. "It's too much," she says like she can't see how wonderful she is. Her posture, her expression, says she believes she's not worthy of such a place, but in truth Sheridan place isn't worthy of her.

"Marry me, Claire."

·Chapter Twenty-Seven·

Even two weeks after Lila's death, the pall still covers the crossroads like a thick blanket of dew. Claire's boys seem more reverent than usual. With Miss Mamie back and grieving, too, she is meaner than ever. Most days when Claire goes to work, Vada keeps the boys quiet and busy at the boardinghouse, but after word of Lila's death, Vada keeps them at Sheridan house. To be honest, Daniel and Reggie do most of the keeping, and Vada stays close to Claire, keeping her hands busy, not saying much.

There are just a few boxes left to sort through. After that, there will be no reason for Vada to stay. But Claire knows the last thing her friend needs is to go back to the boardinghouse and bear the brunt of Miss Mamie's venom. She opens the windows of the bedroom they've used as a storage closet for the last of Reggie's things. A breeze stirs the curtains, carrying the scent of the afternoon shower. The sky is dark, promising steady rains throughout the day, which couldn't be gloomier if it tried.

Vada pushes aside a box marked PRIVATE! DO NOT OPEN, slits the top of another one, and starts sifting through the contents.

"Can I tell you something? Something wonderful?" Claire says in a single breath.

Vada nods and smiles wanly, like she's doubtful any news could be considered good news.

"I know Reggie and I have just known each other a few weeks, but he's so wonderful—I don't know how to say this—we're getting married."

"Oh, Claire." Vada throws her arms around her. "It's an answer to a prayer. When's the wedding?"

"It will just be a little ceremony at Judge Swenson's office, but my boys will soon have the home they deserve. Reggie and I get along. He's funny and thoughtful and he loves my boys."

"Do you love him?" Vada asks hesitantly.

"I adore him, and he is so good with the children." Her eyes tear up at Vada's inference. Claire knows she'll get the same unspoken question from the rest of the crossroads residents. Of course, she barely knows Reggie Sheridan, but what they and Vada really want to know is, will marrying him fill the gaping hole she's had inside of her since Bobby died? "I'm happy, Vada, really I am. Please, be happy for me."

I know I should have been more enthusiastic over Claire's news. She leaves with tears in her eyes and closes the door behind her. What's wrong with me? Isn't this what I begged God for? Before I realize it, I've completely ignored the warning and have sliced open the last box. My fingertips travel across the spines of twenty-six identically bound books. Encyclopedias? Hardly a reason for privacy. I slide the first volume out of the box and finger gold-embossed letters on the leather quarter-bound book. Lesley Faraday 1921. Journals.

The penmanship is artful and perfect. The first pages of Lesley's journal read like a love letter. They are beautiful but private. I snap the book shut. Reggie never said why he left Europe, what happened to Lesley, or why he left her. I pull out random books that are in chronological order, and the expensive binding engraved with the corresponding year is unchanged. The last volume is dated 1946, yet Lesley's name remained unchanged. Did Reggie promise to marry her, too? Twenty-five years of waiting would be enough to make even the most determined fiancée give up.

I pull the last volume out of the box and flip through the blank pages. There is one entry, a single line.

"January 1, 1947. Funny. I always thought we'd be together forever."

I turn the page. A dozen photographs are jammed against the spine of the book like an afterthought. I sift through them, unable to believe what I'm seeing. Is this the future Claire is so happy to embrace? She can't possibly know.

Footsteps thunder up the stairs. Jonathan squeals. "Faster." I snap the book shut and shove it back into the box as the boys burst through the door led by Reggie. Their Air Force squadron buzzes around the room, encircling me, their arms spread wide, dipping from one side to the other. Jonathan is hanging on for dear life to Reggie's back as he leads his men on their mission.

"Captain! Krauts at three o'clock," Daniel screams over the noise of make-believe engines.

"I've got them!" Peter is breathless and red-faced, with arms extended. He balls his fists up and makes good use of his machine gun.

"No you don't." Daniel stops short and pushes his brother. "I've got them."

"We all do," Reggie shouts, and they pepper the room with pretend bullets until they fall into a pile, laughing. Happy.

"It's good to see you, Vada." Reggie stands and lifts Jonathan high in the air, then plops the little guy onto his hip. He gives Vada a peck on the cheek, but she wipes it away. "Thank you for helping out with the house. Although I hope now that I'm settled that won't keep you away. I—" He stops short when he sees the open box.

"Come on, Reggie, you said we'd play until dinner, and it's almost time to eat," Peter says, and he and Daniel drag at Reggie's arms.

"Just a minute, boys." He turns to me, looking like a child who's been found out. "Vada."

I grab my umbrella and run out of the room and down the stairs.

"Wait!" he calls after me.

But I can't stop, can't bear the fact that Claire's happiness is as tenuous as my own. I fling open the front door.

"Vada, let me explain."

The wind sucks the umbrella wrong side out. I throw it aside and sprint down the long driveway that ends at the crossroads. It rains harder. I gulp in air, choking on the downpour. The tears won't stop. For Frank. For Darby. For Claire's soon-to-be-broken heart. Grief knocks me to my knees, and for the first time since Desmond kissed me good-bye, I am homesick. I want Charleston. I want Rosa Lee's arms around me. I want my *murrah*.

Suddenly, I'm weightless. Strong arms scoop me up, carrying me, almost running. Lightning cracks close enough to make the

drenched hairs on my arms stand up. Frank runs faster, until we
are on his doorstep. He throws the screen door open, lays me on
a settee, and backs toward the doorway, beautiful, chest heaving.
I reach for him.

He wipes the rain off of his face with his drenched shirtsleeve
and shakes his head slowly.

"I can't stay here with you, not like this." Frank is so winded,
he can barely talk. "What happened, Vada?"

I shake my head and reach for him again. "Please."

The rain stops like someone shut off the faucet.

"Please," she whispers again.

"No, Vada. I can feel those nosy crossroads bastards with
their faces against their windows, waiting for me to ruin your
good name. Maybe Joe Pike was right about me. Maybe I am
damned for what happened with Lila, but I'd rather die than
make you suffer for what I want."

"Please."

"You don't know how much I want you, how much I want to
stay."

She's a beautiful mess, but the girl who said yes to him just a
few weeks ago hurts so badly, she's no more ready for happily ever
after than Frank is. "Not here. Not like this."

He opens the screen door and plops down on the glider on the
front porch. The faucet turns on again; the rain comes down
harder than before, making the crossroads a blur. *I hate this goddamn place.* He sits in plain view, watching the downpour until
he nods off.

With the exception of the boardinghouse, the crossroads is dark when Vada kisses him awake, softly on the cheek. "What happened to you, Vada?" Frank takes her hand in his. "Are you okay?"

She shakes her head, tells him she can't talk about it right now. She insists on seeing herself off and thanks him for taking care of her.

"Let me walk you home."

"Stay. You've done enough rescuing for one day." She tries to smile. "Really, I'm okay, Frank."

Her sadness terrifies him. He wants to hear her laugh, to squeal with excitement and pin him down with kisses, the way she did in the diner just a few days ago, over a simple postcard. But more than anything, he wants her to be happy. He watches until she disappears into the pitch-black night and the boarding-house goes dark.

His puny house is empty without her, and for a moment, the idea that his house could be like this the rest of his life paralyzes him. He sits down at the small desk, the one his mother wrote her plays and stories at, and takes a postcard out of the drawer. He tries to remember the fancy handwriting, practices mimicking it on a scrap of paper. Satisfied that he can do it, that he should do it, he writes just enough to close the gap on the past and the present and addresses the postcard to Vada. It's a lie. He's not proud of that, but he's willing to risk the consequences to help her move on. To help her be happy.

·Chapter Twenty-Eight·

On and off throughout the morning, Frank eyes the truckers from his cubbyhole. He knows all of them in passing, a couple of them by name. He listens to Tiny chat them up for tips, asking where they're going, what they're hauling, punctuating each question with *shug* or *honey*. Big Jim hasn't been in the diner for a week, and Frank can tell Tiny's more worried than smarting over his absence. Long hauls with even longer hours have gotten a lot of truckers Frank's known over the years killed.

He's nearly burned a fair amount of food this morning, trying to listen to their conversations, and so far not a single driver has been headed north of Georgia.

Tiny puts three more orders on the wheel and hurries back to freshen up the back table's coffees. A stranger in a fancy zoot suit comes in and heads straight for the counter. The man's about Tiny's age, and Frank can tell she thinks he's good-looking, from the way she licks the end of her pencil a couple of times as she takes his order.

"Where you headed, handsome?" Tiny pours his coffee without even looking at the cup and flashes her best smile.

"Chicago." He nods, tight-lipped, and picks up the *Charleston Post* he brought into the diner, to let Tiny know he doesn't want to talk.

But he doesn't know Tiny. "Chicago? Now that's a fer piece," she drawls.

She takes his order and then cracks him like a newly hatched egg. Within fifteen minutes, she has him talking a little, laughing at her playful innuendos.

"Tiny, the back table's ready for their bills," Frank snaps. She waves him off and heads back with a pot of coffee in each hand to hold court with the truckers who adore her. The ones who don't are too afraid of the petite, round fireball's sassy mouth to do anything but yuck it up with the rest of the men.

The guy at the counter catches Frank's eye and nods toward Tiny. "She always like that?"

"Oh, she's toned down a lot over the years." Frank serves the man himself.

He digs right in and nods. "Good crab cake."

"So I'm told." Frank refills the guy's coffee. "I heard you say you're headed to Chicago."

He stops chewing, his manner cold. "Yeah."

Frank nods. "Up Highway 78?"

He takes a swig of coffee. "What's it to you?"

"Nothing. Just curious." The man is still taken aback by Frank's friendly questions, and, to be honest, it doesn't matter to Frank. "What do you do for a living?"

There's a long beat of silence, enough to give Frank pause.

Maybe this isn't such a good idea after all. "Sell insurance." The man shoves another forkful of food into his mouth.

Frank nods and fingers the postcard that's been in his apron pocket all morning. He starts to top off the salesman's cup, but the man shakes his head. He's made quick work of his breakfast and seems to be in more of a hurry than the truckers who come to the diner for Tiny. The man tosses a dollar and two bits onto the counter, drains his coffee cup, and turns to leave.

"Hey, buddy," Frank calls after him, holding the postcard up. "When you pass through Memphis, will you mail this for me?"

"Why? You have a post office."

Frank hands him the card; the man reads it and shrugs. "Vada Hadley, huh? And I take it you're not Miss Kittie Wentworth."

"Long story." Frank wipes his hands on the towel slung over his shoulder. "It's for my girl, Vada."

"She lives here?"

"At the boardinghouse."

"So why the postcard? Why can't you just say what you have to say to this Hadley dame and save yourself the two-cent stamp?"

"I've been down that road." Frank will most likely never see this guy again, so there's no point in telling him about the trip to Memphis, the fight that set him and Vada back. About Lila. "It's better this way. So will you do it?"

"Sure." The man puts the card in the pocket of his expensive-looking suit. "*Buddy.*"

He nods good-bye at Frank as one of the truckers calls out a tired old riddle to Tiny.

"What's the difference between a Peterbilt truck and a porcupine?" She gives the insurance guy a good-bye wink and sashays back to the kitchen. "That's easy. The prick's on the inside of the truck."

·Chapter Twenty-Nine·

I woke up three times since the sun came up but can't get out of bed. My body is sick, achy, cold, but it has nothing to do with the flu. It crushes me to the core to think about Frank and Lila, how she wanted his child so badly, and how he wanted to give that to her. The look on his face when he read Joe Pike's letter was heartbreaking. I never wanted to see him hurt like that and yet, despite him telling me he was just a boy and didn't know what love was, I'll never be able to forget the look on his face that said he'd loved her, worshipped her.

Still, it's selfish to lie here hurt, angry at Frank, jealous of a dead woman. I have to save Claire from making a huge mistake. But isn't a huge mistake with Reggie better than Claire raising the boys at the boardinghouse, or, worse, marrying smelly old Mr. Stanley? No, not if it means Claire's heart will be broken again.

I pull on my Sears dress, hoping it will give me the courage to march over to the palatial Sheridan house and say just the right words to propel Claire out of a future with Reggie, without irreparably crushing her newly mended heart. By the time the screen door slams behind me, I'm resolute to set things right.

I stride toward the long drive covered by an arched canopy of live oaks that leads to the mansion, until my body stops like a horse, dead in its tracks, remembering a place that spooked him. The memory of falling to pieces makes me tremble hard, but Frank saved me. "I owe it to Claire," I whisper and break into a dead run.

By the time I reach the door, I am breathless, beating so hard against the burled wood, my knuckles start to bleed. "Claire. Reggie. Open the door." The door opens, and everything stops. For a moment, I'm not sure what I'm seeing is real. Claire and Reggie are both dressed in Reggie's monogrammed bathrobes, towels wrapped around their heads, their faces covered is some kind of green goo.

"Vada, what's wrong? Is someone chasing you?" Reggie steps out on the porch and looks around the grounds; even in his green Kabuki mask, he looks ferocious.

"Good heavens, Vada." Claire runs her hands down my arms, which hang limp at my sides, like she's checking for broken bones. "Is everything all right?"

Reggie puts his arm around me. "Tell us what's wrong, dear."

"*You*." I finally snap to. "You're what's wrong. You and your promises of marriage to Claire. What about *Lesley*? I saw the photographs of you and that man, and I refuse to let you break Claire's heart like you broke hers."

"Vada, come inside," Claire says, pulling me into the house. "We need to talk."

Reggie motions for me to sit on the settee, but I refuse. "Claire, you can't be serious about going through with this marriage. I never thought I'd be saying this, but please reconsider Mr. Stanley's proposal."

She looks like I've slapped her hard across the face. "Why would you say that to me?"

"Because at least you know what you're getting. I found photographs of Reggie kissing—a man. I'm sure that's why Lesley left him. The poor woman."

"That's enough, Vada. The boys are upstairs playing, they'll hear you." Claire goes to Reggie, who wipes the mask off of his face, and then hands Claire a small, monogrammed hand towel to do the same. Reggie wraps his arms around Claire and folds over her, burying his face in her neck, not crying, but wounded. *Good.*

"Reggie told me about the journals. Those photographs you saw were of him and Lesley."

"Don't tell her," Reggie says softly. "Please. It was just for the two of us to know."

"Please, Reggie, I love you both." Claire crooks her finger under his chin. "You know her secret. It's only right she knows yours."

"*Claire.* You told him? How could you?"

"He already knew, Vada."

Reggie sat down on the settee he'd just offered me. "No matter how much you deny it, you look too much like your mother," he smiles sadly, "but in the end, it was the shoes that gave you away."

"Who I am changes nothing. But what about you, Reggie?"

"Who we are changes everything, my dear."

"Vada." Claire sits down beside me, her voice soothing like when she sets the world right for one of her boys. "Reggie loved Lesley the same way I loved Bobby, but he could never marry him."

"You're saying Lesley *is* a man? I don't understand." In truth, I'm not trying to understand, because I can't possibly see how this could work between Claire and Reggie.

"I was born this way," Reggie begins, threading his fingers in Claire's. "It was easier to live the life I wanted in Europe than stay here and be forced into marrying someone of equal means, someone I didn't love." He looks at Claire, and she nods for him to continue. "It was horrible growing up, hearing the things my parents would say about me. I think they knew I was a homosexual before I did, and they did things to try and straighten me out. But I am who I am."

Claire threads her hand in his. "It's all right. Tell her. She'll understand." Reggie nods, never looking at me.

"My grandmother died and left me a large trust fund. The moment I turned twenty-one, I transferred the money to a bank in Italy, hopped a cruise ship, and never looked back."

"But Claire says you love her, Reggie, that you want to marry her. How can you possibly be a husband to her?"

"Vada, Reggie and I have had the loves of our lives, but they died. I don't want to try to find that with another man, and neither does he. It is a platonic love, and our marriage might not be a conventional one, but we *do* love each other very much. We understand each other. My boys will have a father again, whom they adore, and they'll have opportunities I would never be able to give them. Don't you see? This is an answered prayer."

Reggie kisses her on the forehead. She runs her thumb across his upper lip where he missed some of the green mask. Reggie does the same to her, and then licks his fingers. "Less wrinkles," he laughs softly, "and it's edible."

Honestly, I don't know what God was thinking, but I have to believe, for Claire's sake, that He knows what's best for her. "Reggie, I'm sorry for getting so angry. I love Claire, and I couldn't bear to see her hurt," I say as sincerely as I can after being full of anger, then completely shocked and utterly embarrassed. "You won't tell anyone about me? Not Frank. I'll tell him when I'm ready, and I believe that will be soon. I love him and want to build a life with him here."

"Then we agree to keep each other's secrets?" Reggie asks. "Friends?"

I extend my hand to him. "Friends," I say, and he pulls me in and envelops me in a hug.

Reggie excuses himself, goes upstairs to his bathroom, and turns the water on in the tub. As openly as he lived with Lesley in Italy, it's odd to be able to talk to Claire about *his affliction*, as his mother used to call it. He wonders if Claire would be so understanding if she hadn't lost her husband. Would she be able to accept him the way he is? He wants to believe she would. He's watched her with the boys and can't ever imagine her trying to change them to suit her notions.

When he'd asked Claire to marry him, she was taken aback, especially after she learned about Lesley. He'd tried to make her understand that more than anything, Lesley had wanted a family, but even in Europe, two men raising a child together was frowned upon. Lesley had said he didn't care, that they'd be wonderful parents and their children would be wonderful, too, but Reggie said the children would suffer and he couldn't abide that.

But now, he can have a ready-made family with Claire and her boys. She didn't understand his proposal at first, but she came around. It seemed too good to be true, and, for Reggie, it is. He can finally be a father. He has someone who loves and understands him, sometimes better than Lesley did. And in this place where he was never loved or accepted, he can live out the rest of his days openly and honestly.

He turns off the water. The robe falls to the floor, and he sprawls out in the claw-foot tub, his long legs hanging over the sides. The warm water is soothing, but part of him always remembers the first time his mother caught him in her things. He had her favorite diamond earrings clipped to his lobes, the dangly ones he loved so much, and was in full makeup, or as fully made up as an eight-year-old can be. He grinned at her when she walked into the room, knowing she would think he was beautiful.

She'd jerked him up, locked his mammy out of the bathroom, and ran this very tub so hot, his skin burned for days. Flossie had pounded on the door, begging his mother to let her clean him up, but she never answered. She scrubbed him until he was nearly raw, trying to wash the gay away, before she left him crying on the floor, begging her forgiveness.

This time when the memory comes, he doesn't feel his skin burning. Although the remembrance is still there, it's less potent. Whether it's diluted by time or by Claire's love, he isn't sure, but he knows that he loves her, that he only wants the best for her and the boys, and he can give her that. It was hard telling Vada who he is and what he is, but with Claire beside him, loving him, healing him, he feels like he can do anything. He'll be the best husband he can be, just like he was with Lesley, maybe even better, and if God and Lesley and Claire's husband are looking down on him from heaven, he hopes they are pleased.

·Chapter Thirty·

It's close to ten thirty when the breakfast crowd clears out and the diner is nearly empty. Vada opens the screen door and takes her place at the booth she first sat in the day she walked into Frank's life. She smiles apologetically at him, and he's about to tell Tiny to take a hike when Tiny waves him off.

"I know the drill." Grabbing her purse, she flips the CLOSED sign around on the door, heads back to the postboxes, and asks Hank if he'd like to take a little ride. "I'll lock up, Frank, see you before lunch."

He slides into the booth across from Vada, and she reaches for his hand. "I'm sorry." They say the words at the same time. It's good to hear her laugh, even if it was just a little.

"I'm sorry," Frank says. "I should have told you everything about Lila, but honest to God, Vada, I didn't know how sick she was. I thought Smudge was the one making her like that, and I believed that her getting away from him was a good thing. It was hard watching her so unhappy here, and feeling responsible for her."

"I'm sorry, too, Frank, sorry that you had to take that on as a child."

"It wasn't like I was a little boy, Vada. I was fifteen. I should have known better."

"Wait, Frank, let me finish. What I'm most sorry for is not being there for you when you needed me." He can't look at her. Her hands are on his cheeks, turning him to face her. "I saw you when you read the letter. I know you were deeply affected by it. I love you, Frank, and I want to be there for you. Always."

"I love you." He reaches for her and she crawls over the table. He pulls her into him, cradling her. She rewards him with a long, wet kiss.

I'm breathless, and the familiar feeling between my legs doesn't frighten me anymore. Frank cups my bottom with one hand, holding me in place. His other hand is at the nape of my neck, urging me on, the kiss deepening and rhythmic. He lowers his head and skims the tops of my breasts, searing them with hot, wet kisses, making me moan. His lips travel up my neck, and I feel him bone hard against the small of back. My thighs fall open. Inviting.

"That night by the creek—I wanted to give myself to you, Frank. I've never wanted that with anyone before, but I want that with you. Now."

The kissing stops. "Vada, God knows I want you more than I've ever wanted anything in my life, but I'm not going to mess this up." He presses his forehead against mine, breathing hard.

I kiss him hungrily. "You won't mess things up."

"We have to stop."

My heart is beating so fast, I can barely breathe. "Why?"

"I want you more than anything, but I want to do this right."

"This *is* right, Frank. I know it is."

"You have to get back on the other side of the table, so I can think straight." I wrap my arms around his middle, refusing to move. "Tonight. I'll pick you up at seven. We'll go someplace special, and I'll make love to you all night if you want, but not here. Not now."

I pull away from him just enough to see his face, flushed and beautiful. I know he loves me, that he wants me, and I want him to feel good about what we have together. "Tonight?" I plant a tiny kiss on his temple and follow the line of his cheek until my lips are pressed against his. He nods slowly. "Tonight."

·Chapter Thirty-One·

Frank looks at the clock again, like he can will time forward, but the minutes continue to crawl. It looks like everyone in Colleton County has decided to come to lunch today, and they're not in any hurry to clear out. Tiny didn't quiz him, when she got back with Hank, about what happened with him and Vada. She studied his face, though, and knows him well enough to at least try to hurry the customers out the door, but it's no use. Word got around that Frank baked three cobblers yesterday, and those bastards want nothing more than an excruciatingly leisurely lunch followed up with his damn cobbler. Some with ice cream, some without, but all of them chased with too much conversation and too many cups of coffee.

Ten after two, nobody's leaving, and Frank can't take it anymore. He takes off his apron, strides out from behind the counter, and turns the CLOSED sign face out. He gets some raised eyebrows, particularly from Tiny, before folks go back to savoring their precious dessert. Tiny looks at Frank and cocks her head to the side.

"What?" she mouths.

It's twenty minutes past closing, and if he doesn't leave now, he won't make it to Walterboro in time. "I've got to be somewhere." If Frank says another word, he'll start screaming for the bastards to get the hell out of his diner, and they will probably never come back.

"Go on, Frank. It ain't like I never closed the joint before."

He nods and is out the door before Tiny's smart mouth kicks in. He makes it to Thompson's Department Store in record time and hurries in. The short, dainty man wants Frank to try on the black slacks and baby-blue dress shirt, but there's no time for that. Shoes. He stops in front of the wing-tip display. "Eleven and a half, and make it snappy," he barks at the little man. He does try the shoes on, then pays for his purchase and hurries into the florist, two doors down. "Roses, a dozen." The woman looks up at him like he's lost his mind.

"I don't get much call for roses, mostly mums, for funerals. I have orchids around Mother's Day." She shrugs apologetically.

"What do you have?"

"Not much. Dori Chavis's funeral was just yesterday—all but cleaned me out. I got some Jesus lilies left over."

"Jesus lilies?"

"The white ones, like they have when you get to heaven."

"I'll take them."

She wraps up the flowers and reminds him they are fragile and will be in pieces if he's not careful. Frank pays the woman, and then fires up the Plymouth, headed for the Edisto Motel.

It looks crowded when he pulls into the parking lot. With it being summer, it's doubtful they have any vacancies, but they have a fine restaurant here, which people from all over flock to, so he hopes most of the crowd is here for the good eats. The big woman at the front desk eyes him when he asks for a room. "Just you?" She takes a drag off of her cigarette and nods. "We're a family joint during the summer. If you want to hanky-panky, you'll have to wait till after Labor Day."

"No, ma'am. No hanky-panky." He's not lying, and there's no way in hell he's waiting till after Labor Day. What he wants from Vada is more than touching her, more than just being inside her. In his mind, they're already married, and Frank's ready to make it official the minute Vada is.

She pushes a key across the counter. "Number fifteen. Four bucks. Now."

Frank pays her and pulls the car around to the back of the motel that overlooks the pool, jammed with screaming kids, surrounded by sun-baked parents looking up occasionally to bark orders.

He grabs the key and the flowers off of the seat and opens the door. There is one bed, their bed, a nightstand, a tiny bathroom off to the side. The room smells like stale cigarette smoke, but he knows he won't notice any of that tonight.

He's impressed the Jesus flowers have held up well in the heat of the day. "Shit," Frank hisses. No vase. They'll be a droopy mess by the time he carries her over the threshold.

The restaurant is still busy, the sign promising THE WORLD'S BEST FRIED SHRIMP. Although Frank has his doubts about that, he heads around to the back door like a beggar. The noise from the kitchen frenzy isn't like any he's ever heard before. Through the screen, he counts a dozen people scurrying around to get orders out. Plates of golden fried shrimp, piled high with hush puppies and coleslaw, are doled out as quick as the waitresses can pick them up.

A young colored boy comes out the screen door with a can full of garbage that's as big as he is. He dumps it in the trash pile before he realizes Frank is there. "Help you, sir?"

Frank laughs, almost embarrassed. "Y'all busy in there?"

"Don't you know it." The boy sizes Frank up. "If you're wanting to eat, you got to come around through the front. If you're wanting a job, you can knock on the back door after four and the boss man will talk to you."

"I bought my wife flowers. Forgot the vase. Think you have something in there I could borrow?"

The boy nods. "Wait right there." He comes back with an empty quart-size pickle jar, the lid still on it. "This do?"

Frank nods and thanks the boy with two bits. He hurries back to rinse the makeshift vase out good, so the room won't smell like sweet pickles, too. With everything set, he starts to leave, and then decides to turn down the bed. Maybe not. He flips the spread over the shoddy pillows, but then decides it's okay. Vada has made it clear what she wants, and he can't wait to give it to her.

·Chapter Thirty-Two·

The banging on the bathroom door resumes. "Mr. Stanley, I told you, I'm not coming out anytime soon. I waited for the bathroom for two hours. If you have to use the bathroom, either go outside or ask Miss Mamie to use hers." He stomps off down the hall, swearing at me. *Good*.

I pour more lavender oil in the bathwater and sink down in the tub until the water is up to my chin. I rolled my hair in rags the moment I got back from the diner, while I waited for all three of the bachelors to finish their constitutionals, and I refuse to give up the bathroom until I'm done preening for my night with Frank.

I wonder where he'll take me. I think he knows by now Charleston is out of the question. Maybe one of the hotels we passed on our first date to Walterboro. I know this is fast, but not as fast as the girls I knew in college who met soldiers at the dance hall and went to bed with them just hours later, before their men were shipped out.

The water is almost cold, or as cold as bathwater can be in August. I get out of the tub, wrap a towel around myself, and study my reflection in the mirror. It's too hot for makeup, but I rub a tiny bit of rouge on my cheeks anyway and hope they're not a streaky mess later tonight.

Frank likes my hair down, but it's such a hot day, I don't want it plastered to my neck. I clasp it up in a curly bun and let the tendrils frame my face. *There.* Now, just a touch of lipstick, my little blue scoop-neck Nina Ricci number that matches my eyes, my black Charles Jourdan pumps, and I'm ready to become a woman.

"It's about damn time," Mr. Stanley huffs when I step out of the bathroom. Then he looks at me, and his face twists into the same lewd thing that gawks at Claire all the time.

"Really, Mr. Stanley, neither Claire nor I appreciate your overtures. You're older than God, and even with your pension, there's absolutely nothing appealing about you." I step around him, my heels clicking triumphantly down the hall.

My fingers trail across my neck. My grandmother's necklace would be the perfect touch to any ensemble, but most especially this one. I push the thought out of my mind and head downstairs to wait for Frank on the front porch, so that he knows I'm serious about this, about us.

His car pulls in front of Miss Mamie's. He gets out and strides up the walk, stunningly beautiful, his eyes trained on mine. Miss Mamie comes out onto the porch, but I won't let her spoil this moment I want to remember forever.

"What in God's name?" she hisses, and I want to tell the old bat not to waste her words, because there's nothing that can taint this moment that will lead to losing myself in Frank Darling's arms tonight. "Who in the Sam Hill are they?"

Only then do I see the cars that have pulled in behind Frank's

Plymouth. Two sleek black Cadillacs. I recognize the last custom-made one because it's my father's.

"God, you look beautiful," Frank says, completely unaware my father and a strange man have gotten out of the car. The man says something to my father, who looks around the crossroads in disbelief, and then starts toward the trellis gate. "What's wrong, Vada?" Frank turns to see the object of my gaze. "Who are they?"

The second car door opens, and Justin gets out, stretches his long frame, and looks at me. He's so beautiful, even Miss Mamie sucks in her breath, and I'm reasonably certain she's horribly nearsighted. He nods my way with a thin smile that says he has me now.

"Vada, who are these people?" Frank asks again and reaches for my hand.

"Vada," my father huffs, completely ignoring Frank.

"Wait a minute," Frank says, pointing at the man standing next to my father. "You're the insurance salesman from the diner. What the hell is going on?"

My father glares at me like I'm a naughty child he's ready to spank. "Really, Vada, with your upbringing, I would have thought that you'd have fled to somewhere more civilized than this rural pock."

"Hello, Father," I say, still staring at him with the steely trademark Hadley glare.

"He's your father?" Frank tries to get me to look at him, but I refuse to lose; this is a dance of intimidation. "Mr. Hadley." Frank brushes his hand off on his trousers. "I'm—"

"Frank *Darling*. I know."

Frank nods as Father's tone sinks in. "And I take it you're no insurance salesman."

"Private investigator."

"Enough of this. Vada, get your things. I've come to fetch you." Justin's tone breaks my stare.

"Who do you think you are, talking to her like a dog?" Frank grabs my hand. "She's not going anywhere."

"Her fiancé," Justin bites out, "and I've had quite enough of this game of find-the-bride."

"I knew she was a hussy the moment I laid eyes on her." Miss Mamie stands akimbo. "And a philanderer, to boot. I'm calling the county sheriff this instant," she says as the screen door slams behind her.

"Fiancé? Vada?" Frank waits for me to answer him, but the real battle isn't with Justin.

"I'm *not* leaving, Father. This is my home now, here with Frank."

"Honestly, Vada, you were raised better than this."

"How would you know? You didn't raise me. Desmond and Rosa Lee did. I was just another accessory to your and mother's lives, a way to continue the lineage. You said so yourself when I begged you not to make me marry Justin."

"Vada." Justin steps toward me, and Frank pulls me close. "Look around. You don't belong here. Come home now."

"Whoa, asshole, she's not going anywhere with you." Frank shoves Justin, who promptly begins rolling up his sleeves. He turns his college ring around so that the large dome is a weapon and puts up his dukes. "You want a fight? You've got one." Frank doesn't bother rolling up his sleeves, and throws the first punch.

I step in between them before it goes any further. "Stop it."

"Step aside, Vada, so that I can pummel this country bumpkin to death."

"Move. Vada." Frank's chest is heaving, his knuckles bleeding from where they connected just under Justin's eye.

"No. Stop it. All of you. Father, if you and Mother want to be part of the life I've chosen, a life here with Frank, fine. If not, you can leave. I'm sick of being coerced and manipulated, and I won't have it anymore. Not from you, not from Justin, not from anybody."

"If that's true, my dear, I'm afraid you traded one very comfortable shackle for," he makes a grand sweeping gesture toward the crossroads, "another. Frank *Darling* has done nothing but coerce and manipulate you."

"You don't know anything about Frank. He loves me and would never do anything to hurt me. Unlike you and Mother, he'd never crush who I am to make me what he wants me to be."

Frank wants to kill the bastard, and would have, if Vada hadn't stopped him. As angry as he is, it's hard to sit back and let Vada say her piece, but he knows she needs this.

"You're right, Vada. Your mother and I were heavy-handed with you, rushing into a wedding when you'd barely graduated. For that, I am sorry. But it is a natural progression; I truly believe you belong in Charleston, with Justin."

"Come with me, Vada," the smug jerk coos, and Frank wants to hit him again. "Come home, where you belong."

"She belongs here." Frank's fists are balled up tight by his side. If Vada wasn't here, he'd beat the shit out of this shiny bastard.

"Vada, people do manipulate to get what they want, they do coerce, but the real sin lies in letting them," her father says. "It's obvious you're a grown woman now. You're free to marry whomever you want."

"Matthew," Justin barks.

"I choose Frank." Vada takes Frank's hand.

"Precisely. You've proved my point."

"You're wrong. Frank hasn't manipulated me into anything."

"Perhaps your Mr. Darling would like to explain this."

"Shit." Vada's father pulls the postcard out of his jacket pocket. "Wait. Vada. Let me explain."

"It's a postcard." Vada pushes her father's hand away. "So what?"

"After you left, Vada, I let you have your fun for a while, and then I hired an army of private investigators to find you. Mr. Burton here happened to stop into the diner for breakfast, and Frank asked him to mail this card for him when he passed through Memphis." Her father places the card in her hand again, gently, and closes her fingers around it. "Vada, your mother and I love you, and we are truly sorry for our shortcomings. But we never gave you any false pretenses about our motives. If you truly are done with being coerced, manipulated, I suggest you read the postcard."

She turns the card over slowly and runs her fingers over the address. When she looks at Frank, he knows he did a shitty job trying to mimic the harlot's handwriting, but that's not the worst of it. "Dear Vada." Her voice is trembling with hurt. Anger. "I have found Darby. She is safe and well and happy with her new life, and—"

"Vada. I just wanted to—"

"*Doesn't wish to be contacted.*" She spits out the last words. "Frank. How could you?"

"I shouldn't have written that. I know. But you were so sad and—I'd just found out about Lila. Please, you have to understand."

"Vada, darling. He's no better than the rest of them." The jerk takes her hands in his. "I've been nothing but honest with you about my intentions."

"No. Vada, let me explain." But there's nothing Frank can say to make her understand how terrified he was that night, seeing her so desperately sad. He couldn't lose her like he lost Lila.

She's trembling with anger when she looks away from Frank, silent tears sliding down her beautiful face. The jerk is down on one knee, her hands in his. Oh, hell, he's proposing.

"Vada. No." Frank reaches for her, and she pulls away. "Don't."

"Vada." Justin kisses the backs of her hands and presses them against the swollen place on his cheek. "I never thought I'd say this, but I've missed you. I actually *want* to marry you. Will you do me the honor of being my bride?"

What a cockeyed proposal, and she seems to be considering it. Vada takes one long last look at Frank, to let him know he's responsible for this mess.

"Justin, take me home."

·Chapter Thirty-Three·

Desmond has tears in his eyes when he opens the front door. A half dozen servants are lined up to welcome me home; throwing decorum aside, Rosa Lee dashes to me, wrapping her arms around me, sobbing for joy and for the great sorrow that I've returned. I hold her close and beg her not to cry. "I've missed you so. Please don't cry. I'm home now."

From the foyer, nothing has changed, but Mother stands by the staircase, kindly giving Rosa Lee her due as my real mother.

"Are you all right?" Rosa Lee searches my eyes for the truth.

I nod, because I can't tell her my heart is angry, broken, but she knows. She hugs me again, and then steps back into line.

"Vada?" My mother reaches for me but then pulls back like she's unworthy. I can see I'm not the only one who is hurt. "Can we talk?"

I nod and head to my bedroom. My father follows, but she stops him at the entrance. They've always communicated well without words. He nods and closes the door behind us.

The trunks are still packed, the one with my shoes still open. The white Ferragamos are beside my closet; everything is as I left it, except the wedding dress and the veil are gone. Mother motions for me to sit down on the bed, but instead of standing to lecture me, she sits down beside me.

"Vada. I want you to know that I was only doing what I thought was best for you." She dabs at her eyes with a lace hand-kerchief. "This life, our life, has been this way for so long—it's in the best interest of our lineage to keep the wealth within our small circle. It's how our kind has survived in a world full of people who are more than happy to steal your money and break your heart into a million pieces."

I thread my hand in hers, and she whimpers a little, tears staining her makeup. "Don't cry, Mother."

"I talked to Justin before you left, and—"

"I know you did. I was listening outside the door. What you said meant a lot to me. I think it helped me stand up for myself, which is what I should have done in the first place."

My mother's always been as strong as she is beautiful. It seems wrong to see her so fragile. "I know I'm not very good at it, but I *do* love you."

"I know, Mother. I just wish it hadn't taken so long for me to figure that out." My head is cradled against her neck in a shame-less display of affection, both of us with happy tears. And sad.

The springs creak under our weight, reminding me how much I've missed sleeping in my own bed, and *not* sharing a bathroom. And shoes, God, how I've missed my shoes. Maybe I really do belong here.

A little black Chanel number is where I left it on the back of the closet door that is open and welcomes me home. But it reminds me of Claire. I miss her terribly. I miss the boys, already, especially the little one. I miss the openness of the crossroads and the earthy, musty smell of the open fields after a hard rain—and I miss Frank Darling. Damn him. I miss Frank.

"Vada, sweetheart." Mother holds me while I sob.

I collect myself as best I can. "Justin proposed again."

"Dear, if you don't want to—"

"I know that. He's actually being kind and patient with me, making it hard to say no."

"How is he?" Reggie whispers; his worried look for Daniel warms Claire's heart.

"He'll be fine."

"It breaks my heart to see him so unhappy."

"He's just upset. Vada was his first love. He believes her leaving is his fault because he gave her to Frank." And she was Claire's first real friend in a very long time. "She's a hard one to get over."

"But he'll be okay?" Reggie sounds like he's not so sure.

"Of course. In time." Claire puts her arm around Reggie. She's so grateful to have him. Even if he didn't have a nickel to his name, she'd still love him. He doesn't press her, like other people have, like Vada did, to root Bobby out of her heart, and sometimes she thinks he understands her better than Bobby did. Perhaps it's because he's gay. But Claire believes Reggie understands her because he knows what it's like to find the love of your life and then lose him forever.

Daniel lies across the bed that will soon be his, permanently. Even asleep, his breathing stutters from crying over Vada Hadley. "I'll get him up for supper soon. Maybe he'll eat something this time."

Reggie nods and excuses himself.

She can hear Peter and Jonathan playing outside, but since Vada left, even they have seemed melancholy. Miss Mamie certainly didn't spare any details when she retold the story of Vada's father and her fiancé showing up. Claire understands it was a terrible scene, but it still smarts that Vada left without saying good-bye.

She plops down in the wingback chair beside the bed and touches Daniel's hair softly. He's been so busy acting grown-up since his father died, it's hard to remember he's only twelve. But living here will be wonderful for all of the boys, especially for Daniel. He can be a child again.

"Any better?" Reggie asks hopefully.

"You haven't even been gone fifteen minutes."

"I can't stand seeing him so hurt and not being able to do something about it." The look on Reggie's face reminds her of Bobby, just after Daniel was born. He was awkward, wanting to help but paralyzed by how fragile Daniel was.

"I know. But if you do this, if we raise my boys together, there are going to be a lot of skinned knees and broken hearts we won't be able to fix."

"We'll see about that." Reggie gives her a peck on the cheek. "Judge Swenson is stopping by at six."

"*Reggie.* Why didn't you tell me?" Claire is out of her chair and gathering toys off of the floor. "The house is a mess and there's precious little time to straighten up before he comes. And dinner . . ."

"Relax, Claire. Peter and I will put out some refreshments. When Daniel wakes up, tell him we're getting married tonight." Reggie guides her back to the bedside chair. "When he wakes up, tell him he's home."

·Chapter Thirty-Four·

"Franklin James Darling. You better open this cabin door." Although it's not like he wasn't expecting her, Tiny's incessant banging only makes him more determined to stay put. He hasn't missed a day of work in seven years, but he's sick over losing Vada Hadley and sick over her pretty fiancé he punched. Not that he knocked the guy's lights out. He can't believe she actually has a fiancé. Besides him.

"Life goes on, Frank. It always does. To hell with that girl with her fancy dresses and her hot tea in the summertime. You can't stay lower than a snake's ankles. You got to live, and folks have got to eat. It's Monday morning and time to get back in the kitchen. Things'll get better, Frank. I promise."

He knows that more than anything, it's his silence killing Tiny, but he's not doing it to be mean. He's screamed himself hoarse, cursing the damn geese, the cabin. God. Besides, there's nothing anyone can say that's going to make him feel better.

Hearing Tiny's truck starting back up the dirt road is a relief. He thinks back to that day she brought Vada to him. How beautiful she was, how, for a moment, Vada seemed like she wanted to stay at the cabin instead of going off on some snipe hunt. Even then he knew he could have gotten her to stay, loved her so good, she would have forgotten everything but his name, but no. He just had to try to give her everything she wanted, and the truth is that's not possible. Not with a girl like Vada Hadley.

The only thing that hurts worse than his busted hand is his head. His belly has given up rumbling for food. He can't remember the last time he ate. That would mean sifting back through the events of the last two days, and he'd rather take a boot to the face than remember the particulars that got his hopes up for a lifetime with Vada and then stomped to death by two black Cadillacs and a would-be insurance salesman.

Frank opens the door and stands there for a moment before he ambles toward the rickety little pier that stretches over the riverbank. He knows from taking a flatboat trip with his daddy when he was a kid that this same river ends near the motel he was going to take her. Wing tips and Jesus flowers. Hell, a stinking motel room wouldn't have been good enough for her. *In the end, he wasn't good enough for her.*

If his daddy were here, he'd tell him the same thing Tiny was hollering. He'd tell him to get back in the kitchen. That's what he did when Frank's mother left. He didn't skip a beat. He just kept cooking until he found his peace.

Sitting down on the pier, Frank lets the black water cut around his ankles. Life without Vada is unthinkable, but it's a life, his life. He'll do another night's penance on the cot and head back before the sun comes up tomorrow. Maybe open up the diner.

Everything seems to stop, and the world is dead silent in

agreement. Frank can't even hear his defective heart like he could before Vada Hadley walked into his life. It's too busted up to remind Frank that he was broken to begin with. "What'd you expect?" He whispers the words, glad his voice is shot to hell, and hopes that when he goes back to work, folks will take pity on him and not ask him about the biggest thing that's happened at the crossroads since the preacher caught him with Lila.

By the time the sheriff showed up at Miss Mamie's, the show was over and the Cadillacs were gone. Vada was so angry at Frank, she was trembling, tears spilling down her beautiful face. Before she left with that bastard Justin, she'd glared at Frank like she hoped he'd burn in hell, and he just might, for all of his sins.

Still, it felt like a cruel joke that Frank was on the road back to the sameness of his life in Round O, and there was nothing else to do but go back to the diner until it killed him like it did his daddy, and his daddy before him.

Frank hadn't brought anything with him to the cabin except his troubles, and as much as he'd like to leave them at the cabin, he was stuck like a toad in a hailstorm with them. If he could somehow get time back, if he could do it over again, he sure wouldn't have written that postcard. He will suffer the loss of her all right, till the day he dies. Hell, maybe forever. But to have that little slice of time with her, to be loved by her—even though she left him with a busted heart—it was worth it.

Tiny didn't make a peep when she saw he'd permanently scratched "crab cakes" off all the menus with his bruised hand. Frank nods at her when she puts an order up, not really looking at her. His hand hurts like hell, and he feels pitiful enough without her big brown eyes confirming it. Folks who asked about the inkblot on their menu got shushed, and then Tiny, who has always been in-capable of talking in a low voice, would whisper something to them, while she glanced up at Frank to see if he was going to snap out of his stupor. The offending person always gives Frank an apologetic smile or a little shrug.

"Order up." His gravelly voice is almost back. He shoves two plates of salmon croquettes and grits through the window and stares at them for a moment. He put red and green bell peppers in them so they wouldn't look too much like crab cakes, but sitting there on top of a puddle of hominy grits, it hurts to look at them. Maybe he'd sell bacon and sausage and forget the cakes altogether, or just put more salmon and less flour in the mix to bring out the red color of the fish, maybe brown them a little more.

"We're busier than a one-armed monkey with two peckers," Tiny says, putting four more orders up. "Big Jim's truck just pulled up." Frank knows she's trying real hard, for his sake, not to sound ecstatic that the love of her life just pulled into the park-ing lot. He gets right on the orders, but notices Tiny behind the counter; with her back to the customers, she pinches her cheeks and unbuttons the top button on her uniform. She almost gets a smile out of Frank when she smooths her hands over her bottom. Big Jim won't know what hit him.

Frank wills himself not to look when Big Jim lumbers into the diner. The man's well over fifty, but still a half dozen years younger than Tiny. But it's a force of habit to see who's coming in the door, and even losing Vada Hadley won't cure it. Jim is so shy, his leathery, sunbaked face actually blushes when he sees her. Dolphis learned all about Tiny's hands-off policy the last time Big Jim was here, but when Tiny shows Jim to his seat, he noncha-lantly cups her bottom as he slides into the booth.

He recognizes the look on Big Jim's face and knows it won't

be long until he proposes to Tiny, hopefully after breakfast, because Frank knows she'll say yes on the spot. They'll drive off in the truck, and he'll be left with a diner full of hungry customers and no waitress. He opens three cans of salmon and starts sifting out the bones to make croquettes. He's happy for her.

He cracks two eggs in a mixing bowl. Really, he is. He throws in a handful of diced onion, parsley, and mayonnaise. *Get busy;* he tells himself to hurry past the holy trinity for crab cakes.

He's relieved when he dumps the red fish into the mix, stirs it up fast, too fast, so that it's almost mush. The peppers make the mix look better and unfamiliar. He goes heavy on the Worcestershire sauce and Tabasco, throws in some yellow mustard, and bread crumbs instead of flour, so there's no way they'll look like Vada's crab cakes.

Tiny puts Big Jim's order on the wheel and gives it a whirl. "I got to admit, the croquettes are selling, and they're so good, nary a customer has complained about not having—" She looks at him, and for a moment he's seven again, with a broken heart, only this time he understands why the woman he loves is gone. "You just might have changed the history of the Lowcountry by doing away with crab cakes. But I think we're gonna be just fine with the croquettes. I do."

The look he gives Tiny lets her know her croquette metaphor isn't appreciated. He patties out a dozen cakes, puts them on the grill, and watches a fat dollop of butter meander around the hot surface, bouncing off the cakes like a pinball until it melts into a puddle.

"Morning," Hank says, smiling with his empty coffee cup.

"Morning." Frank flips the cakes and likes how they look, but the crowd is so big this morning, he's about to run out of biscuits. Wouldn't be the first time.

"Guess you heard about Joe Pike," Hank says.

Frank keeps his head down, slopping grits, then a little pat of butter, on each of the six plates in front of him.

"Left town for good, you know. Just the other day. Shame about Lila. She was a nice girl."

Frank almost laughs. There was nothing girlish about Lila Smudge, but when you're ninety like Hank, she probably seemed like one.

"Guess he stayed because he thought she'd come back one day." Hank holds his coffee cup out for Tiny to refill.

"Who're you talking about, Hank?" Tiny asks.

"Lila. Smudge. Joe's gone, you know. For good, he said."

He can feel Tiny's intense stare as she checks to see if Hank's words injured Frank any more than he already is, but he'll not look at her. *Just keep your head down. Keep going.* Let the hard work of the diner numb the pain—not from Lila. He is sorry for what happened to her, but he hurts so badly from knowing he's lost Vada Hadley for good, exhaustion is his only solace.

Tiny fills Hank's cup. "There you go, handsome. And if you're needing any more coffee, just holler at me and I'll come to you."

"Well, that's mighty nice of you, young lady."

As quickly as Frank pushes them through the window, Tiny balances all six plates on her arms. He yanks the next order off the wheel to let her know he's fine. *Just go away.*

"What in the hell?" one of the truckers by the window says. "There's a woman marching this way with a man trailing behind her, and she looks madder than a full-moon dog."

Frank pulls two frying pans off the burners at once and wipes his hands on the towel slung over his shoulder. He starts untying his apron, praying hard that it's Vada.

Claire Greeley comes into the diner with a fury, marches up to his window, and slaps the *Charleston Post* newspaper down. Before he even glances at the paper or can say anything, a man, who he guesses is Reggie Sheridan, comes in with Claire's little one on his hip and Daniel and Peter trailing behind.

"What are you going to do about *this*?" Claire smacks her hand above the fold of the paper. Frank sees the headline and can't read past "Hadley-McLeod Union."

"There's nothing I can do." He reties his apron and goes back to cooking.

"The wedding is Saturday, so you'd better do something fast, because she loves you," Claire bites out. "I know she does."

"If she loved me, Claire, she wouldn't be marrying somebody else."

"Why didn't you fight for her, Frank?"

"I did, Claire, and nearly broke my hand in the process."

"You didn't fight for her." Daniel glares at Frank. "Because you're a coward. And you're a liar. You said if I gave her to you, you'd make her happy. But that was a lie. If she was happy, she would have stayed."

Reggie puts his hand on Daniel's shoulder and draws him close. An opulent gold band that matches the one Claire's wearing says everybody's getting married *but* Frank Darling.

With his mother so riled, the little one starts to fuss, and Reggie bounces him on his hip. When he lays his head against Reggie's chest, every defect of Frank's heart sings he'll never have this with Vada Hadley.

"Daniel." Frank turns the stove off. "I tried to make her happy, but in the end, she wanted what you wanted to give her."

"Then you shouldn't have talked me into giving her to you." Daniel bursts into tears.

"You're a fool, Frank," Claire snaps. "Vada didn't want

money, or even the fancy necklace her grandmother gave her. She only wanted two things: to see her friend Darby again and *you*, Frank Darling. She wanted you."

"She told you that?"

"Yes, all the time, but she didn't have to tell me. I could see it in her face."

"But I screwed up, Claire. Bad."

"She loves you, Frank. She'll forgive you, I know she will. But if you never go after her, she won't know how much you love her. She'll think you don't care about her, that you never cared at all."

He whips off his apron, and for the first time in days, he feels alive.

"So you'll do it?" Daniel asks. "You'll bring her back?"

"Or die trying."

"That's what you said last time."

"Daniel," Claire snaps, "mind your manners. Now, you and Peter take Jonathan home."

"I'll take them," Reggie offers.

"No, Frank will need you," Claire says.

"Thanks, but I know the way to Charleston." Why did Vada tell him she didn't have a boyfriend? How could he be so stupid to believe a girl like her wouldn't have one? "I'll find her, say I'm sorry, do whatever I have to do to get her back."

"Frank, if she's as angry at you as I heard—and, mind you, I'm going by Miss Mamie's version of the story—you can't just barge into the Hadley mansion and haul her away. Maybe you shou—"

"Show her how much I love her." Frank opens the till and takes the money out of the drawer. He hurries into the kitchen and cleans the cash out of the old coffee can. "I'll find Darby O'Doul and bring her back, just like she wanted."

"But if you and Vada couldn't find her before, what makes you think you can find her now?"

"I have to, Claire." When Frank's mind catches up with his body, he looks around the diner to see every customer has stopped eating and is completely enthralled in his business. Even Tiny is silent, a coffeepot in each hand, waiting for him to redeem himself.

"Wait. Take Reggie with you," Claire barks as he starts for the door.

"Me?" Reggie asks. "Why?"

"If Frank is lucky enough to find Darby, surely between your polish and Frank's brawn you can talk her into coming back to Charleston to stop the wedding."

"Claire, dear, I've met Vada's parents before. Believe me, we won't be stopping anything with Frank and an Irish servant girl," Reggie says. "Besides, I'm not even sure it's possible to stop nuptials of this magnitude."

"Of course they can be stopped. Vada did it before, but she'll have to be the one to do it again."

"Thanks, Claire." Frank gives her a peck on the cheek. "But I don't need any help." He nods at Reggie. "No offense."

"None taken."

"Not taking Reggie is foolish, Frank. It's a long trip and you don't have much time. Besides, Reggie can help drive and help you look for Darby."

"Maybe you're right." He nods at Reggie. "All right, you can go."

"Wonderful." Reggie is horrible at pretending to be compliant. "Just how I wanted to spend my week, looking for a bawdy Irish woman."

Down to his bones, Frank is afraid he'll lose Vada forever, but he can't let himself think like that. He's as sure now as he was when he was in Memphis, that the Wentworth woman has known where Darby is all along. And if he's honest, when he was with Vada in Memphis, Frank was more interested in romancing her than actually finding the person most dear to her. No. This time, he won't stop until he gets what he wants, until he gets what Vada wants, and then he'll spend the rest of his life making up for the mess he made. But his feet are cemented to the well-oiled diner floor, like the slightest movement either way might lead to an eternity without Vada Hadley. What if he can't find Darby? And if he finds her and can talk her into coming back to Charleston with him, what if Frank's apology isn't enough?

Tiny is beside Big Jim's booth, and he has his arm around her hips. He pipes up, but Frank's thoughts are too tangled to hear him. He nods at Frank and gives Tiny a little squeeze. "What are you waiting for, Frank? Go get your girl."

·Chapter Thirty-Five·

"Three o'clock, honey." Rosa Lee sits down on the bed beside me.
"Time for dinner."

Her worried look makes me feel guiltier. Even my parents have
been doting on me. I tell them I'm fine, ready to buck up and do
what is required of me by them, by Justin. The last thought makes
my insides clench. I know what he will expect of me, and while
I've resigned myself to this union, I can't imagine wanting him to
touch me the way I wanted Frank to, or begging him to make love
to me.

Justin says I belong with him; the words sound foreign coming
from him, but he genuinely seems to have had a change of heart.
I'm not sure if he's right, but I have been surprised at how natural
it's been to fall back into my old life. Maybe if I continue to let go,
I'll land where I truly belong.

"Come eat something, child. If not for yourself, for me."

But the truth is, my body isn't on Charleston time, where the main meal is served at three o'clock each day. Another reminder of how different this place is from the rest of the world, and how different I am from Charleston.

"All right." I sit up, and Rosa Lee brushes out my hair and then twists it up in a knot. Looking at myself in the cheval mirror, I'm not sure how Justin likes my hair. Frank liked it down, but that doesn't matter anymore. It looks right drawn up into a tight bun. I look older, stately.

"I made all your favorites," Rosa Lee says, and while she goes on about dinner, I can't seem to think of anything but cobbler with homemade vanilla ice cream. Sucking peach juice off of Frank's fingertips.

"Thank you, *Murrah*." Frightened, she looks around to see if anyone heard me. "Don't be afraid, Rosa Lee. I'll speak the way I please. And if it's okay with you—and Desmond, of course—I'd like for you to come live with Justin and I after we're married. But not as servants. He has a carriage house on the property. If you want it, it's yours."

"But Mr. Justin—"

"I'm not a little girl anymore. I make my own decisions now, and if I'm going to marry him, I will have my say in all things."

She gives me an incredulous nod and helps me dress.

"Darling," Mother coos as I enter the dining room. I want to snap at her and demand she call me by another pet name, but I know she's trying to fix things between us. Reggie Sheridan was right. I do look so very much like her. Even our movements are the same.

The doorbell rings before the soup is served, and Desmond shows Justin into the dining room. He kisses the top of my head before taking the seat beside me, lingering for a moment.

"Vada," he says warmly and not curtly like he used to.

"Justin."

Mother gushes over the fact that the whole city has stopped what they're doing to make my wedding happen tomorrow. "Why, Ruthie Rutledge is positively beside herself that Father John moved the time of her wedding back to two so that you and Justin can be married at six. You have your father to thank for that."

"Oh, it was nothing, really," Father laughs. "What is it they say in the Bible? Ask and ye shall receive?"

"Anything you want if your pockets are deep enough," my mother adds, laughing.

Justin takes my hand in his and rubs his lips against the ridges of my knuckles before giving them a chaste kiss. "You're going to be a beautiful bride, Vada."

He seems different, like he really wants this. "Thank you, Justin."

Rosa Lee removes the soup bowls and the tureen and returns with plates piled high with fresh vegetables she got at the market this morning. Mashed potatoes. Fried chicken. The warmer beside my place is filled with a dozen perfect biscuits.

"There's no wine on the table, but I'd like to propose a toast to you, Justin, and to my beautiful daughter, on the eve of her wedding." My father raises his glass of sweet tea. "To health, wealth, and happiness."

"Hear, hear." Justin clinks his glass to mine.

I take a sip. "Mother, I want to thank you for canceling the rehearsal party for tonight. I know you wanted that very much, and I appreciate you graciously bowing to my wishes instead of tradition."

"Hear, hear," Justin says. "Matthew, perhaps we should break out some wine and celebrate my lovely and incredibly agreeable bride."

"You might want to hear me out before you lift a glass, Justin."
He looks playfully aroused. "All right, then. Speak, bride."

"Mother, I love you very much, and I have no say over how
you run your household, but it's wrong for the servants to live in
fear that if they slip and say one Gullah word, they'll be fired."

"*Vada*." She sets her fork down and dabs at her mouth with a
linen napkin. "This was meant to be a consolatory dinner to
bring us all together before your special day. That remark was
quite unnecessary."

"But you're wrong, Mother. It is necessary. Justin deserves to
know what I expect of him before he says, *I do*."

"Vada," Father barks. "This is a dinner, not an ambush."

"No, please, Matthew." Justin is grinning from ear to ear,
laughing. "Let the bride speak. I must hear what's *expected* of me."

"I'm not the same tearstained girl you saw the day before our
last wedding date, Justin."

"No, you are not." Under the table, his hand travels over my
knee, but I stop it before it goes any higher. "I like you a bit
feisty."

"Father, I want you to give Desmond and Rosa Lee their retirement money that you've told them you've been investing all
these years, and I want them to come live with me."

"Vada, they're not slaves," my father huffs. "I can't just give
them to you."

"No they're *not* slaves, but sometimes you treat them that
way. They are loyal servants who have worked long and hard
enough, and if they want, they'll live out the rest of their days in
retirement in the carriage house."

"In *my* carriage house?" Justin isn't laughing anymore.

"No, Justin, *our* carriage house. After tomorrow, I'm your
partner. What I have is yours, and what you have will be mine."

"Matthew, she's lost her mind," Justin says.

"Speak to me, Justin. Not my father."

"All right. Vada Hadley, you're insane."

"Rosa Lee," my mother calls, in an uncharacteristically loud voice. "Please clear the plates and serve the dessert. Now."

As my parents and Justin argue whose fault it is that I have suddenly developed a brain, Rosa Lee's worried look asks if I know what I'm doing.

"I assure you I am quite sane. I look around at the women in our social circle, who are nothing more than well-heeled accessories to their husbands' lives. I don't want that kind of marriage, Justin."

"Tell me, Vada, what kind of marriage *do* you want?"

"I want a husband who listens to me, who values my opinions, and who looks at me as more than just window dressing." Both Father and Justin are red teakettles ready to blow. "And I want to teach."

My father slams the table hard, making the crystal dessert bowls jump. "Vada, no Hadley woman has ever worked. Stop this ridiculous talk this instant." He wags his spoon at my mother. "I told you, Katherine, she should have gone to college here in Charleston, but no, you had to send her off to Radcliffe to have her head filled full of this nonsense."

"There's nothing wrong with teaching, Father. It's an honorable and valuable profession. And there's certainly nothing wrong with a woman working. We might all be speaking German if women didn't do their part during the war. Besides, I want to work."

"Eat your cobbler, Matthew. It's really quite good." My mother takes a dainty little spoonful and pretends everything is fine.

"Well, no wife of mine is going to work, and that's final."

Justin pushes back from the table and throws his linen napkin in his plate.

"Justin, whether I choose to work or choose not to work, I'll consider your opinion, your feelings, but ultimately it's my decision."

"What about all of this what's-mine-is-yours nonsense? Being partners? Doesn't that cut both ways?"

"Yes, but—"

"Don't get up to see me out, Vada. Stay here at the table and run your little show, get it all out now while you can. After tomorrow, I will not only expect you to be more reasonable, more submissive. I'll demand it."

·Chapter Thirty-Six·

Frank didn't bother to change clothes. He and Reggie just jumped in the Plymouth, although Reggie had said he'd rather they take his Cadillac, and the two of them headed up Highway 78, toward Memphis. Frank made it clear that he didn't want to talk and that seemed fine by Reggie, who said he could sleep anywhere and proved it, on and off, with his head thrown against the back of the seat, snoring.

Reggie seems like a good guy. He must be if he took in Claire and her boys. Not that Claire isn't pretty, because she is, but with three boys, she's lucky she didn't end up with Mr. Stanley. Frank smiles at how incensed Vada was when he called Claire the Widow Greeley, even more so when he suggested that accepting Mr. Stanley's proposal might be a good thing.

A car passes in the other direction, going too fast. Frank glances down at the speedometer. It's him who is going too fast. But he can't get to Memphis and then back to Charleston quickly enough to suit him. Better to let off the gas a little, just so he doesn't get pulled over. The car blows past a truck stop Frank thinks wasn't far from the Memphis city limits. He's had almost twelve hours to think about how to go about finding Darby O'Doul, and his best idea is to go back to the cathouse and talk to the harlot.

"How much farther?" Reggie stretches and yawns.

"Less than twenty miles, I think." They pass a road sign confirming Frank's guess, and by his watch, they've made really good time. He hates to admit it, but he's glad to have someone along to help him find Darby. And Reggie's a nice enough guy. "So you and Claire got married?"

"Day before yesterday."

"That's good. She's a good woman."

"Yes, she is, and I'm lucky to have her, and the boys."

Frank slows when he gets to the Memphis-city-limit sign. He hopes he remembers his way back to the harlot's. He doesn't have a plan. He's just going to ask the woman straight-up where Darby is and hope she's not too mad at him to tell him. If she knows. And if she doesn't, he and Reggie will hit the streets again, like he did with Vada. But what if Darby's not in Memphis anymore? He can't let himself think like that. He won't.

"Vada's a lovely girl. Looks just like her mother."

"How well do you know her family?"

"I've met them a couple of times, years ago at parties, that kind of thing."

Frank nods. "Help me look for Adams Street." There's probably a lot he can learn from a guy like Reggie. For one thing, he's a snappy dresser, and he can probably give Frank some pointers when it comes time to talk with the Hadleys and ask Vada's father for her hand before she gives it to that fancy-pants bastard Justin.

"There, on the right," Reggie says, and Frank turns the car down Adams Street and pulls up in front of the cathouse. "I hear music, and there's a valet. They must be having a party."

This is new to Frank. He doesn't feel right handing the keys to the Mayflower over to the guy in the black zoot suit, but Reggie's halfway up the sidewalk and he doesn't have a choice.

Reggie rings the bell, and a tall colored man dressed in a Sunday suit answers the door. "Good evening. Pardon me, gentlemen, but I don't recognize you."

"I'm here to see Kittie Wentworth. She knows me." Frank nods toward Reggie. "He's with me."

"Your name, sir?"

"Frank Darling."

He raises his eyebrows like either he doesn't believe Frank or he's heard about him from the harlot. "Sorry to have to leave you gents standing out here, but I'll be right back."

Reggie buttons the top button on the collar of his shirt and then straightens his shirtsleeves. "Must be quite the party."

"It's a whorehouse."

"No! In this neighborhood?"

"I thought the same thing when I was here with Vada."

"Why didn't you tell me? I love courtesans. They're such fascinating women."

"We're not here for that."

The door opens, and the same gentleman nods them in. "This your first time at the manor?" he asks Reggie.

"At manors as a whole, of course not, but at this one, yes."

"Miss Wentworth likes for her guests to have a few drinks and socialize a little in the parlor first." He points toward the large room where the harlot attempted to show Frank her trophies. A jazzy tune is playing on the hi-fi. "You'll meet all the girls who aren't working right now. Pick one or two, and then head on up-stairs."

"Lovely," Reggie says.

"But Miss Kittie wants to see *you* right now," he says to Frank.

"Give me a minute with my friend." Frank pulls Reggie to the side. "Find out what you can, and I'll go take care of the Wentworth dame."

"What exactly does 'taking care' entail, Frank?"

"I don't know, but I'm convinced she was stringing Vada along and knows something more about Darby than she let on. I'm not leaving here until I know what that is."

Reggie gives a curt nod and heads into the parlor, where a half dozen girls immediately throw themselves at him. *Some help he's going to be.* Frank shakes his head and starts up the stairs.

"Oh, a glass of champagne would be lovely," Reggie says to the tall blonde. He looks around the room at the handful of men; all of them are old, or at least older than Reggie, portly. Most are rather unfortunate-looking. But their suits and the gold and diamond rings on their big fat fingers scream new money.

Lesley used to tease Reggie about always having to be the prettiest man in the room. He wonders if the sadness he feels will ever go away, but suspects it won't. There has always been a part of him that pined for Lesley whenever they were apart, and it's no different after his death. Maybe a half lifetime with Claire and the boys will make the feeling subside, but Reggie hopes it will never go away completely. It's the last bit of Lesley he has to hang on to.

A beautiful girl with green eyes hands him a glass of what is surprisingly good champagne and runs her hand down his leg. "I'm Charity. What's your name, handsome? You like redheads?"

"How rude of me. Reginald Palmer Sheridan the third, but you may call me Reggie. And, of course, I love all of you." He sips on his bubbly as the rest of the courtesans introduce themselves. "Tell me, girls, have you ever been to Rome?"

A sassy brunette named Violet throws back her head and laughs. "No, but I meet a lot of roamin' . . . hands, that is."

All the girls cackle. Reggie nods at the waiter, who promptly refills his glass. "In Rome, what you do is highly valued."

"Oh, don't you worry, Reggie," a stunningly beautiful mulatto girl named Belle purrs. "We're highly valued, the best in the great state of Tennessee. Why don't you let me show you?"

"I'm sure you are, my lovely. As I was saying, the Italians have always held their courtesans in high esteem and have thought of your profession as necessary as lawyers, doctors."

After Reggie holds court for a while, the tall dark waiter nods at one of the girls, and the prettiest one leans forward to reveal breasts that seem awfully large for a woman with such a delicate frame. "Oh, Reggie, I have a thing or two I'd like to teach you. Pick me." As an artist, Lesley rather liked the Botticelli-esque women, but they never held Reggie's interest.

As he converses with the girls, he tries to decide which one is the most savvy and might know more about what goes on at the bordello than who is going to pop the cork on the next bottle of champagne. He settles on the mulatto girl, who seems very bright and might have a bead on the servants, as well as the courtesans, and they start up the gaudy staircase. Her beautiful dark eyes flirt with Reggie until about halfway up, then her look changes. "Why did you pick me?" she asks flatly.

"Because you're especially lovely, Belle."

She shakes her head and pulls him aside at the top of the stairs.

"Look, I know your kind. You're not here to be entertained, and I have to work tonight. What do you want?"

"Can we go to your room?" Reggie pulls two twenty-dollar bills out of his wallet. "Please."

She nods, takes the money, and they start down the long hallway. The moaning and the squeaking of bedsprings competes with the jazz music from downstairs. She opens the door to a large bedroom, and Reggie steps inside. Unlike the rest of the house Reggie has seen, this room is tastefully decorated, well-appointed, and quite different from the rest of the house. "Ah, *siège d'amour*," he says, plopping down astride the sex chair. "I've never seen one of these stateside. This one is quite lovely with the carvings, the gold filigree, a true work of art."

"There's one in every room, but you didn't come here for that."

"No, I guess I didn't." Reggie traces the outline of one of the stirrups. "Do you believe in love, Belle?"

"No," she says flatly.

"A beautiful woman like you? You have to. You must."

"Maybe by the hour." Her hands are on her hips. "I'm going to ask you one more time what you want, and then I'm going to ask you to leave."

"That gentleman you saw me come in with downstairs—"

"Is he your lover? Did you come here for a room?"

"No. Frank's a friend. Well, he's not really a friend, but he's very deeply in love. Frank has all but lost this woman he's mad about, and he's trying desperately to get her back. To do that, he's trying to give her the one thing she wants most in this world."

"Are you sure he's not like you? As good as that man looks, he ought to know what that woman wants."

"Her name is Vada, and she's so very angry at Frank, she's

marrying someone else for spite, and very soon, if this trip is all for naught. A few weeks ago, Vada came here looking for her friend, who I understand got in a bit of trouble with your employer."

"We all walk a tight line here. I've got a good job, and Miss Kittie's hard, but she's fair. I think you'd better go."

"I'm sorry. I told you about Frank and the woman he loves, because I'd hoped to gain your sympathies. So I'll just ask you outright. Do you know Darby O'Doul?" After a long silence, he peels off another twenty and hands it to Belle.

"Yes." She looks at the bills folded up in his hand and nods. He peels off another one.

"Do you know where she is?"

"Yes."

·Chapter Thirty-Seven·

"This is awfully late for cocktails, Vada."

"Relax, Mother. It will be fine."

She pushes the last bobby pin into the bun piled high on top of my head, and pulls a few wispy tendrils around my face. "Pull the black Dior out of the trunk, the dinner dress. That will be perfect."

"We didn't get that one in black. We got it in blue." My first-date dress. With Frank. My nose begins to sting, and I turn away from the mirror so my mother doesn't see. "We got the Pierre Balmain in black."

"I told Rosa Lee to pack your things." My mother rifles through my closet until she finds the chic black dress, the one with the low neckline she complained about when we bought it. "Now, it took some doing by your father to arrange cocktails with Justin tonight. Make the most of it."

I resist the urge to ask her what, exactly, that means as she zips me up, then hands me her diamond earrings. "You know your father gave me these the night before our wedding. I was going to give them to you after you were dressed for yours, but they'll look beautiful on you tonight."

"They're too much, Mother. Really." I close her hand over the earrings and push them back to her, but she knows me well enough. Even in her open palm, they are exquisite, two perfect diamonds in a tastefully beautiful setting, but they aren't appropriate for cocktails with Justin. "I want to keep things simple tonight."

"You'll melt in this heat. Do you want Desmond to drive you?"

"I'll take my car."

"How will that look, the night before you're to be married, your car parked at Justin's house?"

"It'll be fine. I'm not meeting him at his house in town. We'll be at Middleton Place."

"You should have Desmond take you." She looks away from me. "He's the one who drove you the night of your party. Wasn't he?"

I know better than to answer that question.

"Vada?" She sits down on the bed, looking at her hands folded in her lap. "Desmond and, of course, Rosa Lee always knew what you wanted, what to do with you. It wasn't easy watching them do what I couldn't. It still isn't. I've accepted their role in your life, but I want you to know there were times when I wanted to mother you. I just always felt like I was too late."

"I know you did the best you could."

"How can you know that? I'm not even sure I believe it."

"Because you love me, Mother." It's been difficult to watch her twisting in her guilt since I returned home, at war with the side of her that was bred to keep up appearances. Preserve the culture. "And I love you."

My red Cadillac convertible slices down the highway until it comes to the long dirt road lined with century-old magnolias that lead to the house. I drive slowly, feeling each dip and bump, intoxicated by the perfume of the magnolia blossoms. The road stretches past the azalea pool, where two lazy swans glide across the spring-fed waters. All of the gardens are too vast to be seen from the driveway. Tea olives, camellias, and fifty shades of greenery make a fragrant, seductive curtain of swamp lily, bears breeches, and abelia.

Something about Middleton Place has always called to me, and perhaps that's why Justin chose to meet here, rather than the seclusion. Or perhaps he wants me to return to where we were before I ran away, so that we can start over.

The road ends like the bottom of an hourglass, at the front door of the stately redbrick home. I pull alongside Justin's sleek black Caddy that matches mine, and wish I'd come up the loop the wrong way, so that I'd be facing the old slave quarters. This view is a promise of what my life will be like, splitting my time between here and the house in town. The exquisite view that rivals anything Europe has to offer whispers there will be travel. Middleton Place herself sighs, reminding me that when I do come home, it will be to this magnificent vista.

Enchanted, I'm out of the car before I realize it and walking around back toward the glorious view of the Ashley River that graciously bent and widened to show off this place. Chameleon-green marsh grass borders the broad expanse. I step across the boards of the dock, waiting to feel the full force of my jealousy of the river and for the sadness to envelop me. But it doesn't.

Justin's arms wrap around my waist, and he trails the back of my neck with tiny kisses. "You belong here, Vada. You love this place. I know you do."

I'm afraid to answer him. Ashamed. Yes, I do love this place.

"You probably don't remember the first time your parents brought you here. I was twelve, you were four, and even then you were bewitched by this place. Our place."

"There's no denying its beauty."

"Vada, we can be so good together." He turns me to face him and crooks his finger under my chin, nuzzling my lips. He covers my mouth with a dark, wet kiss, and when it's over, I am breathless, my forehead pressed against his. "Come inside, Vada. Come let me love you."

I nod slightly, barely able to breathe, and he picks me up and carries me toward the house.

"Do come in, Frank." Frank stands in the doorway of Kittie Wentworth's boudoir, weighing his options, and there aren't any.

With the exception of Vada's grandmother's necklace, the harlot is naked, sprawled out on the sex chair, with her feet in the stirrups, knees high, legs spread wide. Frank throws her a wad of lace fabric he hopes is a robe. "You should put some clothes on."

"I knew you'd be back." She sits up, astride the chair, and throws the fabric in his face. "It's rude of you not to look at me when I'm speaking to you. Look at me, Frank."

"I don't have time for this." He glares at her, trying hard to ignore her nakedness. "Tell me where Darby is."

"Make. Me." The harlot purrs, her fingers trailing down her neck, across her breasts.

"Was she in on the scam with you?"

"Come on, Frank. It's just you and me here, no silly little girl down the hall whose name is written on your heart.

The last time you were here, I wanted you to come to my room. Now you're here and—"

"Tell me where Darby is now."

"Would it give you great pleasure to know where she is, Frank?"

"Yes. I want to know."

"Pleasure is a give-and-take proposition. Come give the chair a try, and if you can still remember your name when I'm done with you, I'll tell you exactly where she is."

His fists are balled up by his sides. He can't very well beat the information out of the harlot, and wouldn't if he could. She'd bragged about being in bed with the police force and politicians, and he doesn't doubt her. There's nothing for him to hold over the woman's head. But how far is he willing to go for Vada?

The idea of never seeing her again, of her marrying that smug bastard, answers his question.

"I want to unwrap you." The harlot gets off of the chair. She runs her hands down his chest and starts unbuttoning his shirt. "*Slow*-ly."

The word stings, reminding him of Vada. He tells himself he's doing this for her, that he'd do anything for her.

"Now push the shirt off of your shoulders." The harlot inspects him, running her hands over his belly. He tries to think of something, anything, else. "You are a beautiful man, Frank Darling."

"I don't want you. All I care about is Vada."

"Yes," she says with her lips pressed against his ear, her naked body melting into his. "Show me how much you care about her, Frank. How much you want her. Show me all the things you want to do to her."

"This is bullshit," he says, pushing her away. "I'll find another way."

He picks up his shirt just as Reggie opens the door and gives him the high sign.

"You must have gotten yourself in a pretty good bind, Frank." The harlot laughs. "You're trying to fix things again, like you did the last time you were here. Stop wasting your time. You'll never find Darby O'Doul."

Frank pushes past Reggie, buttoning his shirt. "With all due respect, madam," Reggie says, turning down Frank's collar, "we already have."

· Chapter Thirty Eight ·

Frank revs up the Plymouth and heads back the way they came.

"By my calculation, we barely have enough time to nab Darby and make it to Charleston by six," Reggie says.

"Where is she?"

"According to Belle, the courtesan I spoke with, Darby lives with her husband, just outside of a little town called Jasper, Alabama. It's off Highway 78."

"How did you get the information?"

"Well, I wasn't willing to go the lengths you were."

"It wasn't like that. Do you think the girl was being honest?"

"Yes. Belle was very close to Darby and showed me a half dozen postcards she received from her."

"Shit."

"We should be there by one. Is something wrong?"

"Nothing." Damned postcards started this whole mess in the

first place. "No, I just hope her husband is an understanding man and we don't get shot for showing up so late."

"If we wait till closer to dawn, you'll get to Charleston just in time to wish the happy couple well on their honeymoon," Reggie snaps. "Now step on it."

"At least Darby got away from that place."

"Her situation is a bit precarious. It seems she met a circuit preacher and ran away from the bordello around the same time Vada fled Charleston. She started a new life, and her husband doesn't know about her old one. I'd like to be positive, Frank, but there's a good possibility she won't come with us."

"If I have to sling her over my shoulder and carry her all the way to Charleston, she's coming with us."

Frank floors the Plymouth and makes the outskirts of Jasper in less than three hours. "There," Reggie says. "Slow down or you'll miss it." He points to a small dilapidated clapboard building. The sign out front says Jasper Primitive Baptist. "The house is behind the church."

Frank pulls into the washboard parking lot and eases the Mayflower around back. The headlights illuminate a tiny house. A ferocious-sounding dog barks and lights come on in the house just as Frank kills the engine.

"Perhaps we should stay here, Frank, until whoever is inside comes out to greet us. Or shoot us."

"You have a wife now, and a family. Stay here."

"I won't argue with you," Reggie whispers. "What are you going to say to her when her husband answers the door?"

"I have no idea." Frank opens his car door, and the barking intensifies. The front porch is held up with two-by-fours on cinder blocks, bowing from the weight of the overhanging roof. He takes two steps. A gun cocks, freezing him in his tracks.

"Take one more step," the woman says through gritted teeth, "and I'll blow your fucking head off, I will."

Frank keeps his head down and raises his hands in surrender. The dog inside is snarling, banging against one of the flimsy doors of the house that is sure to give way.

"My name is Frank Darling, and I'm looking for Darby. Darby O'Doul."

"At one o'clock in the morning? I think you're looking to meet your maker, and I'm happy to take you there, Mr. Darling."

Slowly, he raises his head. In the slight palmetto moonlight, a young woman about Vada's age stands with her feet spread apart and her rifle aimed at his head like she knows her way around a gun.

"I'd appreciate it if you'd put that gun down, Darby."

"There's no Darby here."

"Vada told me you swore you'd always be there for each other. She needs you now. I need you."

"How do you know Vada?"

"I love her enough to stand here in the dark, not caring if you shoot me, because you're the only hope I have of her not marrying that bastard Justin."

The sound of the car door opening makes both of them freeze. "Tell your friend to stay in the car, or he can carry you home in a box."

Frank nods. "Stay put, Reggie. It's okay."

The words are no sooner out of his mouth when the dog lets out a yelp from the door in the back, which gives way. A thick black German-shepherd-looking dog skids to a stop beside his mistress, growling ominously. She commands the dog to heel and motions toward the house with the gun. "Let me see your face. And keep your hands where I can see them."

The rifle jabs into the small of Frank's back as he moves slowly toward the house. He can feel the warmth of the dog's frenzied bark against his pant legs, daring him to run. Frank stands under the naked lightbulb over the doorway and turns slowly to face her. She is smaller than Vada, beautiful, with steely eyes that make her look formidable, even without the gun.

"You'll have to excuse my keeping this rifle on you. But I meant what I said about dropping you where you stand."

"That's fine." Frank lowers his hands. "I'm not here to hurt you."

"I'll be the judge of that."

"Okay." Frank tries to smile, to put her at ease, but he's too desperate. He catches sight of a sliver of gold on her ring finger. "You're married now."

"A preacher's wife, and I plan to stay that way."

"But you're alone."

"Not entirely. I have a Smith & Wesson to keep me company while my husband's away."

"He knows you worked at a whorehouse?"

"Are you threatening me? In Alabama, that's cause enough to shoot you where you stand."

"No. I'm sorry." He raises his hands again. *Take another tack. A smarter tack.* "Do you know what Vada did for you?"

"Yes, she deserted me. Went off to her fancy fucking college, and I barely heard from her."

"You sure talk different than any preacher's wife I've ever known."

"I doubt you've known many of us, but it does seem that you bring out the Irish in me, Frank Darling."

"Vada regrets leaving you, and she told me so. She loves you so much, she paid off your debt to Miss Wentworth."

"That bitch got hold of Vada?"

"Even when I told her how crazy it was, she was happy to do it. Vada wanted so badly to find you, to say she's sorry, that she gave Wentworth her grandmother's diamond necklace to find you. She did that for you."

"So, what did *you* do to land here on my doorstep?"

"Something stupid. And she's mad at me. Mad enough at me to marry Justin."

"What do you want from me, Frank Darling?" She bites out the words, her gun still trained on him.

"In about eighteen hours, she's going to walk down the aisle of St. Michael's Church. I want you to come back to Charleston and help me talk her out of marrying the wrong guy."

"Why me?"

"You're the best peace offering I know. You're what she wants."

Darby pushes a tendril of her long red hair away from her face with one hand and lowers the rifle. "I won't go with you."

"But—"

"You don't need me, Frank. I know Vada Hadley better than I know myself. If she loves you like you think she does, Vada will stop the wedding herself."

"Please, Darby. I'm begging you."

"Get off my porch and be on your way, Frank Darling. And when you see Vada Hadley, tell her I love her."

·Chapter Thirty-Nine·

"That went well."

"Shut up, Reggie." Frank slams the car door, starts up the Mayflower, and pulls back out onto the road, headed for home.

Around sunup, he pulls into a truck stop. Frank barks at the attendant to fill up the car, and then heads inside to grab something to eat on the road.

"Got some fried-egg sandwiches made up, tuna salad, too. They're not from yesterday, no, I made them fresh, first thing this morning," the wiry little old waitress behind the counter says. Frank orders two Dixie cups of black coffee and one of each sandwich and puts a dollar on the counter.

"Food," Reggie says gratefully, back in the car. "And coffee."

"Hope that's okay. It'll have to be," Frank says, and pulls back onto the highway.

The closer he gets to the Savannah River, separating Georgia from South Carolina, the more the dread in Frank's belly grows.

He's got nothing to keep Vada from marrying Justin and nothing to offer her except love. Until now, he believed that might be enough to stop the bride in her tracks, but without his peace offering, without Darby, he's not so sure.

"Darby is right, you know." Reggie shrugs. "I'm sorry, but she is. And I'm not at all sure when the moment of truth comes, if a girl of Vada's breeding is even capable of choosing a life without luxury, even if that life is full of love."

"Thanks for being so supportive."

"I'm not trying to be hurtful, Frank, I'm trying to help you understand the culture Vada and I come from. Vada's never had to do without anything. All she's had to do is ask for whatever she wanted, and it was delivered on a silver platter. You're asking a lot of her to leave that life."

"You're sure about this?" Mother asks, trying to smile.

"After Justin and I talked a long time last night—yes, I'm sure. It's the first time we've agreed on anything, really. It felt good and makes this seem even more right."

"I don't know where your father is. He should be here by now."

Mother's hand trembles as it skims across the top of one of the trunks that are packed and ready to go.

"You look so beautiful; you always do. I know I should be happy for you, but I can't stop feeling like—I don't know. Like I want to go back to when you were a little girl and do things over again."

"Mother, please don't cry."

She nods and dabs at her tears. "I would be a better mother, the kind of mother you deserved—at least, I hope I would."

"It's time to go," I say softly.

"Do you have a kiss for your old man?" My father appears in the doorway, smiling.

"Yes." Tears spill down my face. I gather them both in my arms and hold them close, grateful for this moment.

"You remember what I've always told you?" he asks softly, wiping my tears away with his thumbs.

"I'm a Hadley."

"And you'll always make your way in this world." He finishes the sentence like a benediction.

"Wake up," Frank says.

Reggie stretches and looks around the crossroads as Frank turns down the long dirt road that leads to Claire and her boys.

"I've kept you from your family long enough." Frank extends his hand. "Thanks for—everything."

"What about Charleston?"

"I have time for a birdbath, a change of clothes, and then—I hope I can find the right words to make her change her mind."

"Good luck, Frank." He opens the car door and pauses. "I hope she chooses you."

Tiny's dust-covered truck is the only vehicle in the dusty parking lot, which probably means that Big Jim did sweep her off her feet. *Damn good for her. She deserves it.* Frank opens the screen door to his house, pushes the door open, and stops just inside.

What if he hadn't stopped the night of the storm? What if he'd made love to Vada like she begged him to? Would things be different?

He looks at his watch. He has fifteen minutes to get on the road again. No more than that. He pulls the new slacks and dress shirt out and lays them on the bed, along with the wing tips and a pair of socks. He strips, steps into the hot shower, and hopes the water will wash away the memory of everything—all the way back to the moment he was getting ready to pick Vada up and take her to the Edisto Motel. He has to think of things that way if he has a prayer of going through with this. There's too many wrongs between that time and now, too many reasons for her to turn him down flat.

Frank's not sure if it's the humidity from the shower mixed with the blazing August day or the fear of losing her, but he can barely breathe. He knows what he's going to say, that he loves her and he knows she loves him. That he can't live without her and doesn't even want to think of what life will be like without her laugh, without her smile, and without those blue eyes that take his breath away. He'll promise her the world and work like a dog to give it to her, if that's what she wants, because his life began the day she walked into his diner.

He can take care of the bastard easily. After the last time they met, her father will be a problem, but Frank's going to focus on Vada, only her, and if her daddy gives them his blessing, fine. If not, he can go straight to hell, because nothing is going to keep Frank Darling from the woman he loves. Except finding his damn car keys.

He rifles through his dirty clothes and starts tearing the place apart, looking everywhere. Shit. How can he be this close to getting her back and have no way to get to Charleston? He runs out to the Mayflower, hoping to God that he left them in the ignition, but no luck. He gets down on his knees and looks underneath the car, but nothing. *Backtrack*. He hurries into the house, scouring the ground, the porch, the living-room floor, everywhere, but he's exhausted, running on no food and bad coffee. He doesn't remember much of anything after he set foot in the door the first time, other than his sole focus was getting Vada back.

He grabs his wallet and sprints to the Mayflower, hoping he remembers what his cousin taught him about hot-wiring a car. He dives as close to the floorboard as his large frame will let him and yanks what he hopes are the correct wires from under the dash. The copper tips of the two wires rub together. Nothing. Cars whiz by as he yanks another wire down and keeps trying, until a half dozen of them splay out like spaghetti on the floor. Shit.

When he opens the door to Tiny's truck, a thick layer of dust flies everywhere. He doesn't bother to shoo it away from his new clothes. Between the dust and the dirt caked on his knees, his clothes are a lost cause anyway. He's grateful the truck is higher than the car, giving him a better view of the wires. He hears a car pull into the lot and wants to scream at them that he's closed, maybe forever. If he doesn't get his ass to Charleston in time to stop that wedding . . .

He racks his brain to remember what was so easy for his cousin, what eventually sent him to prison. Yellow and red? No, red and green? Blue? Shit.

"You seem like you're in a hurry, Frank Darling." The dust is still settling around her bright fire-engine-red car loaded down with suitcases.

He can't believe how beautiful she is. Vada gets out of the car and walks toward him. She came back. Damn it. She came back for him. She wraps her arms around his middle, and he picks her up and takes her mouth in a long, wet kiss. "I thought you were getting married."

"Not today, but soon."

"Soon, like in a few hours, or soon like next week?"

"It depends." She traces his jawline with her finger.

"On what?"

She kisses him again, with such wanting. "On what your answer is."

"My answer?" Crossroads busybodies be damned, he scoops her up and walks toward his house, their house.

He sets her down just inside the doorway. He wants her to be sure she knows what she wants. That she's running to him and not just running away again. She threads her fingers in his hair and raises on her tiptoes to kiss him. Slowly. Sweetly at first, savoring the closeness, the breath they share. She pulls away from him and looks like maybe she's come to her senses, and then shakes her head.

"It wasn't supposed to be like this." She smiles, chin quivering. Tears in her eyes.

"Wasn't supposed to be like what? Tell me, and I'll set everything right."

"I had this all planned out, but—"

"I found Darby for you."

"You did? Where is she? Is she okay?"

"I tried to get her to come back, but she has a new life, and she's pretty good with a gun." He strokes her cheek with the back of his knuckles. "She told me to tell you she loves you. She told me if you loved me, you'd stop the wedding."

She looks down, ashamed. "Frank, I have to tell you something. I was with Justin last night—"

"I don't care. You're here with me now."

"No, hear me out. I thought maybe I belonged in Charleston, with him, but when I told him what I wanted in a marriage—he laughed." She smiles. "Howled, actually."

"He did? Did you tell him you wanted a partner, a man who would be your equal?" He trails kisses down her neck.

"Yes." Her laugh is musical.

"And what did he have to say?" he whispers, his lips skimming the top of her breast.

"Justin said he didn't want me—that with my progressive thinking, I'd be lucky—" He covers her mouth in a long kiss. She pulls his shirttail out and runs her hands up the length of his back. "—if anyone in Charleston—" His hand slides up her thigh; she gasps. "—will have me."

"But you told him you know someone who loves you just the way you are, someone who wants you—more than anything." She nods, her forehead against his, her hands pressed into the small of his back, drawing him closer.

"Yes, but before we go any further, Frank Darling, I have to ask you something." His arms are locked around her.

"God, I love you, Vada. I'm so glad you came back."

"But you have to let go of me for this."

"Never."

"Please, Frank." She tries to use her teacher face, but dissolves into laughter.

It feels wrong to let go of her, even for a second, but he does.

"When you proposed back in Memphis, I said yes, but I was terrified, afraid that loving you meant losing myself, but that's not what happened. In loving you, I discovered who I am and what I want. I want you, Frank, and I can't imagine my life without you." She cups his face in her hands and smiles. "Franklin James Darling? Will you marry me?"

He pulls away just enough for him to see her beautiful face, to get a glimpse of what forever will be like with Vada Hadley. "You already know my answer, Vada," he says. "Besides, I thought it was supposed to be the other way around."

She kisses him tenderly at first, then deeper, passionately. "Okay," she says breathlessly. "Your turn."

"This part, I planned." He gets down on one knee, takes her hand, and places it over his heart. "I never believed in love at first sight. Hell, I'm not even sure I believed in love. But that all changed the moment I looked up from the kitchen and saw you standing in my diner. You changed my life. You changed me for the better. Marry me, Vada Hadley. Say yes to me, and I'll love you forever."

She kneels, melting into his body with a long, sweet kiss.

"Yes."

Recipes

• • • • •

Frank Lee, executive chef at S.N.O.B.
in Charleston, has created recipes
for some of Frank Darling's favorite dishes.
Enjoy!

Slightly North of Broad Devil Crab Cakes

Executive Chef Frank Lee

SERVING SIZE: 4 5-OZ CAKES

Ingredients:

1 pound crab meat

1 tablespoon yellow mustard

1 egg, beaten

4 dashes of Tabasco

¼ cup bell peppers, diced

¼ cup red onion, diced

1 tablespoon Worcestershire sauce

1 lemon, juiced

2 tablespoons chopped parsley

½ tablespoon salt

¼ tablespoon pepper
¼ cup cracker meal or panko bread crumbs

Directions:

Pick crab meat from shell.

Gently mix all ingredients together in large bowl.

Let sit for an hour.

Form into 5-oz cakes.

Heat oil in a large skillet over medium heat. When oil is hot, carefully place crab cakes, in batches, in pan and fry until browned, about 4 to 5 minutes. Carefully flip crab cakes and fry on other side until golden brown, about 4 minutes.

· · · · ·

Slightly North of Broad Fried Chicken

Executive Chef Frank Lee

SERVING SIZE: 10 PIECES

Ingredients:

3 ½ pounds chicken, cut into 10 pieces

½ quart of brine (2 cups water, 2 tablespoons salt,
1 tablespoon sugar, dissolved with 1 tablespoon vinegar)

2 cups buttermilk

2 cups flour

1 tablespoon salt

1 tablespoon pepper

Lard or oil for frying

Directions:

Place chicken in large bowl, cover with brine, and refrigerate overnight.

When ready to cook, transfer chicken from brine to buttermilk.

Heat lard or oil about a ½-inch deep in a 12-inch cast iron skillet to 350 degrees.

Put flour and salt and pepper in brown paper bag. Add one piece of chicken at a time and shake.

Tap off excess flour, fry skin side down. Only 4 to 5 pieces in the pan at the same time, don't over crowd. Cook each piece for about 15 minutes on each side. Be sure to check the temperature and don't burn the chicken.

Drain chicken on newspaper bag or brown paper bag. Enjoy!

· · · · ·

Slightly North of Broad Fried Okra

Executive Chef Frank Lee

SERVING SIZE: 2 POUNDS OF FRIED OKRA

Ingredients:

2 pounds of fresh, tender okra

½ cup buttermilk

4 dashes of Tabasco

1 egg

½ cup corn meal

½ cup flour

Salt and pepper
Lard or oil of your choice

Directions:

Wash and trim okra into 1-inch-thick barrels.

Mix buttermilk, egg, tabasco in medium-sized bowl.

Mix dry ingredients in another medium bowl.

Put enough oil or lard in 10-inch cast iron skillet for a depth of ½ inch, heat skillet to medium heat, 325 degrees.

Coat okra in small batches in the corn meal mix, fry until golden brown, about 4 minutes.

Drain on newspaper or brown paper bags.

· · · · ·

Slightly North of Broad Peach Cobbler

Executive Chef Frank Lee

SERVING SIZE: 4–5 SERVINGS

Peach filling

4 large peaches

1 cup bourbon

½ cup sorghum syrup or brown sugar

½ teaspoon vanilla

Topping

¼ pound butter

1 cup sugar

1 whole egg
½ cup sour cream
¼ teaspoon salt
1 teaspoon baking powder
1 cup flour
½ teaspoon cinnamon

Directions:

For the Topping:

Cream the butter and sugar. Add the egg, fold in sour cream.
Sift dry ingredients together, and then fold into wet.

For the Cobbler:

Macerate the peaches with bourbon, sorghum, and vanilla for at least 30 minutes or overnight.

Add fruit and juice into appropriate baking dish. Top with cobbler topping.

Bake at 325 degrees for 40–50 minutes.

Tips:

Use ripe local peaches and good sipping bourbon.

If using White Lily self-rising flour, baking powder can be omitted.

Cobbler topping best used immediately to capture the rising quality of the baking powder.

Serve hot with vanilla ice cream.

·····

Slightly North of Broad Salmon Croquettes

Executive Chef Frank Lee

SERVING SIZE: 4 5-OZ CAKES

Ingredients:

1 pound cooked or raw salmon

½ cup sour cream

1 egg

1 tablespoon lemon juice

½ tablespoon salt

1 tablespoon chopped capers with some juice

4 dashes of Tabasco

1 cup panko or dry bread crumbs (divided into ½ cups)

1 tablespoon fresh dill

½ cup parsley

¼ cup red onion, diced

Directions:

In medium-sized bowl, beat egg with sour cream and add crumbled cooked salmon or minced fresh salmon.

Reserving ½ cup bread crumbs, add all ingredients, mix together, and refrigerate for an hour.

Form all ingredients into cakes.

Coat in reserved bread crumbs and pan fry in olive oil or butter, about 2 minutes on each side.